# BRIDGE OF SOULS

## GREG F. GIFUNE
## SANDY DeLUCA

## JOURNALSTONE
YOUR LINK TO ARTIST TALENT

ISBN: 978-1-68510-065-0 (sc)
ISBN: 978-1-68510-066-7 (ebook)
Library of Congress Catalog Number: 2022940904

First printing edition: August 19, 2022
Published by JournalStone Publishing in the United States of America.
Cover Design and Layout: Don Noble
Edited by Sean Leonard
Proofreading and Interior Layout by Scarlett R. Algee

JournalStone Publishing
3205 Sassafras Trail
Carbondale, Illinois 62901

JournalStone books may be ordered through booksellers or by contacting:
JournalStone | www.journalstone.com

"And besides all this, between us and you there is a great chasm fixed, so that those who wish to come over from here to you will not be able, and that none may cross over from there to us."
—Luke 16:26

# BRIDGE OF SOULS

# PROLOGUE

EVERYTHING WAS SHADOWS NOW.

The old woman's mind wandered. From what, she could no longer remember, as only a wisp of distant memory remained. Moment to moment, things faded and blurred, only to refocus in her mind completely out of context. Her mind had betrayed her long ago, and soon thereafter, her body did the same. She hated her diseased mind, but the confusion and fear was something she'd grown used to. After all, what choice did she have?

Earlier, one of the women that cared for her—she couldn't recall her name, although she knew it as well as her own—helped her out of bed and placed her in her wheelchair. Then she placed a blanket over her legs and wheeled her to the window so she could see outside. She liked to watch the birds in the courtyard just beyond the window. She enjoyed watching the squirrels as well, and often sat there motionless and silent for hours, doing just that. Now and then, if she was lucky, even a bunny or two hopped by, and that always made her smile. She loved animals. Their innocence and profound wisdom fascinated her. In many ways she envied them. There was something so peaceful about watching the trees and the grass and the little critters out there. It brought her back, reminded her of when she was a little girl playing outdoors.

Existence was truly a wonder.

The room was small, consisting of just a bed, a night table, a standing bureau, and a chair. The adjacent bathroom sat empty and dark. A photograph of her child hung on one wall, but the rest of the wall space in the room was filled with crucifixes and crosses. An old set of rosary beads dangled from a particularly large crucifix on the wall over her bed. She couldn't always remember why these things were so important to her, but in those rare instances when she did, she wished she hadn't.

With an arthritically gnarled hand, the woman reached up and gently rubbed her eyes. Stricken with cataracts, she didn't see as well as she once had, but as she did each time she was out of bed, she looked at the little ceramic angel on her windowsill. It was very old, cracked and worn, a part of it containing a message broken off and lost. Though just a cheap little thing given to her years ago, it was very important to her. She couldn't remember why, she just knew it meant the world to her.

The old woman looked out the window again. Her eyes had not failed her this time. It was nighttime. At first she'd feared her vision had gotten worse and that perhaps she'd finally gone completely blind, but that wasn't it at all. It took her mind a few seconds to catch up, but when it did she realized just how dark it was out there. That's why she couldn't see anything beyond the window. In fact, it was storming. Rain gushed and poured across the glass, blurring it like a dream.

She knew there were winged creatures out there in the night, and they weren't birds. They were something far worse. She just couldn't see them yet.

But were they real or simply phantoms—boogeymen—from her nightmares?

Thunder rumbled, startling her. A flash of memory, there then maddeningly slipping from her grasp before she could fully understand it…

Again, her tired eyes looked to the little angel on the windowsill.

So much had changed since she first received that trinket. But had those changes come about naturally, or with deliberate malice? Had they come about normally, as time passed, or had they been perpetrated by unseen forces bent on controlling and ultimately destroying her?

The old woman had no idea what any of that meant, only that such thoughts ran through her withered mind often. Sometimes she saw things in her mind too, strange, horrifying things that slithered and played out before her like a movie in her head. Stories, lives, timelines, brief glimpses of how she'd come to be here, tales told and imagined, both recalled and purposely implanted by those things she knew even now watched her in the night. Those things that gathered around her bed in the darkness, red eyes glowing as if on fire. Glimpses of real events, of a life and people she swore she'd once known, or just more bad dreams in a mind twisted and diseased?

She was no longer sure.

Had she ever been?

The shadows along her limited peripheral vision shifted, crept closer, and she knew she was no longer alone in the room. Staring straight ahead, the old woman continued to watch the rain glide along the window before her. The little angel figurine reflected in the bottom portion of the dark glass looked as if it were melting, becoming something else from some other time, some other night.

*Sleep…*

Horrible whispers circled her like the predators they were, and at the very edges of her perception, she could've sworn she heard the distant cries of a baby.

Thunder raged, and the world blurred through the old woman's tears.

She looked to the little angel's worn, stained and chipped face. It watched her impassively, frozen in forced silence.

Forever trapped in its creator's cruel grasp.

# CHAPTER ONE

IT SEEMED AN ODD time for angels.

All the color in the world was dead, and yet, as a gray winter day morphed into a brutally cold and starless night, there seemed to be something unusual in the air, something extraordinary.

A man…

*George.* She was sure his name was…


George stood at the head of the sales floor and gazed through the enormous front window. Snowflakes danced in the breeze, spiraling about though not amounting to much in terms of accumulation. He watched them fall across the vast and nearly empty parking lot like tiny feathers, or perhaps the ashes from bodies burned and scattered to the winds long ago, reborn in the vaporous and smoky pools of streetlamps.

Except for the security lights, the store was dark, which brought the night awaiting him into clearer focus. There was at once something comforting and unsettling about that. The rest of his staff had left, but this was George's last night, so once the goodbyes had been said, he decided to stay behind a while. Never again would he set foot in this store, sit in his office, or interact with his customers and coworkers, yet that was the least of it. He'd spent twenty years with the company, the last fifteen in this store specifically, and although there was once a time when he couldn't imagine his life being any different, he'd already mourned this loss, and leaving it all behind gave him a sense of bittersweet freedom.

Like a free-fall into night.

After locking up, George stepped out into the cold. Beneath the glow of a nearby Red Lobster sign, he crossed the plaza parking lot and headed for his car. Traffic on the street beyond was slower than usual, the area quiet and nearly deserted, and the snow blowing about was heavier and wetter than he'd expected. As he made his way to his Chevy, which was parked beneath a light post at the rear of the lot, he aimed his fob, and with a press of the appropriate buttons, unlocked and started his car while still a few feet away.

Just then, George hesitated and looked to the sky.

Flakes tumbled all around him, descending in beautiful twisting curtains. He opened his mouth and stuck out his tongue. How many times had he done that as a child? How many times had he watched snow fall with wonder and awe, never realizing that one night, in some dark and distant future, as a grown and aging man, he'd be doing the exact same thing? Instead, like countless others, he'd wandered through his life as if he'd been dropped into it mistakenly, often blissfully unaware of the tragedy headed straight for him.

George looked back at the bookstore one last time.

He'd been marking time for so long it felt strange to be anticipating anything different. All those days and nights—years—of hard work, what the hell was the point? He'd tried to build something, a life, and he had to a degree. But so what? A simple man, a good, loyal, and loving man, George had tried his best. Hadn't he? Though his life was far from perfect, he'd been happy once, that much was true. He must've been. If not, having it torn away would never have been so painful.

And no question, life—at least as he'd known it—was gone.

As if to remind him that the final nail in the coffin had finally been driven home, it was then that the call came.

The angels his mother had always assured him would one day come for her had apparently arrived, and there, in the cold and snow and quiet, on this night of final things, of completion, that seemed appropriate. There were no bright lights, heavenly horns, or religious visions dancing in the night sky, only the abrupt ring of his cellphone, and the strange knowledge of exactly who was on the other end of that call.

George reached into his coat pocket, retrieved his phone, and with a press of a button, brought it to his ear. "Yes?"

\* \* \* \*

In the evenings, most residents were asleep.

The nursing home was quiet, so George moved carefully, negotiating his way around the various wheelchairs, gurneys, and housekeeping carts littering the dimly lit hallways. Occasional groans or whimpers drifted from the rooms, but it was the smells that disturbed him most. They struck the moment he was on the ward, hitting him as he passed particular rooms, though oftentimes the entire floor reeked of excrement. Human beings lying in their own filth as the steady and annoying buzz of call alarms echoed incessantly.

As he reached the nurse's station, a CNA in flowery scrubs hurried past without making eye contact. Behind the counter, a lone nurse sat before a computer monitor, her pale face bathed in the eerie glow from the screen. She looked up, recognized George, and offered a weary, cartoonish frown.

"I'm so sorry, Mr. Gage." She stood and quickly referred to her wristwatch. "She was pronounced about half an hour ago. I've been in touch with the funeral home listed for her final arrangements. They're on their way."

George nodded, glancing down the hallway in the direction of his mother's room. "Is she still…"

"Yes, she is."

"Is it all right if I go to her room?"

"Of course, and if I can help with—"

"Thank you."

As George turned, he saw another man approaching the station. A mousey, nervous sort, he looked troubled, lost in the way that so many people with loved ones here did.

*Maybe I'm not the only one faced with the death of a loved one in this awful place tonight,* he thought. *I wonder if the poor soul got a call just like I did.*

When George arrived at the small room, the bed closest to the door was empty. His mother's roommate had died a few days before. Her bed was made, neatly awaiting its next occupant. The other bed was still occupied, though by something no longer quite his mother. Then again, his mother hadn't really been his mother in a very long time.

As he moved closer, he saw that her eyes were closed. Horribly pale, she didn't appear to be sleeping, as people often said of the dead. In fact, the body lying in that bed barely resembled a human being at all. She'd lived in this place for some time, yet George already felt no trace of her here. He never really had.

Reaching down, he carefully rested his hand against her forehead. Cold, it felt more like the synthetic flesh of a mannequin than something that, until recently, was alive. George slid his hand up to her cotton-white hair, which was combed back in a severe manner. She'd never worn it like that outside this place. Soft, it at least *felt* familiar, reminding him of the times he'd gently stroked her hair and lied through his teeth, assuring her everything was going to be all right.

With a sigh equal parts grief and guilty relief, George sank into the chair next to the bed like a slowly deflating balloon. As his eyes filled with tears, he placed his hands in his lap, sat quietly, and waited for the mortician to arrive.

\* \* \* \*

Later, once the body was removed and George found himself alone in the room, he began to collect his mother's belongings.

In the drawers of the modest nightstand, he found a pad of lined paper with some scribblings on it, a badly worn copy of the Bible, two dog-eared paperback romance novels, and the last purse his mother had owned, a light brown faux leather bag with a detachable strap. Along with a small stuffed bunny rabbit, the few clothes in the bureau, and two framed photographs on the wall—one of George as a little boy and one of his late father—these things constituted his mother's possessions. A lifetime whittled down to a handful of meager items, most of which would likely end up in the trash.

At once, an array of emotions washed over him, and again, his eyes filled with tears. George had grown used to this sort of thing the last few years, since it tended to happen whenever he came to this place. That's not to say it got any easier. It didn't. In fact, it got decidedly worse. It was simply familiar, a painful sense of helplessness with which he'd grown accustomed.

Shadows drifted, moved along the walls as the light from the hallway shifted. Somewhere not so far away, a high-pitched alarm from another room sounded. It signaled a resident was calling for help, needed to be taken to the bathroom, had fallen, or perhaps needed basic assistance of some sort.

It seemed to go on forever, unanswered.

"She was a special lady."

Startled, George looked up and saw a woman in blue scrubs standing in the doorway, her raven hair pulled into a ponytail and held in place with a clip in the shape of a butterfly. She looked no older than thirty, and her face was devoid of makeup, her large brown eyes sad and tired. She had a peculiar stance, like she couldn't decide whether to cross into the room or stay where she was.

"Mrs. Gage," the woman said, her voice soft.

"Yes." George forced a smile, or something similar. "She was. Thank you."

"Are you Georgie, her son?"

Only his mother had called him *Georgie*. "Yes," he said, clearing his throat.

"She talked about you a lot. You were her pride and joy."

He stood there stupidly, unsure of how to respond.

"I'm a CNA here." She drew a deep breath. "I've taken care of Mrs. Gage since she got here. We haven't met before because I work the overnight shift. One of the downsides to working overnights is you don't get to meet a lot of the families or loved ones, those lucky enough to still have any, that is."

George walked to the doorway and extended his hand. "George Gage."

"Magdalena Carlino," she said, shaking his hand.

"Were you with my mother when she died?"

"Yes."

"Was she, I mean— Did she— Was she in any—"

"She died peacefully."

Although comforting to hear that, he'd been informed his mother had died of a massive heart attack, so it was rather difficult to believe. "When they called she'd…" He released her hand and turned back to the small room with a single window his mother had called home for the past three years. "She was already gone."

"I'm very sorry, Mr. Gage."

"At least she wasn't alone. Thank you for being with her."

"It's my job. But with Mrs. Gage it was more than that."

"I appreciate you caring for her, Magdalena. More than you know."

"It was my pleasure. Even though she struggled with dementia, she was lucid sometimes. Good days and bad, you know? We spent time together almost every night. She had trouble sleeping sometimes, even with her medications, so I sat with her when I could."

"I'm sure your company meant a great deal to her."

"She was a sweet woman, a good woman. I'm going to miss her."

"Yes," George said softly. "So am I."

The beeping down the hall finally ceased, leaving behind an unnerving silence. An air of discomfort hung in the air, but that was nothing new.

"I'm sorry I bothered you, Mr. Gage, I just wanted to—"

"You haven't bothered me at all. And please, call me George."

Magdalena smiled self-consciously. "I should go now."

"I'm sorry if I've kept you, thanks again for taking the time to see me."

"No, you didn't keep me. I wanted to talk to you before I left."

"Thank you. I'm glad you did."

Still straddling the doorway, Magdalena started to leave then hesitated.

"Is there something more?" George asked.

Magdalena's nervousness turned to distress. "She was the first resident I ever really bonded with, and especially at the end, well, she told me some things."

"What kind of things?" he asked. When Magdalena didn't answer, George said, "Did she say something to you when she died?"

"She wasn't awake when she passed." Magdalena glanced in both directions down the hallway, making certain no one else was within earshot. "Mr. Gage, did—"

"George."

Magdalena gave an uncomfortable nod. "Did she ever talk to you about what she saw, about what she heard?"

"I'm not sure what you mean."

"The last few weeks she said she was seeing and hearing things."

"With her dementia that wasn't unusual."

"I mean when she was lucid."

"I don't understand."

"I shouldn't have said anything, I—"

"No, it's fine." The memory of his mother's face staring at him flashed across his mind's eye, her frustration and confusion turning to sorrow, and then something that more closely resembled terror. "What did she say to you?"

Wringing her hands, Magdalena checked the hallway again.

"Was there something wrong?" George pressed. "Did something happen?"

The young woman's dark eyes brimmed with fear. "It's not unusual for residents to, well, at the end, or close to it, sometimes they say strange things."

George knew if he pushed too hard it might seem unnecessarily aggressive and make things worse, so he tried to speak as calmly and evenly as he could. "Listen, I need to get my mother's things in order, but that won't take long. Maybe we could talk some more in a minute. Would you like to get a cup of coffee or something?"

Magdalena blushed. "I'm married, have a child."

"No, I didn't mean it like that." George was stunned she'd taken it that way. "I don't know how old you are, but—"

"I'm thirty-one."

He glanced at the plain gold wedding band on her left index finger. "Well, I just turned fifty-nine a few months ago. I'm old enough to be your father, which makes me too old for you, at least by my standards. While I'm flattered and a little embarrassed, I promise I'm not hitting on you. Having just lost my mother, trust me, that's about the last thing on my mind right now."

"Of course, I—I don't know what I was thinking. I'm sorry if I offended you."

"Not in the least, it's fine. You just seem uneasy, and I thought maybe you'd be more comfortable talking somewhere else, that's all."

Magdalena finally stepped into the room. This time when she spoke it was just above a whisper. "Mrs. Gage was seeing and hearing things at night, things in the hall and standing in the doorway, voices in the darkness when she was trying to sleep. Sometimes she said they were even in her dreams. She was very frightened."

"Magdalena, my mother wasn't in her right mind."

"Sometimes she was. She was lucid when these things were happening."

"Her doctor says that's exactly when those with dementia struggle the most, because when they're lucid they realize how nonsensical their thoughts are."

"There's something I think you need to see," she said.

Magdalena drifted to the nightstand next to his mother's bed and hesitantly reached for the notepad George had found earlier. After pulling back the top sheet with the scribblings on it, she handed it to him.

On the second sheet were several unsophisticated and shaky drawings of something dark. Distorted faces of some sort, certainly not human, with fierce eyes; the drawings looked as if they'd been made quickly, frantically. The strokes were long and ragged, black splotches from which the eyes protruded like light bursting through a patch of night. Horrific, the faces appeared *tortured*. On the next page were crude drawings of what appeared to be more of the strange dark beings.

"What the hell is all this?" George asked.

"It's what she was seeing. That's what she said to me."

He glanced down at them again. "What are they?"

"She wasn't sure." Magdalena blessed herself. "But they terrified her."

"I'm not surprised, they're awfully scary looking."

"She told me the things she was hearing at night were them too."

George flipped the sheets back into place, covering the hideous drawings. "You can't possibly believe my mother was really seeing such things."

"Many people come here to die, Mr. Gage. There's a lot of death between these walls. Strange things happen in this place all the time, especially at night. When residents are close to the other side, many see and hear things the rest of us can't. Sometimes I think it's just because their heads aren't right anymore. But sometimes I think it's something...*else*. Sometimes I think they're telling the truth. I know your mother saw and heard those things."

"In her state of mind it's hardly surprising," George said, tossing the pad on the bed. "Look, thanks for telling me, but I've got to gather her things and get going. I'd rather not be here any longer than necessary. I'm sure you understand."

Magdalena bowed her head but said nothing and remained where she was.

"Was there something else?" George asked.

"She had a phone," Magdalena said rather abruptly.

George looked around, saw it on the nightstand. "Yes. There." He pointed to a flip phone. A basic model she'd been able to use without getting confused, it had an oversized keypad she could see clearly, and it disconnected calls when closed. "I got it for her so she could call me whenever she needed to."

"Don't forget to take it with you," she said, her dark eyes burning with intensity. "You wouldn't want to leave it behind by mistake."

"I won't." George looked at her for more, but she offered nothing further.

Magdalena's eyes moistened. "I had to wait for you. It's my last night here. They're making cuts, laying people off, and jobs like mine are always the first to go."

"I'm sorry to hear that."

"Mr. Gage, she made me promise her, so I *have* to do it. I couldn't leave without telling you. The last thing I said to that sweet old woman can't be a lie. I could never live with myself. Your mother said if anything happened to her before your next visit that I should tell you about what she was seeing and hearing."

"All right," George said patiently. "You've done that."

Magdalena stepped into the shadowy hallway, then turned back. "She said: *Tell him to listen. You tell my Georgie to listen...so he can* hear."

# CHAPTER TWO

A SECOND MAN...THROUGH the tears...yes, she remembered now...

The microwave timer sounded, snatching Winston from his world of dreams. With a sigh, he stood, removed the 99-cent chicken potpie from the microwave, and placed it on the kitchen table next to his glass of chocolate milk. His mother had been gone for months, but there were still two places set at the table, complete with inexpensive placemats, napkins, and silverware. The kitchen was outfitted in a rooster theme. There were roosters everywhere. His mother loved the country kitchen look and liked the house kept a certain way, so since she'd been admitted to the nursing home, Winston hadn't changed a thing. She'd be upset if he had, but that wasn't the real reason. He knew it was virtually impossible, though somewhere deep down he'd been hoping his mother might come home and things could go back to the way they'd been before. And if she did, everything would be exactly as she'd left it and ready for her return. Not that his life before was so wonderful—it wasn't—but at least there had been moments of joy, however fleeting.

*I'm not afraid*, he thought.

But he was. He always was. Always had been, always would be.

Amidst the silence of the big old house he'd lived in his entire life, Winston sat at the kitchen table and sullenly ate his dinner. It wasn't very good, but he finished every bite, because as his mother always said, there were people starving all over the world and to waste food was shameful.

*And be sure to drink your milk, Winston.*

Once he'd finished, he washed his dishes then put them away, as he'd been taught. Next, he emptied the trash, wiped down the counters with a sponge, and turned off the lights, leaving only the small bulb from the stove on.

He climbed the stairs in darkness, stopping at the first door, his mother's bedroom. Other than to clean, he hadn't been in there since they took her away. Even now he felt uncomfortable crossing the threshold. Tentatively, he opened the door, flipped the wall switch, and took a quick peek.

Everything was just as she left it. Even her bed was turned down.

Winston closed the door and moved down the hallway to his room. Everything was in place, as it always was, but he stood there a moment and took it all in. For fifty-three years he'd lived in that room, and all of his things reflected that. His books and games and comics and even some toys from his childhood he treasured, many of them still in the original packaging, they were all pieces of his life, his past. But not his future, he knew that now. He'd never known anything else, and the days ahead terrified him. But he had to be strong, because he'd promised his mother he would be, and as she used to say, a man was nothing without his word. Still, he'd never been on his own before, and although he was embarrassed by that, he was also terrified. Even if he could make it on his own, what was the point? He had no friends, no wife or girlfriend, no one. There wasn't anyone he could turn to who understood him or even liked him. And now that his mother had been taken away, he was alone.

Truly, totally, horribly *alone…*

His eyes moved to his desk, an array of computers atop it, all the monitors dark. They were Winston's only real link to the outside world, his profession, his entertainment, his connection, his *everything*. He spent a while longer looking at his room and taking in all the history displayed before his eyes. Then he stepped back into the hallway and slowly shut the door.

Downstairs in the front closet, he found his winter coat, hat, and mittens. Slipping them on, he left the house, locked the door behind him, and walked the four blocks to the bus stop.

The neighborhood had changed drastically from what it once was. When Winston was a child, it was much nicer, far safer, and the homes better kept. Over the years the area steadily declined. These days, most houses sported bars on the windows and heavy security front doors that looked like something out of a prison movie. Other properties were abandoned, foreclosed on or condemned, and several buildings had been demolished in recent years, leaving behind empty lots littered with debris and garbage. Where once an occasional homeless person appeared in the shadows of dusk, there were now too many to count, lost souls warming themselves around makeshift fires in metal barrels or huddled in doorways and alleys, wrapped in tattered clothes and living in cardboard boxes. Gangs roamed the streets, drug deals took place out in the open at all hours of the day and night, nearly everything in the neighborhood was spray-painted with graffiti, and even the park he enjoyed as a child, and had gone to for years as an adult with his mother for walks or to just sit on the benches and feed the pigeons or squirrels, was no longer safe. Sirens screamed around the clock, as police cars, ambulances, and fire trucks raced through the streets. It wasn't unusual to hear random gunshots after dark most nights. Just two weeks before, a block from Winston's home, an assassin in a passing car shot a young man to death on his front steps. The television news said something about a gang-related drug deal gone wrong, but Winston didn't know about such things. He'd never even had a sip of alcohol, much less done drugs. He'd always tried his best to be a good boy. Even now, he tried.

Ignoring a kid in a bandana and a filthy Red Sox jacket calling to him from the corner, Winston hurried along the street, head down and hands stuffed deep into his coat pockets. He neither slowed nor stopped until he reached the bus stop. Once there, he found an older woman sitting on the bench, her purse in her lap. He'd seen her around the neighborhood before, but didn't say anything. Instead he offered a polite smile, then quickly looked away and shuffled his feet against the cold.

Moments later, a dilapidated city bus turned the corner, and with a loud hiss of air brakes, lurched to a stop.

As his mother taught him, Winston let the woman board first.

*Always mind your manners*, she'd told him from the time he was a little boy. *And always be a gentleman.*

Yes, Momma, always.

Following the woman, he climbed the steps then paid his fare. Choosing a seat near the driver, he settled in.

After a few miles he arrived at his stop, a small plaza that was home to a gas station, a coffee shop, and a couple other businesses. From there, like always, he hired an Uber to take him the rest of the way, through the heavily wooded rural roads which eventually led to the secluded nursing home where his mother had lived for the last several months. No one called them nursing homes anymore though. He learned that early on, when one of the nurses corrected him. *Long-term health care and rehabilitation facilities*, that's what they were called now. But there would be no rehabilitation for his mother. She would die there, and worse, she'd likely never even realize it.

Maybe that was better. Winston couldn't be sure. His head filled with conflicting thoughts as he closed on Matheson Manor—a name so falsely grandiose that Winston found it offensive—and entered through the sliding glass front doors.

The large reception desk in the lobby was dark and unmanned, but Winston signed the register anyway then moved down the hall toward his mother's room.

When he reached the nurse's station, a dejected-looking man was finishing up a conversation with the nurse. Once he moved away, she turned to Winston and offered a tired smile. "Running late tonight, hon? It's past visiting hours."

"I'm sorry," he replied. "I'll be quiet and sure not to wake Mrs. Harrelson."

"Your mom has the room to herself. We lost Mrs. Harrelson last night."

"Oh." Winston felt his face flush. He hadn't known the woman with whom his mother had shared a room well, but she'd always been pleasant. "Can I still…"

"Of course, but your mother's having a tough time tonight, so be prepared as best you can, okay? She hasn't been terribly lucid the last few days." The nurse noticed him rubbing his hands together. "Still awful out there, huh?"

"It's very cold. And now it's snowing too."

"We both need a vacation," she said with a wink. "Somewhere warm, right?"

Winston smiled nervously. "I won't be long."

She cocked her head toward the hallway. "Go ahead."

Winston shuffled off, ignoring the mostly open doors on either side of him, until he reached his mother's room. Hesitating in the doorway, he found her propped up in bed, a television suspended from the corner of the ceiling playing an old black-and-white movie starring Cary Grant.

She looked horrible. Old and frail, so drawn, she'd become little more than a skeleton in a nightgown wasting away to nothing, dying slowly in a place with no soul and with which she had no personal connection.

*It's all so cruel*, he thought, *so unnecessary*.

"Hello, Momma," he said, stepping into the room.

His mother's head lolled to the side, her dark eyes squinting through the shadows, as if she couldn't quite make him out. "Who's there?"

"It's me, Momma."

"Are you a salesman of some kind?"

Winston slid into the chair next to her bed. He wanted nothing more than to take her hand and hold it a while, but knew in her present

21

condition that wouldn't be a good idea. He could never be sure how she'd react these days. "I'm your son."

"And don't try any of that fancy sales talk. I'm not some bumpkin." She looked him over, and with a roll of her eyes, turned back to the television. "I shouldn't be watching this movie, but I love Cary Grant. So *dashing*, isn't he? Still, I've got dishes to do and a house to tend to. My son Winston counts on me. He's a lost soul, poor boy, but he loves his mother and that's what's important. Don't you think it's important that a boy loves his mother?"

"Yes. I do love you, Momma."

"Good, every boy should love his mother. I hope she appreciates it and showers you with her love as well, because there's nothing as warm and wonderful as a mother's love." She smiled, albeit slightly. "I'll have you know I enjoy gravy on my mashed potatoes, but I do *not* care for lima beans. I'll tell you that straightaway."

Winston closed his eyes. "I know, Momma," he said, nearly whispering.

"I've got laundry to do and dinner to make. I have a young son and he's out back playing. His father, useless as he was, is gone. Just picked up one day and ran off like a coward. Never saw or heard from him again. It's just my boy and me now."

Fighting emotion, Winston risked it. He reached out and gently rested his hand on hers. She was cold and brittle and slowly dying, it seemed to Winston. Morphing into something no longer wholly human…

She looked down at his hand, then back at him, and from somewhere deep in her eyes came a faint flicker of recognition. "Winston?"

"Yes. It's me."

"What are you doing up? Why are you out of bed?"

"I wanted to see you," he said, emotion catching in his throat. "I love you."

"I love you too, son. Now go back to bed, you have school tomorrow."

Although this woman bore little resemblance to the one he'd known his entire life, he forced himself to maintain eye contact with her. Where once love and wisdom and understanding resided, there was now only confusion and fear. Always so meticulously groomed, she looked a mess, her hair no longer dyed but reduced to its natural shocking white. Her salon hairdo no more, she looked instead as if she were wearing some sort of frizzy fright wig. She wore no makeup, and her once polished and manicured fingernails were cut short, cracked, and discolored.

*She'd be appalled by her appearance*, Winston thought, *mortified*.

He leaned in and kissed her forehead. Never sure if this would be the last time he'd ever see his mother, he remained there a moment, his lips pressed to her cool, paper-thin flesh. She wasn't coming out of this place alive, and for the first time, he'd be without her. It still didn't seem possible, but that's what was coming, and like a runaway train barreling down on him, its path was inescapable.

"I'll see you in the morning," he told her. "Sleep well, Momma."

"I don't sleep anymore," she said, suddenly coherent. "Not with *them* here."

"Who do you mean?" he asked.

"They think I don't know they're there," she said in a quiet, conspiratorial tone. "But I do. I *hear* them. Sometimes I even see them."

Winston nodded as if he understood. *Just more madness*, he thought.

"So I don't sleep," she continued. "I just wait."

"What are you waiting for, Momma?"

She looked at him with hopelessness bordering on abject panic. "I can't remember."

Somewhere down the hallway a person groaned. It was a horrible sound of surrender, a cry for mercy in a place where clemency and death were kin.

An alarm sounded from a distant room, signaling a resident needed assistance. That awful, grating sound had become so familiar to him, Winston was certain he'd never forget it, even long after he stopped coming here.

"It's late," Winston said. "I'm going to go now. Goodnight, Momma."

But his mother had already looked away, her attention drawn to a shadowy, allegedly empty corner of the room. Her face twisted into a grimace of equal parts confusion and eerie recognition, the way one might look if someone they knew but didn't expect suddenly entered a room.

"I hear you," she said to the shadows. "I *hear* you, you bastards."

Winston followed her gaze to the corner of the room, but of course there was nothing there.

"You have to listen very carefully," she said, turning back to him, her eyes wild now with so many emotions it was hard to settle on one. "Do you understand? When it's quiet and you're sleeping—or they *think* you are—that's when they come. If you listen, you can hear them. They think I can't. But I can."

He gently touched her face. "Everything's going to be all right, Momma."

Winston could tell by the look in his mother's eyes that they both knew he was lying. But it didn't seem to matter.

Somehow, even if just for a short while, it was better to believe.

# CHAPTER THREE

THE SHARP PAIN IN Magdalena's temple worsened, bringing the world back into harsh focus. "I understand we're past due," she said, attempting to maintain some semblance of composure as she pressed the phone tight against her ear. "But I can't pay the total amount right now."

"There's nothing I can do about that," the woman on the other end replied.

"It's snowing out. It's cold in here and we're out of propane. We don't have any heat, do you understand? This is an emergency. Can't you just—"

"If you can make a payment of—"

"I've told you what I can pay four times," Magdalena said.

"And *I* have told *you* that your past-due balance of three hundred and twenty-two dollars must be paid *in full* before we can schedule further deliveries."

"All I've got is two hundred. If you'll accept payment over the phone, I can pay you that right now, either by electronic check or debit card. And I promise to—"

"Ma'am, your account has been past due for several months now."

"I realize that." Magdalena fought tears, but she knew hers was a losing battle. "I'm just asking if you could give me a break this one time. I've been trying my best to pay something every month, but my husband, he—"

The woman on the line sighed into the phone.

"Look," Magdalena said, "I have a child here, okay? She's only five, and I—"

"Mrs. Carlino, we've sent you numerous notices. You've had several prior opportunities to set up payment plans so this could be avoided. You chose not to do that. You ignored the options we offered. Now your account has been flagged."

"*Flagged?* What the hell does that mean?"

"It means no more deliveries can be made to your address until your entire balance has been paid. *That* is what it means."

"But I've tried to explain to you, I didn't know anything about any payment options. You must've spoken to my husband. Don't you think I would've agreed to anything that would've prevented us from running out of propane and being without heat in the dead of winter?"

"Ma'am, please, I have no idea what you would or would not have agreed to. But here's what I do know. If you pay your past-due amount in full, I can have a truck out to you in the morning. I might even be able to have one there tonight on an emergency basis if we can get this done before all our trucks have returned to base. But your bill *must* be paid first. I'm sorry, now there's nothing more I can do."

Magdalena closed her eyes, and with her free hand, rubbed at the pain shooting through her temple. "We don't have any heat," she nearly whispered.

Silence answered her.

"Please. Can't you help me just this once? I need help, do you understand? I'm—for God's sake, I—I'm asking for your help."

"I've explained our policies numerous times now, ma'am."

"Are you a mother?"

"I don't see what that—"

"Do you have children?"

After a moment the woman answered. "Yes, I have two kids, all right?"

"Then you're a mom just like me. I have a daughter. She's only five and my husband, he's—"

"Mrs. Carlino, I'm sorry, but I can't help you any further."

"You mean you *won't*."

"If you pay your past-due amount, I can—"

Magdalena felt a tear roll along her cheek. "I literally don't have it."

"Then I'm not sure what to tell you."

"If you just give me a few days, just a couple days, that's all I'm asking. I got laid off this week, but my first unemployment check should be in soon. Plus, I've got some interviews next week. I'm a CNA. My husband is—he's out of the picture at the moment—but I can get you the whole amount if you can wait just a while longer. I promise I'll be able to pay all of it."

"Frankly, neither your choice of profession nor your marital woes are our fault or responsibility, ma'am."

"My *God*, what is the matter with you?" Magdalena felt sick to her stomach. "Can't we just talk like human beings? I'm asking for your help, I just—"

"Mrs. Carlino, I see no point in continuing to go round in circles like this."

"Yeah, you're right, there isn't," she said evenly. "Go *fuck* yourself, you heartless bitch."

Before the woman could respond, Magdalena hung up, brought trembling hands to her face, and did her best to prevent the tears from getting any worse. If she gave in, if she let herself go even this one time, hers would be a complete collapse, a total implosion from which she would likely never recover.

For more than a year now, in an attempt to make as much money as possible, she'd picked up as many night shifts as she could. Her husband Mitch had worked sporadically as a mechanic, but had left a few months prior. One morning he got up, packed a bag, and announced he was leaving, going out to the west coast. They hadn't been happy in a long while, and he'd never been much of a husband or father, but Magdalena never imagined that was how it would end. He just got on his motorcycle one morning and left. *He* couldn't take any more, he'd said. *He'd* had enough. If it hadn't been so heartbreaking it would've been funny.

"You don't love me anymore?" she'd asked. "Don't you care about me at all?"

"Come on, Mags, we been going through the motions for a long time. It ain't just me, baby, we both know it. Like you still give a flying fuck."

"What about Kaley?"

"A kid needs her mother. She'll be fine."

"You're her father."

"So?" he'd said with a shrug. "It's not like she's never gonna see me again."

Had Magdalena been a violent person, she'd have killed him right then in their kitchen. Instead, she told him to go, to get out and stay out. And he did. She hadn't heard from him since. Not even so much as a phone call to their daughter. So now she was left holding the bag and having to make up fantasy scenarios to help explain to a sad little girl who missed her daddy why he wasn't there anymore.

Until Mitch left, even though Magdalena had almost always brought in more income, he'd insisted on handling the money and all of the bills. Once he was gone, she knew why. They were broke, he'd spent through what little they had on a regular basis, and many of their bills had gone unpaid for months. It had taken nearly every dime she had just to keep the lights on.

Magdalena was raised Catholic and taught to forgive, but when it came to that son of a bitch, she was still working on it.

Month after month she'd pushed on despite her mental, emotional, and even physical exhaustion, held her emotions in check, done her best to repair the finances, to get the bills paid, juggling one in favor of another—*robbing Peter to pay Paul*, as her mother used to say—doing anything and everything in her power to keep her and her daughter afloat. And all the while she braced for that next threatening phone call to arrive, the next knock on her door from the postman bringing yet another registered letter, the next mortifying envelope in her mailbox with a bright red stripe across the top indicating it was a past-due bill. There was never a break, never any escaping this hell, not even for a little while. Even when she was at work, it was on her mind, worrying her, constantly gnawing away and reminding her that no matter how hard she worked she'd only make enough money that shift to put a small dent in what had become a nearly insurmountable problem, a tempest that grew worse and worse, stronger and stronger with every minute that passed.

If she allowed herself to sink beneath the surface tonight, she'd surely drown, so she steeled herself and drew a series of deep breaths. "It'll be okay. I just have to keep the faith." She looked away from the stacks of unpaid bills and collection notices littering the kitchen table. "Keep it together, girl, you can do this."

The gold band on her finger caught her attention. She wanted nothing more than to take it off, to get it away from her, but then she'd have to explain it to Kaley. The kid never missed a trick. Still, the idea of being rid of it was so appealing she nearly pulled it off and threw it across the room. She went for her cigarettes instead, and despite her trembling hands, managed to light one. She'd tried to quit several times before, and had almost made it this time, until—

"Why are you crying, Mommy?"

Magdalena turned to see her daughter Kaley standing at the mouth of the hallway adjacent to the kitchen. Clad in her Winnie the Pooh onesie, complete with feet, one hand clutched her newest toy, a small stuffed panda bear, while the other rubbed at her sleepy eyes.

"They're happy tears," Magdalena said, standing and quickly wiping them away. "I was just thinking about something happy, that's all. What are you doing up, sweetie? It's late."

Kaley shuffled her feet. "I'm cold."

As her heart sank, Magdalena hurried to her daughter and scooped her up. "I'll turn the heat up," she said, moving back down the narrow hallway toward Kaley's bedroom. "But first we'll get you tucked back in bed nice and tight, okay?"

Clinging to her mother, she rested her head on her shoulder. "Okay."

Magdalena reached the bedroom and, with a small nightlight providing just enough illumination for her to see what she was doing, gently returned Kaley to bed. "I'll get you another blanket from the closet and add it to the pile," she said, forcing a big smile as she pulled the covers tight.

Kaley snuggled up with her stuffed panda, which she'd named Amanda—*Amanda the Panda*—only moments after she got it. It originally belonged to Mrs. Gage, who upon hearing that Magdalena had a young daughter at home insisted she bring it to her. Employees weren't allowed to accept gifts from residents, but the woman had been so adamant Magdalena had told no one and broken the rules that one time. From the moment she brought the stuffed panda home, Kaley adored it and had been carrying it around and playing with it for days.

Magdalena pulled a blanket down from the shelf in the closet and threw it across her daughter. "You and Amanda snuggle up and get right back to sleep now."

"That's what they said too."

"What who said, sweetie?" she asked, as she smoothed the blanket out.

"The men."

With everything else on Magdalena's mind, it took a couple seconds for her daughter's response to register. "What men?"

"They said I should go back to sleep too."

Magdalena sat down on the edge of the bed. "Who told you that?"

"The men did." Kaley held Amanda close.

"What men are you talking about, sweetie?"

"I couldn't see them but I heard them. They said to go back to sleep too."

"They did, huh?" Magdalena arched an eyebrow, playing along. "They must've known it's way past your bedtime."

"They were talking real quiet but they woke me up anyways."

The imagination of a five-year-old never ceased to amaze, but Kaley seemed so sincere it was a bit troubling. "Are you being silly?" Magdalena asked.

Kaley shook her head no.

"Are you pretending with Mommy right now?"

"No," Kaley said through a quiet yawn. "I asked them what they were doing and they said I should be quiet and go back to sleep like a good girl. I went and got you instead though, 'cause I was cold."

With a slight twinge of discomfort, Magdalena asked, "Kaley, there's no one else here except you and me. What men are you talking about?"

Kaley smiled, as if the answer to her mother's question was so obvious there was no need to respond.

"*Sweetie*," Magdalena pressed, "I need you to answer Mommy honestly, do you understand? Who are these men you're talking about?"

Closing her sleepy eyes, Kaley said, "The men that live in Amanda's tummy."

# CHAPTER FOUR

ONCE GEORGE LEFT MATHESON Manor Nursing and Rehabilitation Center, he sat in the parking lot a while, watching the snow fall through the darkness. Alone in his car, he began to weep. He'd already cried countless tears over the last few years, as the mourning process for his mother began long before her death. She'd been slowly receding—dying—right before his eyes for months, and with each visit, there were fewer traces of his mother in the woman he came to see. Of course there had never been a chance of reversals or miracle cures. Once his mother went into that awful place, she was never coming out alive, and although she didn't realize that for a while (and perhaps never truly had), George did right from the start. The doctors explained that the reality was she would slowly get worse and worse, and that was exactly what happened. Her death, in some ways, was far more merciful than the alternative. The last thing George wanted was for her to linger on and on until she became a drooling zombie in a wheelchair staring out the window all day. And while it was excruciating to lose his mother, her death also brought with it a strong sense of relief. George felt guilty about that, but her ordeal was finally over. She was at peace now. Pain and fear could no longer touch her.

Just the same, he'd had it with death and dying. A year before, George's wife Maureen had passed as well. Diagnosed with pancreatic cancer, she lived only two years from the day of her diagnosis, and her quality of life during that time was, at best, harrowing. George had felt relief then as well, alongside the agony of losing her, because the woman he had spent his life with, a woman he truly, deeply loved, was finally free of the suffering and indignities that horrible disease had drowned her in.

Now, for the first time in his nearly sixty years, George was truly, desperately alone, and though he'd tried his best to prepare himself, he had no idea what to do with that reality. He and Maureen had no children. He'd just taken an early retirement, and the only two people he could call family were no more.

Just like that, his life had no direction or meaning.

For months George thought about moving away, but where would he go? He even considered selling everything, buying a small mobile home and spending the remainder of his days on the road, crisscrossing the country like some lonely old vagabond, but at the end of the day that didn't really appeal to him either.

Not much did. Staying or going, what the hell was the difference now?

"I feel like there's no point to me anymore," he muttered, his voice an empty and emotionless echo in the quiet of the dark car.

With a deep breath, George wiped his eyes, started the Chevy, and pulled away from the facility. *At least I'll never have to see this place again*, he thought.

After driving through miles of woodlands, the dark, lonely, winding rural roads eventually led him to a well-lit intersection. Normally, he'd have turned right and headed for home, but on this night George sat there a while, gazing through the snow at the small coffee shop directly across from him. The shop and a nearby self-service gas station were the only things still open, and though he was exhausted, the idea of going home to that empty little house was terribly depressing.

George had driven by that same coffee shop numerous times but had never gone in. *Maybe I'll give it a try*, he thought. *I could get a cup of tea.*

Once the light changed, he drove straight across to the coffee shop, pulled up in front and parked. A large front window revealed only two patrons inside, a long lunch counter with stools, and a small area that housed a few tables and chairs. It was a modest, no-nonsense little place, but looked clean and even inviting on such a cold winter night.

George glanced over at the small cardboard box filled with his mother's belongings on the seat next to him. Gently, he let his hand rest on the edge of the box. In his mind he saw his mother happy and smiling, frozen in time before all this, as if that simple act had somehow conjured her healthy living self. He hoped this might illicit a warm feeling, but instead he felt only the dreadful pain of loss.

Then visions of Maureen flooded his mind and he was weeping again.

"Christ," he said through a heavy sigh, frantically pawing at his eyes.

George shut the car off, and with it, the hot air blowing from the heater. He looked around, suddenly gripped with the uncomfortable feeling that someone was watching him. With the snow, visibility was low, and he couldn't see much beyond the reaches of the lights from the coffee shop and adjacent gas station. Yet he could not shake that uniquely unsettling feeling.

*The last few weeks she was seeing and hearing things…*

Magdalena's words rang in his ears as the memory of her frightened face flashed across his mind's eye.

*Mrs. Gage was seeing things in the hall and standing in the doorway…*

The fact that dementia was often hereditary was not lost on George, and since his mother's diagnosis he'd been focused on such things, and worried more than he probably should have when it came to basic memory loss and strange thoughts that sometimes crept into his head. While his doctor had assured him a certain degree of such things were normal with age, and that tests had shown he was fine, George knew it was also possible for the same horror that had ravaged his mother's mind to be lurking, as yet undetected, in his own. Once one acknowledged that as even a slight possibility, it became impossible to ever cavalierly discard such thoughts again.

*Sometimes she said they were even in her dreams…*

George's eyes scanned the parking lot and gas station, then slowly panned their way back. If someone *was* watching him, he couldn't see any sign of them, so he dismissed it. But the feeling remained.

*You're still picking up the pieces after losing Maureen and now you've lost your mother just a couple hours ago,* he thought. *For God's sake, give yourself a break.*

George considered heading home. The way it was coming down, the snow wasn't likely to let up for a while, so the longer he stayed out the worse the roads and driving conditions were going to get.

*I don't care,* he thought. *I'm going in. A hot cup of tea might do me good.*

\* \* \* \*

George stepped through the entrance to the Hot Cup and was immediately greeted by a burst of heat, the smell of freshly roasted coffee and assorted baked goods, and the ring of a little bell from somewhere above him that signaled his arrival. Shaking excess snow and ice from his coat, he wiped his feet on a small square of industrial carpet just inside the door then pulled his gloves free. It was brighter here than he expected, and it took a moment for his eyes to adjust to the fluorescent overhead lights. Once they had, he noticed a couple of young women behind the counter. One, a redhead positioned at the register, flashed a bright and welcoming smile. The other fiddled with her phone and didn't seem to notice him.

"Nasty out there," the redhead said.

GREG F. GIFUNE & SANDY DELUCA

"Sure is." George took a look around.

At one of the nearby tables, a rail-thin bald guy in a turtleneck and slacks sat sipping coffee. Furiously tapping away on a laptop with his free hand, his eyes glared at the screen with the intensity of an air traffic controller struggling to bring a troubled jetliner in for a crash landing.

The only other patron was a man about George's age sitting at a table near the back. After a second or two he recognized him as the same person he'd seen at the nursing home earlier. Sitting with his elbows on the table, the man held a steaming mug with both hands and stared off into space, as if in a trance. On the table before him was a dog-eared paperback.

"What can I get you?" the redhead asked.

Stuffing his gloves into his coat pocket, George strode to the counter and looked up at the menu boards on the wall. There were dozens of exotically detailed choices, and though he'd originally intended on getting decaffeinated tea, the smell of the freshly roasted beans convinced him a hot cup of coffee sounded even better. Normally George never drank coffee so late, as it kept him up, but he didn't plan on sleeping much tonight anyway, so he asked, "Would it be possible to get a regular old cup of black coffee? Maybe something not too strong, like a breakfast blend?"

The woman smiled patiently. "Sure, no problem, what size would you like?"

He scanned the board again. There were terms listed he assumed were sizes, but he had no idea what they meant. "Do you have mediums?"

"We do," she chuckled. "Can I get you anything else?"

Directly behind her were shelves of donuts, croissants, muffins, and pastries. "One of those glazed donuts, please."

Once he'd paid, George took his coffee and donut, then made his way to a table not far from the mousey little man he'd seen at the nursing home. As he moved by, the man seemed to snap out of his trance and notice him as well. George gave a quick nod, which the man awkwardly returned with one of his own.

Once he settled in a couple tables away, George found the coffee scalding, so he decided to let it sit a while and eat his donut instead. Though not terribly hungry, he devoured the entire thing in just a few bites. Plucking a napkin from a silver holder on his table, George wiped his mouth and, perhaps mistakenly, made eye contact with the man again.

The man quickly looked away and took a sip from his mug.

George was not the kind of person that pushed himself on others, and in that moment, sociable was about the last thing he felt. He had no idea what it was, but something about this man drew George to him, and before he could stop himself, he began to speak. "Excuse me, I don't mean to be a bother, but did I see you earlier at Matheson Manor?"

Although clearly uncomfortable by the sudden question, the man responded in a quiet, almost childlike voice. "Yes. My mother is a resident there."

George thought the man's cadence odd, like someone who had only recently learned the language and still spoke with a deliberate and uncertain delivery, but he detected no accent, so George chalked it up to nerves. The man was definitely the anxious, painfully awkward type.

"My mother was too," George said. "She passed away tonight."

The man's expression shifted to one of genuine compassion. "I'm so sorry," he said. "That's awful, to lose one's mother. You have my deepest condolences."

"Thank you," George said. What he thought was: *What the hell are you doing? You damn fool, why would you blurt that out to some stranger in a coffee shop?*

George tried his coffee in the hopes it might shut him up, but it was still too hot to drink.

The man stared at him, as if expecting something more.

"In a way, it was for the best really," George told him. "She'd been suffering from advanced dementia for quite a while."

"I understand," the man said. "My mother has it too."

"I'm sorry to hear that."

The man took a sip from his mug. "It's very…difficult."

"Yes. It is." George cleared his throat. "Very."

An awkward silence followed, and then George suddenly found himself rising from his chair, rounding his table, and leaning closer to the man, his hand extended. "I'm George. George Gage."

At first the man seemed taken aback by the move, but he managed a twitchy smile and held out his hand as well. "Winston Tucker."

"Pleasure," George said as they shook. The man's grip was weak, his palm sweaty, so he released his hand and stood there a second. Then he slowly drifted back toward his own table.

"People don't really understand what it's like unless they experience it firsthand," Winston said. "The dementia, I mean."

George stopped and looked back at him. "That's very true."

"I would not wish it on anyone."

George pointed to the chair across from him. "Do you mind?"

"Please." Winston motioned to the chair as well.

After gathering his things, George joined the man at his table. "I don't do this sort of thing normally, but, well, I guess it's kind of a strange night."

Winston didn't seem sure how to respond to that. After a moment he indicated his mug and said, "The hot chocolate is very good here."

"The coffee may be too, but it's so hot I won't know for sure until tomorrow."

Although he nodded politely, Winston seemed to miss the attempt at humor.

George wasn't the least bit offended. There wasn't anything at all funny about this night. His comment had more to do with annoyance than wit. Laughing was about the last thing he felt like doing just then, especially when the only thoughts in his head were of his mother lying dead in her bed, or being transported in the dark to some slab at the local funeral home until such time as she could be shipped off to a local crematorium. Her remains would be returned to him in an ornamental urn full of ash and chips of bone. Visions of her cold body slowly drifting through an incinerator toward a wall of flames flashed in his mind, followed by those of a faceless man raking through the ash and embers with a steel shovel, breaking down the last of her the same as one would the remnants of any fire.

"I know it's only a matter of time for my mother. I've tried to prepare but…"

Winston's meek voice brought George back from the nightmares crawling through his brain. Yet they remained at the periphery of his mind's eye, lingering and lying in wait like the horribly ghoulish things they were.

"Sometimes she says the *strangest* things," Winston added.

*Like something watching from her doorway and whispering to her at night?*

"In the few months she's been there she's gotten worse quickly." Winston looked like he was going to have another sip of hot chocolate, but put the mug down on the table before him instead. "I don't usually visit so late, but sometimes it's…"

"I understand." George stared at the steam rising from his coffee. "I wanted to see her, of course, but I still had to drag myself to that place every single time."

The little man adjusted his eyeglasses, pushing them higher on the bridge of his narrow nose. "It's very hard to see someone deteriorate like that, day after day."

"Yes, it is," George said, as memories of Maureen just hours before her death took hold of him. He would never forget the look in her fading eyes that day, one of such abject sorrow and worry, and not for herself, but for him. It was scorched into his brain like a scar, which was exactly what it was. "And to know there isn't a damn thing you can do to help them or stop it makes it all so much worse. It's that feeling of complete *helplessness*, you know?"

"I do. Far more than I wish I did." Winston looked at the front window and the falling snow beyond. "I could've gone in earlier but I got caught up with work and let that distract me. It doesn't make it any easier, but sometimes putting it off is really all you *can* do."

"True." George made a third run at his coffee. This time he was able to take a couple quick sips. "What do you do for work, Winston?"

"I'm self-employed, freelance computer work."

"There must be a lot of opportunities in that these days."

"I'm fortunate to have several clients. I have an office in my..." Winston hesitated, as if he'd forgotten the rest of what he had planned to say. "At my house, I—I work mostly from home. What do you do?"

"Not much now."

Winston raised an eyebrow.

"I just retired," George explained. "Today was my last day."

"You don't look old enough to retire."

"It's an early retirement. I managed a bookstore over at the Red Lobster Plaza on North Street, worked for the company for years."

"Books-A-Mania," Winston said. "I go there sometimes. It's wonderful, particularly for a chain store. I've always loved books, I'm a voracious reader. Mother started reading to me when I was very young, and taught me to read even before I began school. *Smart people read.* That's what she always says."

"That's great." George managed a smile. The man struck him as the type that didn't speak much, but now that he'd been given the chance had probably already said more in the last few minutes than he had in ages. "I'm going to miss the job in some ways, but the last couple years have been trying, to say the least. It was time to do something—anything—else. I lost my wife last year, and now, tonight with my mother passing, the last vestiges of my old life are gone. Everything changes now. I just can't figure out if that's good or bad. Time will tell, I guess. It always does."

The musical ringtone from a nearby phone sounded, startling them.

As the bald guy with the laptop a few tables over answered his cell, the music ceased. "Edith, how *are* you?" he said with more volume than seemed necessary. "I'm doing my damnedest to finish the new poem! It's been *strangling* me all week!"

*If I don't get out of here soon,* George thought, *that poem won't be the only thing strangling you.* "Thanks for listening, Winston." He rose to his feet. "It was nice to meet you, but I should go."

"Me too, the last bus is coming through any minute."

George looked out at the snow. "Are you sure buses are still running in this?"

"Yes, it's fine." He stood and offered his hand. "I'm very sorry for your loss."

"Thank you," George said as they shook. "I'll keep you and your mom in my thoughts. Take care."

Bringing his coffee with him, George crossed back through the shop to the door, hesitating a moment to watch the snowy night through the glass. It still felt like something was looking back, and right at him, from deep within that darkness and snow, but he couldn't make any sense of it.

Exhausted, and with a nearly suffocating sense of sorrow, George pushed the door open and stepped out into the night. Even as the cold air hit him, and the flakes tickled his face, nothing felt quite real. Everything seemed slightly...off.

He wondered if things would ever be normal for him again. As he stood next to his car and looked up at the snow-filled sky, George couldn't be sure if he even knew what normal was anymore.

Swirls of snowflakes danced in the darkness all around him.

*Are you out there, Mom? Is Maureen there too, showing you the way so you won't be so scared? Are all the bonds and restraints of this world a thing of the past now? Have you found yourself again? Will you and Maureen wait for me, together? Do I matter that much? Or do the dead have more important things to attend to?*

Without warning, a streak of fear surged through him.

Shaken, he steadied himself against the car, worried he might otherwise fall.

It was one thing to be afraid of the unknown, of what might lie ahead now that his life had changed so drastically. But it was something else entirely to be frightened of the night, to inexplicably fear the terrible things it might conceal.

And this, it seemed to George, felt decidedly like the latter.

# CHAPTER FIVE

EXCEPT FOR A SCRAGGLY man sitting near the back, Winston was the only other passenger on the bus. Positioned close to the driver, as was his custom, Winston tried to ignore the man, who was muttering to himself and frantically looking around as if to be certain no one else had joined them. Although the man wore a long, heavy winter coat and untied winter boots, beneath his coat he appeared to have nothing on but what looked like a faded hospital johnny. Even at a distance he had the appearance of a crazed, recently escaped mental patient.

"Takes all kinds," the driver said with a wry smile, his weary but pleasant eyes finding Winston in his large rearview mirror. "That's what they say, isn't it?"

Winston nodded, then looked away. Although he'd tried his entire life to overcome it, his social anxiety rarely waned. He wanted nothing more than to be the kind of person who could offer a smooth smile and a witty reply, but the angst was always there, like a great wall blocking him from acting and reacting in ways most people considered normal and took for granted. The closest Winston had come to feeling comfortable with human interaction in a long while was earlier at the coffee shop when he'd spoken with George Gage. He knew he'd struggled and been painfully awkward even then, of course, but at least he was able to converse with the man and not feel as if he were about to come out of his skin. Winston's typical reaction was to extricate himself from such situations until his anxiety passed, but for some reason his usual need to flee hadn't kicked in.

Maybe that's why he'd been thinking about George ever since.

He tried to imagine what it might be like if they were friends. Winston had never really had friends, so he couldn't be sure exactly, but he'd observed others and their friendships over the years. It looked nice, foreign as it was to him, and though it often seemed an insurmountable hurdle, Winston still held out hope that he might one day experience it firsthand.

"It's not like I'm the only one!" the man suddenly shouted, still swinging his head back and forth in one direction then the next. "I'm not crazy!"

"Gonna need you to do me a favor and simmer down, pal," the driver said in a firm but compassionate tone. "Can't have any disruptions on the bus, okay?"

The man folded his arms, tucked his chin to his chest, and quietly mumbled a string of unintelligible sentences.

"Poor soul," the driver said to Winston. "I try to be patient with that sort. There but the grace of God go I, am I right?"

*Mother used to say that*, Winston thought. *Be grateful for your blessings, and never speak ill of the downtrodden, because there but the grace of God go I.*

The tired, pleasant eyes found him again. "Not much for conversation?"

"No," Winston managed, fidgeting about in his seat. "Sorry."

"No reason to be sorry, my friend. Like I said, all kinds, right?"

Thankfully the strange man rescued him from having to respond any further by suddenly giving the pull-cord a yank, signaling the driver he wanted to get off the bus. They'd long since crossed into the more urban part of town, and despite the weather, the traffic was a bit heavier here, so the driver's attention shifted from Winston to carefully changing lanes. Once he had, he pulled the bus over, slowly easing his way to the curb before rolling to a stop.

As he ambled up the aisle, the man stopped at Winston's seat and looked over at him. At first Winston tried to avoid eye contact, but the man just stood there staring at him.

"You all set, my friend?" the driver asked, turning in his seat and looking over his shoulder at the man. "You wanted off, didn't you?"

The man ignored him, and instead leaned closer to Winston, allowing his coat to fall open enough for him to see an IV hookup still in the bend of his arm. "You've seen them too, haven't you?" he said softly.

Winston shook his head no, trying not to react to how strong the smell of body odor and urine had become with the man so close to him.

"*Haven't* you?" the man pressed.

"No," Winston blurted, having no idea what the man was talking about.

"I think we're supposed to," the man said. "I think they want us to. It's all part of it. Whatever they gave us, it makes us—"

"On or off, bud," the driver said. "Got to make a decision, okay?"

The man pulled his coat closed and turned to the driver as if he'd just heard him. With a sad nod he shuffled away and stumbled down the steps to the street.

As the doors closed behind him, the driver pulled away. "Don't let that upset you," he said. "The guy's obviously not right in the head and talking nonsense."

Winston didn't respond, but the man *had* upset him. What in the world was he talking about, and why had he singled him out? He could've just as easily said such things to the driver. *Why me?* he wondered.

*I hear you,* his mother had said earlier. *I hear you, you bastards.*

"I sure hope the poor fella's got somewhere to go tonight," the driver said. "It's not fit for man or beast out there."

*You have to listen very carefully. If you listen, you can hear them.*

Could these things be connected? Winston didn't see how. In fact, it was absurd to even consider it, but he couldn't shake the feeling that the man's words were more than the deranged ramblings of a lost and mentally disturbed soul trying to sort things out in his own tattered mind.

Yet wasn't that exactly what his mother had attempted earlier?

Winston leaned his forehead against the window and watched the city streets pass as the bus lurched through the night. *Nothing seems real,* he thought.

But this was no dream. The only question was: What did it all mean?

Were these things connected somehow? Was some form of synchronicity at play? Were the peculiar things his mother said, his impromptu meeting with George Gage, and the homeless man's babblings all meant to happen just as they had on this strange night? Did they have actual meaning? Wasn't it far more likely that due to emotional and mental exhaustion he was seeing connections where none existed?

*Of course it is,* he thought. *Don't be ridiculous.*

Before he could give it more thought, the bus again rolled to a stop.

"End of the line," the driver said with a smile.

Winston slid out of his seat, hurried to the steps, and muttered, "Goodnight," as he exited the bus. He heard the doors close behind him, and although his first instinct was to begin the walk home, something told him to look back. When he did, the driver was still smiling at him. Eyes once pleasant now seemed menacing.

The driver gave a playful wave, then pulled away.

As the bus barreled off into the night, there appeared to be someone standing at the large rear window staring directly at him. The interior light blinked off then on then off again, making it impossible for Winston to discern much else, but someone *was* standing there. No. Not someone. Some*thing*…

On a bus that, except for the driver, should've been empty.

*Obviously you didn't realize someone else was onboard*, he thought.

Doing his best to believe that, Winston turned into an oncoming burst of icy wind and began the four-block walk home.

The neighborhood was quiet and unusually still, there was no one else on the street, and the only sounds were those of his footfalls crunching snow and ice as he made his way along the treacherous sidewalk. The snow continued to fall, but was lighter and appeared to be winding down, while the cold had only gotten worse, locking everything down in a deep-freeze that cut like a razor and chilled him to his core.

When he reached the final block, Winston noticed a car parked diagonally across the street from his house. It was not unusual for cars to be parked on either side of the street, but this one had its lights on despite the fact that it was parked and not running.

Stranger still, the moment he saw the car—or perhaps the moment its occupants saw him—the lights went out.

Winston came to an abrupt halt. Despite the cold, he stood there a moment, watching the car. Was it waiting for him? Who would be outside his home like that at this hour, or at any hour, for that matter? No one ever came to see him here. He couldn't remember the last time anyone had visited, and it was far too late for it to be business-related.

The car remained dark.

Hit with a violent shiver, Winston hurried to the house and up the porch steps to the front door. As he slid the key into the lock, he glanced back at the car. Nothing had changed. No one got out and the lights remained extinguished.

*It's probably nothing, someone just happened to turn the lights off when I rounded the corner*, he thought. *I need to get in the house before I freeze to death.*

Once inside, Winston engaged a series of locks on the front door. Without turning on any lights, he moved to the front window and looked out at the street.

The car was still there, but from this angle, and with the change in light, he was able to make out a silhouette sitting perfectly still behind the wheel. Far as he could tell, the driver was the lone occupant of the car, but rather than looking at the house, the silhouette faced forward and appeared to be staring straight ahead.

*Maybe it's not there for me at all*, Winston thought, feeling his heartrate slow. *After all, why would it be?*

Still, there was something odd about it. And why hadn't the driver moved so much as a muscle the entire time Winston was watching him?

He knew it was probably silly to remain in darkness and shadow, but there had been a series of late-night home-invasion burglaries in the area over the last few weeks, and as his mother had always said, one could never be too careful when it came to safeguarding against such things. If something *was* going on, Winston didn't want whoever was watching to be able to see inside, so rather than turn on any lights, he activated the flashlight app on his phone and let it guide him through the dark house.

Climbing the stairs, he made his way to his bedroom then extinguished the flashlight. Heart racing, he warily approached the lone bedroom window and took another look.

Everything out there remained the same: cold, dark, and vaguely threatening.

But the car was gone.

# CHAPTER SIX

A DISTORTED VOICE CRACKLED from the radio on the police officer's shoulder. A startling and aggressive sound, it seemed unnecessarily loud and abrupt. With a sigh of disinterested nonchalance, the cop muttered something equally unintelligible into it, his eyes trained on Magdalena throughout.

"Could you turn that down a little, please?" she asked. "It took a while to get my daughter to sleep tonight and I don't want it to wake her."

He stared at her a moment, as if he hadn't quite understood what she'd said. "So," he sighed, fiddling with the unit, "as I was explaining, I checked around outside. I found no sign of a disturbance. Nothing's been compromised or tampered with, and all windows are intact. There's no evidence anyone broke in or even attempted to—none—and since we've got snow on the ground out there, if someone was trespassing on your property they would've left footprints. There were none."

Magdalena wrapped her arms around herself to combat the cold in the room. "I don't understand it," she said. "Then how did those men get in here?"

"I seriously doubt anyone *got in here*. In fact, I'm sure of it."

"But Officer…" Magdalena hesitated. She'd forgotten his name.

"Rutherford," he said before she could read his nametag.

"Officer Rutherford, yes, I'm sorry. You heard the voices."

"What I heard, ma'am, were some voices on a child's toy. Problem is, there's no way to know exactly *when* those recordings were made, or if they were directed toward, or even specifically related to, your child."

"You heard her have an exchange with them. I can play it for you again if—"

"What's to say they didn't come with the stuffed animal?" He flashed a rather condescending smile. "I think there's a good chance your daughter was playing, talking back to prerecorded messages that already existed like *go to sleep* or *clean your room*, that kind of thing."

Magdalena looked at Amanda the Panda sitting on the counter. She'd managed to get it away from Kaley once she'd fallen asleep so she could play it for him. "I didn't even realize the thing had a record function," she told him. "It wasn't until Kaley showed me that if you press one paw it records. The other one stops it and then plays it back. The speaker's in the tummy. She told me she'd heard the men talking to her, but she was half asleep, so she decided to record the voices so she could listen later."

The cop arched an eyebrow. "Is your daughter accustomed to hearing strange voices in her bedroom at night?"

"Of course not, I—"

"Seems to me something like that would terrify a small child, no? Hell, I'm a grown man and if I heard voices I didn't know talking to me in the dark, it'd scare the bejesus out of me."

"Kids are funny sometimes. Kaley sleeps like a log. She said they told her there was no reason to be scared and that she should go back to sleep, I—well—you heard the recording. She doesn't even fully understand how recordings work. She thinks they live in Amanda's tummy. Maybe she was asleep, came awake, and was so out of it she just went back to sleep and didn't wake up until later when she was cold."

The minute the words left her mouth she regretted it, but Magdalena tried to downplay it as best she could.

"It is pretty cold in here," Rutherford said.

"I turned the heat up not long before you got here," she said, hoping he'd bought it. "Unfortunately sometimes these older trailers take a while to warm up."

Rutherford nodded, apparently finding her response acceptable. "Okay, so anyway, I'm just saying it seems unlikely your daughter would've thought to record these men before she drifted back to sleep, see what I mean? Maybe she was playing a game, or maybe those recordings were already on there, came with the toy, and Kaley likes to pretend there are—"

"Yes, I see where you're going with this, I get it."

"But you don't buy it, do you? I can tell from the look on your face."

"I'm just spooked, that's all."

"I understand." Another voice crackled through the unit on Rutherford's shoulder. He turned it down. "But even if there were men in here—which I'm not at all convinced is the case—troubling as that may be, it didn't happen tonight. Now, you mentioned your husband watches your daughter when you work nights?"

"He did, yes, but he's been…away…for a few weeks now. Mrs. Bucci—she lives in the trailer next door—has been taking her during my night shifts recently. But she lives alone."

"Did your husband ever have friends here when he watched Kaley?"

Magdalena shuddered as she remembered the guys Mitch hung out with, usually strangers he befriended at local bars, and how she'd come home from a long night's work to find one or two dozing in a recliner or smoking a joint out in the yard. She'd become so alarmed by this behavior that she'd worried for Kaley's safety and began dropping her with Mrs. Bucci long before Mitch left, though there seemed no reason to share this with the policeman. "His friends did come around when I was at work sometimes, but—"

"Well, there you go then. They could very well be responsible. Or could be that your neighbor had somebody over one of those nights, right? Did your daughter take her toy with her to Mrs.— Sorry, what was her name?"

"Bucci. Yes, she did. Kaley takes Amanda with her everywhere, it's her favorite toy."

"The bottom line is those voices couldn't have been recorded tonight because I checked the trailer top to bottom and there's no one in here but us and your daughter. And outside, there's no evidence anyone's been anywhere near your home. So here's my point. Is it more likely a couple men broke in, completely undetected and without leaving footprints outside in the snow, and were then mistakenly recorded by your daughter while they told her to go back to sleep? Or that those voices were recorded at some earlier point in time and are just your husband's friends or someone that was visiting Mrs. Bucci? Or even that they're some sort of prefab recordings you didn't even realize the toy came with? I know this jarred you, Mrs. Carlino, and understandably so, but if you just stop and think about it, which of those possibilities seems more likely to you?"

"Yes," Magdalena said, forcing a smile. "You're right."

A sudden burst of wind rocked the trailer, causing it to creak then settle.

"Bad out there," Rutherford said. "At any rate, you said yourself the toy was a gift and didn't come new in the box, right? You didn't even realize it had the capability of recording and playing messages. The thing was lying around when you weren't here. Your husband had friends coming and going. Your daughter took it with her to your neighbor's trailer. So who's to say what might have already been on there? We've got a lot of possibilities here, Mrs. Carlino, but I can assure you none of them point to a break-in."

Magdalena held her hands down at her sides, hopeful the policeman wouldn't notice how badly they'd begun to shake. "Okay, well, thank you for—"

"It's creepy, I get it," Rutherford said, drifting toward the door. "Until you realize it's likely all just a silly misunderstanding. Maybe try to relax for the evening, take it easy. Put your feet up, have a cocktail, get a good night of sleep."

She thanked Rutherford again then showed him out. Once she'd closed and locked the door behind him, she fell back against it and hugged herself. The only reason she'd called the police in the first place was to make sure no one had broken in, and now she was certain that hadn't been the case.

But that left only one option. One she'd been hoping against hope she wouldn't have to consider.

*Deep down you already knew*, she thought, trembling. *You just didn't want to.*

Although the voices weren't exact matches, there was no longer any point in denying the cryptic recordings on poor Mrs. Gage's phone had been eerily similar.

Too similar, in fact, to discount.

\* \* \* \*

Wind and rain pummeled the trailer, rattling glass, steel, wood, and aluminum as nearby trees swayed and bent amidst the onslaught. Heavy bursts of icy wind whistled, sending chilly drafts through the poorly insulated windows and turning the trailer even colder. Magdalena didn't mind snow or rain. In fact she liked storms. It was the wind that frightened her most, and even though she'd been through plenty of New England storms in her life—from Nor'easters to hurricanes to blizzards to floods—it was only recently that the area had started to experience small but powerful tornados as well. Prior they'd been almost unheard of in these parts.

Still, even though the park was low income and most units were rundown rentals like theirs, not long after she and Mitch moved in, Mrs. Bucci had told her the area was relatively safe and thankfully not in a flood zone. "Plus you've got a pretty good trailer there, kid," the old woman had told her. "It's older, like mine, and it may not be much to look at, but they built them better back then, that's why they still hold up while the fancy-shmancy ones don't. And don't worry about that old tree out front. It's been around forever, even since before I got here. It bends but never breaks. Might lose a branch now and then, but the tree itself is sturdy, believe you me, it's not going anywhere."

As Magdalena watched the storm through her bay window, that same old tree swayed in the wind. Mrs. Bucci's assurances aside, the damn thing always looked like it was one or two heavy gusts away from toppling over. Fighting her growing anxiety, Magdalena looked away from the towering pine and decided to check on Kaley.

She found her sleeping peacefully, so Magdalena covered her with another blanket, then sat down gently on the side of the bed and stroked her daughter's hair. Kaley stirred, mumbled incoherently, then went quiet and still.

Moments later Magdalena was back in the kitchen. She grabbed a bottle of Jack Daniel's that Mitch had left behind and poured herself a drink. She'd never been a heavy drinker, but she needed to take the stress off, and within seconds of her first few sips, she could feel the warmth of the liquor moving through her.

With a heavy sigh, Magdalena looked at the half empty bottle and a stack of unpaid bills on the kitchen table. That's all that was left of her husband after all the time they'd been together. She'd met him right after high school, and had been immediately taken with him and his whole bad boy motorcycle-riding routine. Little did she know then that he'd come and go in and out of her life for the next several years.

And he'd break her heart every time.

Her marriage to Mitch even derailed her education. Magdalena had always wanted to be a nurse, but because Mitch only had sporadic income, she needed to work, so school had to wait. She got her certification and became a CNA, telling herself it would only be temporary. Once things settled down and Mitch found steady work, she could go back and become an RN. That was several years ago now, and the longer that dream waited, the more it faded away. *Like so much else*, she thought. And now, with these latest rounds of layoffs, she'd even lost that job.

Though the wind kept up, the rain had switched over to snow again. Heavy wet flakes stuck to the windowpanes, and something in the distance cracked, like a branch snapping free from a tree, probably a few lots down.

Her gaze drifted to Amanda the Panda sitting on the table next to her. Hesitantly, she reached for it, remembering the night Mrs. Gage had insisted she take it the moment she'd learned Magdalena had a little girl.

"It belonged to one of my roommates who passed," she'd explained. "Her son got it for her. She wanted me to have it because she knew I thought it was adorable. But I won't be here long, and besides, it just sits on my windowsill. She should be enjoyed, so you take her home to Kaley."

Magdalena stared at the panda. Just a harmless stuffed animal, and yet...

She pressed the play button.

At first, white noise crackled, and then she heard Kaley's sleepy voice.

"What are you doing?" she asked groggily, clearly not fully awake.

"It's all right," a strange electronic-sounding voice answered, robotically and with no discernible emotion. "You need to be quiet now, everything is okay."

"Sleep," a second male voice said, with the same eerily detached and artificial tone.

*What the fuck?* Magdalena thought. *Who sounds like that?*

A spike of fear surged through her as she tossed the toy back onto the table. She finished her drink in a single gulp then poured herself another, but her hands would not stop shaking. After lighting a cigarette, she collapsed into a chair near the bay window.

When Mrs. Gage started experiencing the strange sightings and hearing things, she'd been having trouble sleeping. When even the meds didn't work, Magdalena helped her download an app that monitored her sleep patterns so she might better understand why she was so restless at night. It wasn't unusual for residents struggling with dementia to experience periods of sleeplessness, but when they'd listened to the playback it was obvious she was sleeping more than she'd thought. There were, however, deeply troubling things on the recordings as well.

Strange voices Magdalena had originally chalked up to people on staff coming in and out of the room, sometimes talking quietly when they came in pairs. But the deeper Mrs. Gage fell down the rabbit hole of strange entities watching her from the hallways and phantoms creeping into her room in the middle of the night, the more things the app began to pick up. There were strange bursts of white noise, odd clicking sounds and voices, usually male and always monotone, flat like the ones recorded by the stuffed panda.

In one encounter, Magdalena remembered Mrs. Gage sounding as if she had come awake and asking who was there.

*Sleep,* the voice had said.

*Who are you?*

*Sleep...*

*Why are you here?*

*It's all a dream. Sleep...*

It had frightened her then because, while she couldn't prove it was staff, she thought that very unlikely. She worked the night shift herself and knew everyone on staff, from the nurses to the other CNAs to housekeeping and even the kitchen workers. Not wanting to feed into Mrs. Gage's fear, Magdalena had tried to downplay it, but she made sure the recordings on the old woman's phone were saved. It's why she'd told her son to make sure he took her phone with him. Partly because she didn't want it mistakenly left behind, but the real point had been her hope that at some point George might find the messages and listen to them. Maybe he could make sense of them, though that seemed doubtful.

"Because they don't make any sense," she mumbled.

And now, whatever had come to see that old dying woman had come here as well, to Magdalena's home. They had to be connected, but what could they possibly want?

Wind lashed the trailer. It creaked and moaned, then went quiet.

As a chill coursed through her, Magdalena's eyes slowly panned across the room, watching for things that weren't there, that *couldn't* be there.

*In my house, they—whoever they are—they were in my house, in my child's* room. *And it's my fault—I brought this on us, I—or did they follow me here?*

Either way, they *had* been here. And if they'd managed to get in undetected and without leaving any physical evidence, what was to say they couldn't do that again? Maybe they could do it whenever they wanted to, which meant they could return at any moment and there wasn't a damn thing she could do to stop them.

Or what if they never really left? Could they be here now, hidden?

*No*, she thought. *Officer Rutherford searched the whole place.*

His condescending smile slowly drifted past her mind's eye.

Not that she could blame him. She wasn't even sure *she* believed it.

Whatever *it* was...whatever *this* was.

Magdalena took a drag on her cigarette and snuggled deeper into the chair. From her position she could see out into the night and, with the slightest turn of her head, the entire trailer except for her bedroom and Kaley's.

*It's all right. It's just the two of us here.*

*They come at night*, Mrs. Gage had said, her faced twisted with terror and confusion, those sad eyes filled with uncertainty. *They think I don't see and hear them, but I do.*

The drawings the old woman had made came to Magdalena next. Those horrible, hideous drawings...

Terror filled her, so she took a sip of JD. "Get ahold of yourself, Mags. You're a survivor. You've got to figure this out."

She just wasn't sure she could do it alone.

If anyone could help, it was probably George. He *was* Mrs. Gage's son, after all. But did she have the right to further involve him in this? Would he think she was crazy too? She wondered what he was doing just then. He seemed like such a nice man, broken and suffering, but a good man, a decent man. And even though they'd never met before, there was something uncannily familiar about him. Regardless, maybe he could help.

It felt wrong to pull him into this, but it was also possible he was already involved and simply didn't realize it yet.

Magdalena looked through the window at the night and all the snow blowing about, as inside her an even fiercer storm raged, one of uncertainty and fear, grim anticipation, paranoia, and barely contained panic.

She knew she wouldn't be getting much sleep, if any at all, so she'd just sit with her bottle and her cigarettes and ride out the storm as best she could.

But it was going to be a very long night.

# CHAPTER SEVEN

DESPITE HOW STRESSED AND tired George was, and although the prospect of returning to that empty, maddeningly quiet house was about the last thing he felt like doing, there seemed little else to do at that point but go home. Since leaving the coffee shop he'd driven around aimlessly, perhaps foolishly, in the storm, killing time and putting off the inevitable. He was about to embark on an entirely new chapter in his life, and that, coupled with the odd drawings his mother had made before her death and the disconcerting conversation he'd had with Magdalena, had left him more shaken than he'd originally realized.

Maybe it was all just too much to deal with in a single night.

With a sigh, he set out for home. The drive was as treacherous as the weather suggested, and turned out to be something of a white-knuckle ride through the wind, snow, and freezing rain.

As the commercial streets turned to quieter, darker, more residential parts of town, George struggled to concentrate on the road and keep his mind blank. He didn't want to think any more about it—not his mother's death, the things she'd been experiencing, or the things Magdalena had told him—but those thoughts refused to leave him alone. He couldn't stop them from firing through his mind no matter how hard he tried. It almost felt as if someone, or maybe some*thing*, was preventing him from doing so.

"Ridiculous," he muttered, squinting his eyes and leaning closer to the windshield as the wipers squeaked across the slushy glass. "Don't be absurd."

About five minutes later, George finally reached the side street where he'd lived with his wife, Maureen. Their house, same as the others on their street, was a ranch with a paved narrow driveway, a one-stall garage, a modest, perfectly square patch of front lawn, and a small fenced-in back yard. It sat waiting for him in long shadows, the windows filled with dull yellow light. George was pleased to see the timers he'd installed were working properly. It was hard enough coming home to an empty house, never mind a dark one.

Like the hundreds of other nights when he'd worked the closing shift, George wearily climbed from his car, hurried through the icy rain down the driveway to the mailbox, retrieved the usual stack of bills and advertisement flyers, then crossed the yard to the front door, careful not to lose his footing along the way.

Once inside he hesitated, looked to the living room and imagined Maureen there like she'd been so many nights before.

"There you are," she'd say.

"Here I am," he'd respond, tossing the mail on the kitchen counter. "Where else would I ever want to be?"

"I was worried about you," she'd say. "I always worry until you get home safely, you know that."

"Nothing to worry about," George would say. "I'm here now, safe and sound."

George's eyes locked on the TV on the far wall. Dark, empty, reflecting his image back to him: a sad, disheveled, lonely old man dripping ice and rainwater from his coat. He looked away to the couch, where Maureen would always be curled up, watching a movie or one of her favorite shows. She'd be clad in a nightgown, slippers, and bathrobe, and she'd look over at him and smile the same smile that had dazzled him all those years before when they first met. Then she'd pat the couch cushion and he'd go to her and sit close.

George could almost feel her arms wrap around him as she rested her head on his shoulder and whispered, "I'm so glad you're home."

"Me too," he'd say softly.

She'd raise her head and look at him longingly. "Can I have a *real* kiss now?"

George shuffled into the kitchen, and along with the mail, placed the box of his mother's belongings on the table. He removed his coat, shook it, then hung it in the front closet. He looked back at the empty living room.

*A shower*, he thought. *I'll take a nice hot shower.*

He moved down the hallway and slipped into the bedroom. Something that had once served as a sanctuary was now just another reminder of all that had been lost and how horribly alone he was. From their wedding photographs to later shots of them on vacations or at various points in their life together, the room was a shrine to their marriage, their love. Those things meant the world to him, but now they came with daggers. They *hurt*. They weren't supposed to, but they did.

He settled on a photograph of his mother at the corner of the bureau.

*Such loss,* he thought. *So much death, and yet, I'm still here, left behind. Why?*

At least with his mother, painful as it was, he'd lived his life assuming he'd most likely outlive his parents. But not his wife, never his wife, never Maureen, she was supposed to outlive him.

*And God knows she deserved to.*

Their marriage hadn't been perfect, they'd had their ups and downs like any couple that had been together for decades, but he realized now more than ever just how good it had been.

George turned away from the photos of his wife and mother, his past, and undressed in silence.

Once in the shower and beneath the hot water, he closed his eyes and pretended it was his pain he was washing away. He knew better, of course, but it was a pleasant fantasy.

Maureen's beautiful eyes drifted through his mind.

*I can still feel you with me sometimes,* he thought. *But I know you're gone.*

Maybe he was gone too. Certainly Maureen had taken a big part of him with her to wherever she'd gone.

As they had been for months, his emotions were all over the place, and his sorrow eventually turned to anger. He pushed the water from his eyes and glared down at the shower drain and the water and soap circling it. Wasn't losing the love of his life enough for a while? Couldn't he at least try to recover from that before losing his mother as well? If a greater consciousness existed, surely it was capable of preventing such things. And if that were true, then why hadn't it?

It felt like a punishment, his having to go through this.

George placed his hands on the walls of the shower and let the hot water pound the back of his neck until his rage weakened and dissipated.

But the sorrow refused to let go.

\* \* \* \*

After his shower, George changed into his pajamas. Then he threw on a heavy robe and a pair of slippers and went back out into the kitchen. He grabbed a bottle of beer from the fridge, then sat at the table and stared at the box of his mother's belongings a while. Except for the constant ticking of ice and rain against the windows, and the occasional bursts of strong winds, the house remained deathly quiet. Visions of those hideous drawings blinked in his mind. Those were the last things he wanted to think about just then, so he had a sip of beer and rummaged around in the box a bit, passing over the notepad and instead settling on his mother's cellphone.

He pulled it free of the box and held it in his hand a moment, remembering when he'd gotten it for her. He also recalled the increasingly disturbing calls she made to him from this phone. The more her mind deteriorated, the more confused she'd become, her voice shaking with fear.

*Why am I in this awful place?*

*You need to be, Mom. It's going to be okay.*

*Come and get me, I—I want to get out of this place! I don't belong here!*

*Mom, calm down, you—*

*Why would you do this to me? Why have you abandoned me like this?*

*It's not like that, Mom, I—*

*Why can't I come and live with you and Maureen?*

*Mom, Maureen died.*

*Maureen died? My sister's dead?*

*Maureen was my wife, Mom, your daughter-in-law, not your sister.*

*Please don't leave me here, Georgie. Please come get me.*

*You need to be there because I can't provide you with the care you need. It's not safe for you to be anywhere else. Please try to understand.*

*I don't need any care! I need to get out of here! How could you leave me here?*

Those calls had nearly killed him, and remembering them now broke his heart all over again.

Pushing the memories aside, he made a mental note to call the carrier and have service to his mother's phone disconnected. But he decided to go through the phone first to see if there was anything on it worth saving.

After another sip of beer, he checked the photographs. His mother had never mastered using the camera, but there were a few pictures on the camera roll, so he brought them up and shuffled through them.

The first two shots were what looked like the floor of her room, mostly likely taken mistakenly. The next was a picture of one of her roommates not long before she died. The third was a selfie of his mother and Magdalena. It was a nice picture and centered perfectly, which meant Magdalena had taken it.

*She must've done so during one of the nights she had some time to spend with her,* he thought.

Both women were smiling in the photograph, but even with a smile on her face his mother looked troubled and forgotten. It left George wishing he could go right into that camera and give her a hug, apologize for having to put her in that place and explain again that he'd had no choice.

*Forgive me,* he thought. *Hopefully now you understand.*

He looked at Magdalena. She was an attractive woman, but had an air of sadness about her too. Although young, she had the look of a person for whom life had not been easy. Looking into her eyes now, he remembered how she'd made it a point to tell him not to forget the phone.

George closed the photos and looked through the handful of other apps on the phone, finding nothing of any significance or value.

Until he landed on one titled: SLEEP RECORDINGS

"The hell is this thing?" he mumbled, opening the app.

The heading read: ALL RECORDINGS, and beneath that were four different recordings, numbered and listed in order, by date. The longest was twelve minutes in length. The next was a little over ten minutes, and the last two were one minute and thirty-nine seconds and fourteen seconds in length.

He clicked on the ABOUT button and quickly read a paragraph that explained the app was designed to record while a person was sleeping. It was sound-activated and would come on when there were any discernible sounds, then record until they stopped. The app was designed for people that were experiencing interrupted sleep patterns or general sleeping issues. It allowed them to hear if they were snoring excessively, suffering from sleep apnea, or any other dangerous sleep deprivations.

George knew his mother sometimes had trouble sleeping through the night, which one of her doctors had explained was not that unusual with people in the throes of dementia, but he had no idea she had such an application on her phone, much less actually used it.

Yet he knew there was no way his mother had found this app, downloaded it, and used it on her own. She would've had no idea how to do any of that. She could barely operate the phone as it was. Making a call took her three or four attempts to get the right number, even when George had put his number on speed dial and repeatedly told her which button to press. And it certainly wasn't something that came with the phone, which meant someone had done it for her, and activated it once she'd gone to sleep at least four times.

It had to be Magdalena. The question was why.

*Mrs. Gage was hearing things…*

George's finger hovered over the first recording.

*…voices in the darkness when she was trying to sleep…she was very frightened.*

The look on Magdalena's face and the intensity in those dark eyes when she told him not to forget his mother's phone was jarring even in memory.

*You damn fool,* he thought. *She was trying to tell you something.*

With his free hand he grabbed the beer bottle and took a long drink. Sitting there staring at the phone, George drew a deep breath and let it out slowly.

Then he hit PLAY.

# CHAPTER EIGHT

WINSTON STIFLED A YAWN, closed the science fiction paperback novel he'd been reading and placed it on the table. A cup of steaming hot tea he'd prepared sat before him on a placemat. At the end of each day, after dinner and once the dishes had been done, he and his mother would sit at the kitchen table together and chat over a cup of hot tea. Sometimes they'd read and not say so much as a word for an hour or more. In those quiet moments, simply being with each other had always comforted them both.

Now the place across from Winston sat empty.

As if the incident on the bus and then that strange car parked in front of the house weren't enough, Winston's constant worry for not only his mother's wellbeing, but also his own, had left him exhausted. He was disappointed in himself for allowing such intrusive thoughts to distract and alarm him, especially since they'd caused him to stop reading several times so he could hurry into the front room to check the windows. Each time he found nothing out of the ordinary out there, but he didn't know how to avoid or turn his worries off. They seemed as much a part of him now as his mother's companionship had once been.

The snow had turned to rain and the wind had picked up, causing every little noise to seem suspect. Even those sounds he could easily explain left him rattled.

Winston didn't even want his tea now—not really—but he'd already made it and couldn't let it go to waste. That would be wrong. *Sinful,* his mother called it. *It is absolutely sinful to waste food or drink when there are people starving to death and dying of thirst all over this planet each and every day.*

He blew on the tea then took a sip. His mother always prepared it with a dollop of honey, but he'd run out a few days ago.

*She'd be so disappointed in me,* he thought.

With a sigh, he put down his cup and saucer. It was very late, well past his bedtime, and although he was tired, Winston knew he wouldn't be able to sleep, not with so much on his mind. Every time he closed his eyes he was bombarded with visions of his mother, alone, forgotten and hopelessly lost in the darkest corridors of her muddled, dying mind. And now, since his encounter with the strange man on the bus, his mother's words continued to repeat in his head as well.

*I hear you. I hear you, you bastards.*

It was ridiculous to think that some crazy man on a city bus could be talking about the same deranged ramblings that had spilled from his mother's mouth earlier, but Winston remembered them quite clearly. They were eerily similar.

*You've seen them too, haven't you? Haven't you?*

Why had he assumed Winston knew what he was talking about?

This all seemed so farfetched, so ridiculous.

*You have to listen very carefully*, his mother had told him.

How could some homeless man and Winston's mother share the same disturbing knowledge?

*You have to listen very carefully.*

None of it made a bit of sense.

*If you listen, you can hear them.*

Flashes of the silhouette in the back of the bus as it pulled away came to him next. Winston shook his head. Hard as he tried to make sense of it, he couldn't. He and the other man were the only two passengers on that bus. Of this he was certain. There was the driver, the other man, and himself, period. At that point, any attempts he made to convince himself otherwise required outright denial.

*Then who was it?* What *was it? And regardless, how was it possible?*

Winston sat up straight in his chair.

*I don't sleep anymore*, she'd told him.

He'd been slouching, and his mother didn't approve of that.

*Not with* them *here.*

He took a quick look around the dimly lit kitchen, also taking in as much of the adjacent room as he could.

*They think I don't know they're there, but I do.*

Winston rose to his feet.

*I hear them.*

Had he heard something just then, or was it only the wind and rain slamming the house?

*Sometimes I even see them.*

He did his best to think of something else, something more pleasant, but was unable to concentrate on anything. Until he remembered the man he'd met tonight.

George. What a nice fellow. He was having a bad time too. The poor man had lost his mother only an hour or so before, yet there he was taking time to speak with Winston.

*What will I do when that day comes? When she finally dies, what will I do?*

George could've kept to himself, or talked to the other man on the phone or one of the women behind the counter, but he didn't. He *chose* Winston. And on the very night he'd lost his mother. That had to mean something, didn't it?

*Did he see something in me?*

At the far counter, Winston stopped and stared at a particular drawer.

*You're a sad and pathetic little man, Winston Tucker. He chose you because you were sitting there like the useless blob you are, some nobody he could talk to and never have to see again. He doesn't want to be your friend. No one does.*

It was a drawer he and his mother rarely opened. In fact, he couldn't even remember the last time he'd opened it, that's how long it had been. But he'd been thinking about doing so for some time. Unlike the other drawers, cabinets, and cupboards in the kitchen, it only housed a single item.

Before he could change his mind, he stepped forward and opened the drawer.

And there it was, just as he knew it would be.

As Winston gazed at the old revolver, something deep inside him shifted; something instinctual and darkly primal. With a trembling hand, he reached in and picked it up.

The gun was heavy and alien, some foreign *thing* that didn't belong in his grasp. His mother had owned the gun since Winston was a little boy, having purchased it when his father left. She'd always said she disliked guns and didn't really want one in the house, but she was a woman alone with a young boy, and she believed it was a necessary evil in today's world.

*Today's world*, he thought. He could almost hear her say that.

As far as Winston knew, his mother had never fired it. He hadn't either. He was relatively certain no one had.

*It wouldn't be so difficult really.*

This was not the first time Winston had considered anything so drastic, but it was the first time he'd taken it this far.

*You know exactly what you're thinking about doing, don't deny it.*

Winston tried to convince himself it was because of everything that had happened, and the things running through his mind nonstop. But it wasn't quite that simple.

*You've been thinking about this more and more every day.*

Before his mother became ill she'd have never forgiven such a thing. Now, well, she wouldn't even understand what had happened. The nurses and doctors could explain it to her endlessly and she still wouldn't get it.

*You could do it right now.*

And even if she did, it would be short-lived. She'd never fully comprehend it. How could she process the suicide of her only child when more than half the time she didn't recognize him when he was standing right in front of her?

*You could put it to your temple or in your mouth and pull the trigger.*

Wind crashed against the house.

*You could spray your brains all over her lovely rooster-filled kitchen, and no one would care. No one would even notice you were gone, much less miss you.*

Winston knew his body wouldn't be found for quite a while. Maybe once a few of his work contracts started getting antsy because of a lack of communication, or if the nursing home realized he hadn't been there in a while, or when some of the bills weren't paid, maybe then someone might make an attempt to find out what was wrong. But that would take weeks, possibly even months, and God only knew how much longer it might be before the authorities actually came and checked the house.

"What am I supposed to do?" he muttered, embarrassed by the weakness in his voice. "I don't know what to do."

*You can't make it by yourself.*

He wasn't even sure he wanted to.

And now strange things were happening. The man on the bus, the silhouette of someone who couldn't be there, the car out front, the strange things his mother had said that clearly connected to the crazed man's ramblings. That was bad enough, but what if the explanation for it was more horrifying than anything he could imagine?

*Dementia is often hereditary.*

He'd read that, spent hours researching it and trying to understand. Could it be that his mind had become infected with the same insidious disease that was ravaging his mother's brain?

*Maybe that's all this is, confusion due to an early onset of dementia.*

Suddenly lightheaded, Winston returned the revolver to the drawer and steadied himself against the counter until the dizzy spell was gone.

*Do it, you little wimp. Pick it up again and do it this time.*

He stared at the gun.

But when his mother's face came to him, twisted with emotion, her eyes begging him not to do anything so horrific, Winston slid shut the drawer and, riddled with guilt and shame, forced himself back to the kitchen table.

*Try to get through tonight*, he told himself. *You need rest.*

He sank back into his chair and placed his hands on either side of the teacup. The warmth was soothing.

His thoughts returned to the gun, and just how close he'd come to taking his life. Until tonight he'd thought about it—seriously even—but he'd never taken it any further. He'd never opened the drawer. He'd never held the gun in his hand.

*What if next time—*

In a sudden crazed rush, a wave of emotion struck him with such violence he put his head on the table and wept uncontrollably.

When it was finally over, Winston wiped his eyes then staggered over to the sink and poured what remained of his tea down the drain. He wanted to throw the cup and saucer against the wall or down to the floor. He wanted them to shatter into pieces. But he couldn't bring himself to do it.

Placing the cup and saucer carefully in the sink, he looked at them a while. Was he really going to leave them there without washing them? How scandalous. His mother always said dishes should be done and the kitchen cleaned before bed because no one should wake up to either.

*I'm a grown man. I can do whatever I like.*

With a sigh, Winston ran the water, rinsed them out, then dried and put them away in the appropriate cupboard.

Once he'd neatly folded the dishtowel and returned it to its proper place over the stove handle, he shut the lights off and stood in the dark kitchen a moment.

*Maybe I should try to get some sleep. I could at least try.*

What was it his mother had said earlier about sleep?

*I don't sleep. I just wait.*

He could do the same. He could just wait.

*You have to listen very carefully.*

He did listen.

The hum of the refrigerator…the tick of an old nearby wall clock…the wind and rain battering the house…the slow and steady cadence of his breathing…

Was that all?

Or was there something more…there…just beyond his comprehension?

Still leaning against the counter, Winston slowly sank down onto the floor and sat there watching the darkness and shadows drift through this old house he knew so well.

And though he couldn't define it, or even explain it, for the first time since they'd taken his mother away, Winston felt like he might not be alone within the walls of the only home he'd ever known.

# CHAPTER NINE

ICE CLICKING AGAINST THE window in heavy sprays tore Magdalena from sleep. Despite being convinced she'd never be able to nod off, she'd apparently done just that.

*Too much Jack Daniel's can do that to a girl*, she thought, *among other things.*

Liquor usually gave her bad dreams, especially when she was younger, and tonight had been no exception. She'd dreamed of running through a snowy forest, avoiding tangled, low-hanging branches, brambles, and weeds, as an eerie mist rose from the earth. Overhead, barely visible through the dark treetops, ravens soared, screeching as if in agony.

She didn't know how she knew, but Magdalena was certain she was being chased deeper into the stormy night by dark unseen *things*, their voices not human but whispering to her from *inside* her head.

As they came into view in the night sky, a feeding frenzy of black flapping wings and whirling snow, the screams of the damned echoed through the forest and she stopped dead in her tracks.

A piercing pain in the bend of her arm, and then the smell of burning flesh filled her nostrils, death wafting closer.

Blood and gore exploded all around her, bone and tissue blending with the icy snow and rain.

Magdalena screamed and stumbled away, her hands running over her body frantically to make sure she was still intact. But as she staggered through the darkness, it was Kaley she thought of, not herself.

"Are you all right?" she called out. "Kaley—baby—where are you?"

*She's ours as much as you are...*

Magdalena nearly fell, spinning back toward that horror she hoped to never have to see again. But this was her *child* it was talking about.

"If you so much as *think* about my daughter," she screamed into the night, trying to maintain her balance in the wind, "I'll kill you! Do you hear me? I'll fucking kill you!"

*Do you see them, Magdalena? Tell us what you see...*

Magdalena ran for the trailer. When she finally reached it and burst through the door, she closed and locked it behind her then fell back against it in an attempt to catch her breath.

*Kaley*, she thought. *I have to check on Kaley.*

Why then did she retrieve the card the policeman had left instead, grab her cell and call the number with shaking hands?

"Rutherford," a man answered.

"Officer, I—something's in the woods and I—"

A burst of white noise replied, followed by a string of undecipherable words that sounded more artificial than human.

"Officer Rutherford, are you there?"

*"Sleep, Magdalena."*

The next thing she remembered was coming awake in the chair. It took her a moment to realize she was awake, but when she did she let out a heavy sigh of relief. "Jesus Christ," she whispered, bringing a hand to her face. She listened to the storm a moment, and then looked around, grateful to see the power hadn't gone out. If it held until daylight, at least she could make coffee and cook her daughter some breakfast.

Remnants of the nightmare blinked through her mind, but as Magdalena's head cleared and the distance between the waking world and the realm of dreams widened, her thoughts turned to more practical things. Come morning, maybe she'd check to see if she qualified for emergency heating assistance. She vaguely recalled Mrs. Bucci telling her she'd been getting it on and off for a few years. Surely a single mother, now unemployed and with a small child, could qualify.

But for now it was still cold in the trailer, colder than it should've been. Magdalena shivered, and guiltily thought of the prospect of expecting Kaley to spend even one more day without heat.

*The hell with pride*, she thought. *If there's help out there, I'm getting it.*

The clock on the kitchen counter read: 1:28 a.m. She remembered glancing at the time around midnight, just after she'd last checked on Kaley and had then settled back in her chair and had yet another glass of JD.

Had she really slept for over an hour?

A soft murmur emerged from her daughter's room. Her eyes shifted to Amanda the Panda, still where she'd left her on the table. It was probably just Kaley, but fear momentarily froze her in place as sounds of the storm intensified. A lamp flickered on then off. The trailer rattled and what sounded like a stray cat howling erupted somewhere not far outside her window.

A gust of wind shook the trailer, and Magdalena turned, noticing the rickety bookcase on the nearby wall, a thing that Mitch had picked up at a flea market a few months before.

"Something where you can stack all those books you've got," he'd said. "I'll paint it and fix the shelves, tighten everything up so it's not so shaky. It'll look nice."

Of course, he never did any of those things, and the last burst of wind had shaken it so badly a coin tumbled from one of the shelves to the floor. A penny Kaley had found the day prior; she'd nestled it between a paperback and a small figurine for safe keeping. Finding the penny had cheered Kaley up after she'd been disappointed during their trip to the local thrift store that day. Magdalena had been searching for bargain books to read to Kaley before bed, but when Kaley spotted a small doll sitting atop the store's worn shelves, a vintage doll dressed in a tattered cape and a black lace dress with hems frayed, she wanted that instead of a book.

Even at a discounted price, Magdalena couldn't afford it. "Maybe next time, okay?" she said, her heart breaking. "Today I can only get you a book."

Tears filled Kaley's eyes as she chose a book, one about elves and fairies that lived in a magical forest. She was always such a good kid, and it killed Magdalena to have to deny her something most people could've easily afforded. But there was nothing she could do. Not yet.

As they headed for the car, Magdalena desperately searching for some way to make it up to her, Kaley spotted a shiny new penny in the parking lot. Her face lit up, excited the way only small children get over seemingly inconsequential things.

"Look, Mommy!" Kaley said, squatting down to pick it up. "It's a penny!"

"Awesome!" she said, playing along. "And it looks brand new too."

Kaley nodded, smiling as she held it up for her mother to see. "Mrs. Bucci says that when you find a penny it means angels are watching over you."

But now, as that same shiny penny rolled toward Magdalena, stopping when it reached her right foot and falling onto its side, there was something almost menacing about it.

*Those aren't angels, honey...*

Magdalena rose from her chair, picked up the penny, and looked it over.

*Nothing to be afraid of,* she thought. *It's the same penny as before.*

She placed it back on the shelf and was about to check on Kaley again when she heard something outside. A voice—she was sure of it—muffled by distance and the storm, but a voice nonetheless.

Moving quickly, she went to the kitchen, grabbed a steak knife from the counter, and crept back toward the windows. Staying just to the side of them, she squinted, watching the darkness.

And then, once again, there came the unmistakable sound of a voice.

"Here, kitty…"

A familiar voice but not quite right…

"Come on, Gypsy, you're all wet."

Magdalena leaned closer to the blurred window. The lot was dark, but there were lights on in Mrs. Bucci's trailer. That wasn't unusual, even at this time of night, since she tended to keep some lights on regardless of the hour. Sometimes it was because the old woman often had trouble sleeping, and sometimes, Mrs. Bucci once explained, keeping a few lights on made her feel safer at night.

"Come on, kitty."

Suddenly, a single outside lantern flickered on a few feet away from Magdalena's trailer. It hadn't worked in months, something else Mitch had promised to fix but never did. Yet now the dull yellow light had come on, casting a sickly glow over the area, enough to reveal a figure bent over just outside Mrs. Bucci's trailer.

It was hard to make out much detail, but Magdalena saw a hand gently patting a small black shape she recognized as Mrs. Bucci's cat, Gypsy. That voice, though, it wasn't Mrs. Bucci, but a man's.

"Come inside now," the figure said, slowly lifting the cat into its arms.

Magdalena could only make out a silhouette, but it was definitely a man's.

"Come out of the storm, you're soaked," the man said, as from inside Mrs. Bucci's trailer her phone began to ring. "I think that crazy woman's calling again."

Heart racing, Magdalena watched as the figure moved toward Mrs. Bucci's trailer, but then another gust of wind struck, plastering her windows with icy slush, and the dull yellow light went out, plunging everything back into darkness.

Unsure of what to do, Magdalena waited, watching the night. Should she call Mrs. Bucci? What if she was mistaken? Maybe someone was staying the night for some reason and had simply gone out to bring Gypsy inside or—

*Sleep…*

Behind her, from Kaley's room, came the sound of shuffling footsteps. Magdalena whipped around, knife in hand, and charged for her daughter's bedroom.

She burst into the room, the knife raised.

There was no one there but Kaley, who lay sound asleep in bed, cuddled up in her blankets.

*I'm losing it*, Magdalena thought. *I'm losing my mind.*

And then from behind her, black wings exploded from the darkness, wrapping around her and yanking her back against whatever stood there in the shadows.

Paralyzed with fear, she tried to lift the knife, to attack whatever had a hold of her, but she couldn't move, couldn't even scream. Even when she felt its hot putrid breath against the side of her face and its grip tighten.

"*Please*," she gasped. "Don't hurt my child."

*Sleep…*

She closed her eyes, and when they reopened she was back in her chair in front of the windows.

"Get away!" she snapped, flailing about.

But she was alone.

Magdalena tumbled from the chair, landed on her feet, and whirled around, looking for the intruder. Until she realized she'd been dreaming the entire time, and had only thought she'd woken up. Out of breath and covered in a thick sheen of perspiration despite the cold, she looked to the windows.

No dull yellow light. No silhouette. No Gypsy.

She opened her hands. No steak knife.

*Kaley!*

Magdalena ran to her daughter's room. Just as in the dream, she was sound asleep and bundled up under numerous blankets.

Still shaking, Magdalena carefully crawled into bed next to Kaley, pulling the blankets in tight around them. Her daughter let out a soft murmur then snuggled closer.

*It's going to be all right*, Magdalena told herself. *It's going to be all right.*

But she couldn't be sure if she was trying to convince herself, or the things she feared were still hiding just beyond the shadows and in the darkest corners of her soul.

# CHAPTER TEN

GEORGE BROUGHT THE BOTTLE to his lips and took a long drink. The cold beer felt good going down, ironically rather sobering, given the situation. Placing the bottle back on the table, he eyed his mother's phone. He'd listened once to the recordings the sleep app had made, and the prospect of listening again wasn't exactly something he was looking forward to. But he knew he had to do it.

A harmless phone had now become an ominous instrument of fear and paranoia, because the things contained within it, the things he'd heard, couldn't be right. Whatever his mother had experienced in her last nights in that nursing home was not normal. It couldn't be. The things he heard on those recordings had to be some sort of anomaly, a mistake, something taken wildly out of context or—

*The last few weeks she said she was seeing and hearing things.*

Glancing around the kitchen, at the windows and darkness beyond, George did his best to ignore the tension building from deep within him. He was alone in the house, yet the same feeling he'd experienced earlier was back, and stronger than before. An uncanny sensation of being watched—*observed*—that he couldn't shake.

*Why are you doing this to yourself? Go to bed, you're exhausted, try to sleep.*

George opened the sleep app again.

*Mom's only been gone a few hours,* he thought. *You're still processing that and not in the right frame of mind to handle this bullshit right now, much less look into it or make any sort of judgments.*

His finger hovered over the link to one of the recordings.

The two longest segments, which totaled approximately twelve minutes on one and a little over ten minutes on the other, were almost exclusively sounds on the unit that had triggered the app. Recorded first, they offered nothing unusual, just various segmented recordings of machines beeping, call alarms sounding, carts rolling along the hallway, and several episodes of his mother snoring or moaning softly in her sleep. The only voices either had picked up were what sounded like nurses or

CNAs chatting as they walked by the room or came in to check on her throughout the night. George suspected Magdalena was still perfecting its use at that point, and had eventually figured out how to either better position the phone or fine-tune the app, because the last two recordings, while significantly shorter, were the ones that had rattled him.

He hit PLAY.

This recording, the third, contained a few segments that totaled only a minute and thirty-nine seconds. The first several times it came on to record, it was the same as the first two recordings, nothing unusual. But then the second to last segment—which ran just over nineteen seconds—began with his mother's voice. She sounded so groggy George assumed she was either half asleep or had been disturbed somehow and was talking while still deeply asleep.

"Who are you?" she asked, words slurred.

"Sleep," a strange artificial-sounding male voice answered in monotone.

"I thought...I was asleep."

"Sleep..."

"What are you doing to me?"

"Sleep," a second male voice said.

This was followed by another quick segment that only lasted five seconds. George could hear the emotionless male voices again, but this time the words were muffled, garbled, and he couldn't figure out what they were saying.

The rest of the segments on that recording were normal, explainable sounds and noises.

George finished his beer and hit PLAY on the final recording.

This one was only fourteen seconds in length, but it had a single recording on it. Again, the app had come on very late at night, and his mother had either been partially awakened by the intruders or was talking to them in her sleep.

"You think I can't see you," his mother said, in a quiet, singsong voice. "But I can. I *can* see you."

"Sleep," one of the same flat male voices responded.

"Why are you here?" his mother asked, the tone of her voice becoming more agitated and afraid. "You don't...you don't *belong* here."

"*Sleep...*"

The recording ended, but George left the app open. Slumped in his chair at the kitchen table, he stared at the phone, still trying to make sense of this.

With a sigh, he pushed himself up and back to his feet. But he was still unsure of what to do or think, so he paced a bit by the sink. Finally, he returned to the table, closed the app, and tossed the phone back into the box with his mother's other things.

George grabbed another beer from the fridge, twisted off the cap, and took a long pull. "Okay," he said. "Okay, use your head, think. Two people, both male, using some kind of device, talking to her in the middle of the night, they—they must be staff, right? They have to be. Who else would be there at that hour?"

*I'll give that place a call, get ahold of the administrator and play these for him,* George thought. *Then he can explain to me what the hell these two men were doing in my mother's room talking nonsense to her in the middle of the night.*

Clearly the voices were human. Weren't they? Void of any emotion and kind of robotic, maybe they were just jokers disguising their voices for some reason.

*You're letting the things Magdalena told you and those drawings Mom made frighten you,* he thought. *Calm down. Think rationally.*

Fine, so if they were just a couple weird staff members, what in God's name were they doing in her room?

*Sleep…*

Why did it all seem so oddly, vaguely familiar?

"The hell was going on in that place?" he muttered.

Anger slowly began to overtake his fear. Who were these men? Certainly they weren't doctors, so what the hell were they doing in his mother's room in the middle of the night? How were they able to do that without any staff noticing or hearing them? And if they were, in fact, staff members, why were they there at such a late hour, and what were they doing hovering around his mother's bed to the point that they at least partially awakened her?

*Whatever they were up to, they wanted her to sleep through it,* George thought. *I should get a lawyer and sue their asses. I'll own that place.*

The entire thing was ludicrous.

Taking his beer with him, George drifted into the living room. He was still too wired to sit down, so he wandered around the room, trying to figure out what to do, what to think, how to react. He'd never been an indecisive man. He prided himself on being in control. He was rational, practical, realistic, a man not easily rattled or prone to flights of fantasy. He believed in science, and was skeptical of things that go bump in the night and silly ghost stories. Yet now he found himself reeling, his mind a jumble of disjointed thoughts and unspecified fears.

A photograph on the wall caught his attention. He'd taken it, and had a clear memory of the day he'd done so. One of his favorite photographs, it featured his mother and his wife together, sitting out on the back deck on a beautiful summer day. Both smiling at the camera and looking vibrant, healthy and happy.

Two years later, they'd both be gone.

It hit him again. She really was gone. They both were.

*You think I can't see you. But I can.*

"What happened to you in that place?" he asked the woman in the photo.

*I can see you.*

"What did they do to you?"

Magdalena had told him his mother had said, "Tell him to listen. You tell my Georgie to listen...so he can hear."

George reached out and touched the photograph, his fingertip resting against his mother's cheek. "I'm trying, Mom. I'm trying to listen. What were you telling me? What did you want me to hear?"

*Were you abused by these people? Was this the only way your crippled mind could make sense of it and tell me?*

His mother's smiling face gave no answer.

The storm raged on, spraying the windows with icy rain.

George turned away. He couldn't look at her any longer without the emotion welling up in the base of his throat.

He guzzled down the remainder of his beer, then set the bottle down on the coffee table just as his phone began to ring.

Startled, George whirled around and hurried back into the kitchen, but his phone was where he'd left it on the counter, the screen dark.

The ringing was coming from the box on the kitchen table where he'd just tossed his mother's phone. Incredulous, he snatched it up and checked the screen.

UNKNOWN CALLER

*Who the hell is calling her phone at this hour?*

George accepted the call, but didn't say anything. The line was quiet.

"Hello?"

Silence...

"Is someone there? Who's calling? Do you have any idea what time it is?"

A sudden shriek exploded through the phone.

Recoiling, George jerked his head back and away from the sound.

As the phone dropped and bounced along the tile floor, he brought a hand to his ear. The shriek was so piercing it had left that entire side of his head ringing.

*What do you see, George? What are you hearing?*

And then, just as suddenly, the shrieking stopped, taking the strange questions filling his head along with it.

But another sound emanated from the phone now.

Heart racing, George closed on the phone and, with shaking hands, picked it up. His ear was still buzzing, so this time he hit the speaker function.

Odd sounds burst forth, eerie electronic sounds, pulses and beats followed by pops of static, white noise, and what could only be described as *growls*.

From somewhere deep within those sounds, as if trapped and lost in the storm of static and pulses, George swore he could hear a distant voice speaking. But it was so faint he couldn't make out any specific words.

"Who is this?" he snapped. "Who's there? Answer me!"

Just as suddenly, what sounded like human screams bellowed from the speaker, cries of horror wrapped within a chorus of alien electronic noises and bursts of deafening static.

And then, through the chaos, a single whispered word…

*Sleep…*

There, then gone so quickly; he immediately questioned whether he'd actually heard it at all as another round of white noise followed. He hadn't activated the feature, yet the phone vibrated, startling him so badly he nearly dropped it again.

Managing to hang onto the phone, George watched as the screen went dark and the call disconnected. He checked the call register, clicked RECENT, and pulled up the last incoming call.

UNKNOWN NUMBER

It felt like an electrical charge was crackling through his veins, and the shaking in his hands quickly became a trembling throughout his entire body.

He put the phone down, this time leaving it face-up on the table rather than in the box, and watched the black screen, waiting for it to ring and come to life again.

It didn't.

*She was very frightened.*

George found his way back into the living room.

*Magdalena, my mother wasn't in her right mind.*

He collapsed onto the couch and put his face in his hands.

*She was afraid.*

Wind rocked the house.

*Yes, you said that.*

George dropped his hands. His eyes shifted, looked in the direction of the kitchen.

*She had a phone.*

He listened.

*Don't forget to take it with you.*

Heart still racing, George closed his eyes and took a few deep breaths. He needed sleep desperately, but that seemed unlikely.

Regardless, at least for tonight, the couch would have to do.

*Try to think clearly*, he told himself. *What in the world is going on here?*

Whatever had happened—whatever *was* happening—had nothing to do with abusive staff members, lawyers, or nursing home administrators. He knew that now.

This was something else. Something…more…

And he needed to get to the bottom of it.

Visions of Magdalena came to him, standing in his mother's room at the nursing home, and how she sounded so nervous and uncomfortable. How she looked so…*frightened.*

He just needed to get himself through tonight, because once the light of a new day dawned, George knew exactly what he was going to do.

# CHAPTER ELEVEN

THE ICY RAIN AND heavy winds from the night before had stopped at dawn. Since then, the temperature had plummeted, locking everything down in a deep freeze.

Magdalena pulled into the driveway of her friend Esther Jarrett's house. She stared at the dark Cape Cod, its shades drawn tight, and wondered if she'd made a mistake coming here. A former coworker and career CNA that had trained Magdalena, Esther not only knew every inch of Matheson Manor, she knew the business inside and out. Despite her personal problems, Esther was by far the best CNA Magdalena had ever known. She was also a no-nonsense person with a low threshold for bullshit. Though tough as nails, Esther had a big heart and a great, albeit sometimes dark, sense of humor.

She'd also abruptly left her job at Matheson without explanation nearly a week before. Completely out of character for a senior CNA that had weathered numerous storms at work for more than a decade, she'd seen enough adversity and bad days within those nursing home walls to last a lifetime, and she'd never buckled. She always survived.

Until one night shift Magdalena had taken off because she wasn't feeling well. When she went in the next night, she learned that Esther had quit, left right in the middle of her shift, walked off the unit and gone home.

Magdalena had tried calling her several times, but it always went straight to voicemail. She left numerous messages but none were returned. Eventually, she started getting a message saying the line was no longer in service. At the time, Magdalena had decided to give her some space, unsure of what exactly had happened, but now she felt a bit guilty for not stopping by to check on her sooner.

And she couldn't help but wonder if Esther's sudden departure had something to do with what was going on.

*Whatever that is*, she thought.

Magdalena remembered the conversation she had with Joan Irving, a fellow CNA she'd known for a few years, the day after Esther quit. She found her in the break room having a cup of coffee just prior to their shift.

"Joan," Magdalena said, sliding into the chair next to her, "what the hell happened with Esther last night?"

Joan kept her voice low, not wanting others nearby to hear her. "I don't know, Mags. She just walked out, quit right on the spot. Cleared out her locker and bolted."

"I've been trying to call her but it keeps going right to voicemail."

"I ran into her in the hallway when she was leaving and I knew something was wrong. I could tell from the look on her face. Like she seen the Devil or something, for real. So I tried to calm her down, get her to talk to me, fill me in on what was going on, you know? But she just kept walking and mumbling something about how she couldn't take it anymore and she was done."

"She didn't say what was wrong? Did she have an argument with someone or—"

"I don't think it was anything like that." Joan sipped her coffee and combed a wisp of dirty-blonde hair behind her ear with a finger. "I talked to a couple girls at the nurse's station on her unit. They said she lost her shit and there was no talking to her. Happened out of the blue, they said. Like something spooked her so bad she couldn't deal with it."

"Spooked? *Esther*? She's not afraid of anything."

"I know, right?"

"Did they say anything else? Did Esther?"

"Girl, all I can tell you is I never seen her like that before. To be honest, outside of a horror movie I ain't never seen *nobody* like that. And I hope I never do again. She was scared, Mags, *really* scared."

As the memory of Joan's troubled face faded, Magdalena rubbed her eyes. They were sore and burning and heavy from a decided lack of sleep.

*Why did you leave without an explanation, Esther? What scared you that bad?*

A part of her wanted to just back out of the driveway and forget this.

"Fuck it." She lit a cigarette, gathered her composure, and took several quick puffs before crushing the cigarette in the ashtray. "If Kaley's in danger, I need to find out what's going on."

She glanced once more at the old Cape, noting the handful of newspapers piled up on the front step. To look at the dark house and small property it sat on, one would think no one even lived there anymore.

With no idea how she'd be received, or if the house had been abandoned, Magdalena stepped out of the car into the bitter cold and hurried to the front door.

She rang the bell, but no one answered. Seconds from ringing it again, she heard the sudden sound of coughing and approaching footfalls.

The door opened slowly, and the smell of liquor and spoiled food wafted toward her. Esther—in sweatpants and a pajama top stained with what looked like spaghetti sauce and oil—stumbled into view. An attractive woman in her early forties, with wavy red hair and startling green eyes, the lines in her face and around her mouth looked deeper than the last time Magdalena had seen her, and her once beautifully styled hair was pinned up sloppily.

"Mags, that you?" she said, eyes squinting against the daylight as if she hadn't been exposed to it in a while.

"Hi," Magdalena said awkwardly, trying not to react to the smell. "I've—"

"What are you doing here?" Drunk, Esther swayed in the doorway, her words slurred. Although she offered a relieved smile, her eyes told a different story.

They were filled with terror.

Magdalena knew Esther liked her vodka, and often talked about going out to small clubs on the weekends she didn't work—*Couple adult beverages and a few dances with a guy or two, then I head home. Most times alone, sometimes with company. Just do it to unwind.*

"I wanted to—"

"Come in out of the cold. Christ, fucking freezing out here." She swung an arm between them, apparently designating the area as *out here.*

Magdalena gently took hold of her arm in an attempt to steady her as they stepped inside and closed the door behind them.

"Are you all right?" Esther asked.

"They laid me off yesterday."

"Rotten fuckers, tell me Denise doesn't still have a job."

Magdalena couldn't help but smile. Denise was an infamously lazy and disagreeable CNA they'd worked with that no one liked. "They let her go too."

"Okay, so at least something good happened then. You get your unemployment?" She wagged a finger at her. "You make sure you get your unemployment."

"Are *you* all right? I've been calling and meaning to stop by, but—"

"Don't worry about it."

"Maybe we should get you some coffee."

"And ruin this perfectly good drunk? Hell's wrong with you?" Esther pulled away, yanking her arm free. "Don't worry about me, kid. I've been on worse binges than this one."

"Why are you binging? What's wrong? What happened at work, why did you quit like that? They said you just walked off the unit with no explanation."

"Sometimes breaking open a few bottles of vodka helps take the edge off," Esther said, as if she hadn't heard her. She directed Magdalena to the living room, where empty food containers and spent bottles of vodka were piled on the coffee table and on an end table by an overstuffed chair.

"Stolichnaya and Beluga Noble," Magdalena said in an attempt to lighten the mood. "Keeping the Russians in business, I see."

Esther laughed lightly, almost sadly. "Hey, I ever tell you about that Russian dude I dated back in the day? Bastard was sexy as hell and mean as could be. *The Madonna and Child* tattoo on my back, it's a thieves' amulet—Russian—means that you're a child of prison—been a criminal from an early age. Got it to match his, can you believe it? The stupid shit we do when we're young, huh?" She leaned closer and put a hand next to her mouth, as if to block others from hearing. "That tattoo actually has a deeper meaning too, which I would explain to you, but you don't know about that part of my past, so I won't."

Magdalena remembered seeing the tattoo when Esther changed out of her scrubs a few times at the nursing home. There were others too, psychedelic designs on her arms and legs. "That Russian, is he still around?"

"He got killed, drug deal gone wrong a couple years after we split up." She stared not at Magdalena, but beyond her at nothing. Or perhaps things only her memories could provide. "He was a piece of shit, but I loved him. I would've gone down with him if I'd stuck around."

At the nursing home, Esther had joked about men she'd met when she frequented the clubs, trying to comfort Magdalena when Mitch had left and trying to get her to go with her. It was just a small slice of Esther's personal life she'd revealed, and even then, the details were sparse. This was the first she'd heard of a dead Russian boyfriend.

"Better to be a solo act, that's what I think," Esther slurred. "Besides, men are slobs too, and I like a tidy house, don't need someone crapping up my digs."

Ironic, since the house was far from tidy at the moment. The furniture hadn't been dusted in a while and the floor was littered with dirty clothes and scattered scraps of paper, a discarded shopping list, strange geometric drawings—probably doodles absently constructed in

Esther's drunken stupor—and there was a stale smell permeating the whole place. This woman had always been a neat freak. What happened?

Esther waved at a couch that was littered with what appeared to be reasonably recent cigarette holes in the upholstery. "Sit down. Can I get you anything?"

Magdalena shook her head and, after finding a safe spot, sat on the couch. "I'm fine, thanks. I just need to talk to you."

"Yeah," she said through bleary eyes. "I bet."

"What's wrong, Esther? What happened at work, why did you quit?"

Esther flopped into an overstuffed chair, arms and legs dangling, her hair popping loose from the pins. Her eyes darted to the shaded windows, and then she put a finger to her lips. "Had the phone shut off," she said. "I'm tired of being harassed."

"Who's harassing you?"

Esther shrugged, wouldn't look at her.

"Joan told me when you left Matheson you just stormed out all of a sudden."

"*Joan*," Esther said through a brief, quiet, drunken laugh. "Sweet kid, but she looks like a rodent. Seriously, tell me she doesn't look like a fucking rodent. And the poor thing's got the brains to match."

Magdalena offered an obligatory smile. "She's worried about you too, you know."

"Sorry, I…" Esther pawed at her eyes.

"What happened at the nursing home, Esther?"

"*You* tell me, kid. Looks like you haven't slept much yourself."

"I've had a tough time lately."

Esther nodded, as if she'd just remembered. "You're better off without that loser Mitch. Same as I was better off without Pavel the crazy Russian."

"I'm not here about Mitch."

"No?" she smirked. "Then what are you here about, Mags?"

"I wanted to make sure you were all right."

"I'm fabulous, as you can plainly see. What else you got, kid?"

Magdalena sat forward, hoping to focus Esther up. "I don't know if I'm going nuts, but somebody may have broken into my trailer and tried messing with my kid."

"Somebody tried to hurt Kaley?" Concern washed over Esther's face.

"I've got to know what's going on, Esther, and maybe I'm wrong, but I have a gut feeling you have the answers I need. You were at Matheson so long, you saw so much."

"Too long," she said softly.

"I don't want you to think I'm crazy, but—"

"Kid, I'm so drunk right now you could tell me you turned water into wine and I'd ask for the recipe. Knock yourself out."

"I called the police. The officer treated me like I was insane."

"Well, fuck him then. Shit, I dropped acid fourteen times when I was younger. Saw God once. He was just standing there looking at me from the bedroom doorway. By the way—you heard it here first—he kinda looks like Pee-wee Herman. Go figure. Point is, I've just about seen and heard it all, so go ahead and hit me." Esther reached for a nearby bottle of Stolichnaya, opened it then took a long drink. "I got all day." She wiped her mouth, still clutching the bottle with her other hand. "What's going on?"

"You remember Mrs. Gage, we—"

"Yeah," she said, "sweet old girl."

"Yes, she was. She passed. You know we sort of got close."

"You had a soft spot for her, it happens."

"She was hearing things, seeing things."

"I saw the drawings."

"You saw those?"

Esther nodded. "She was drawing them one night and dropped the pad, couldn't reach it from bed, so she hit her call button and I was the first one to show up. I picked it up for her, saw what was on there and asked her why she was drawing scary stuff. She said they were in the hallways at night, in her room."

"You never told me."

"Figured you'd bring it up if it was something you wanted to talk about."

"It was upsetting her so bad I got her this sleep app for her phone," Magdalena explained. "And it recorded these...voices."

Esther had another pull of vodka then rested the bottle in her lap.

"She said it was them."

"And did you believe her?" Esther asked.

"I do now."

"What convinced you?"

"She had this little stuffed panda. When she heard about Kaley, she insisted I take it and give it to her. She didn't mean any harm, she was just happy to hear I had a daughter and thought she'd enjoy it. So I gave it to her. I had no idea the thing had a recording device inside it. It's just a toy, meant for kids to be able to make recordings the panda can play back and—"

"Now they're on there too, the same voices." Esther cocked her head, as if she'd heard something in the distance. "Aren't they?"

Magdalena nodded.

"Been having crazy nightmares?"

"Yes."

"When I saw you pull up," Esther said, speaking slowly and deliberately, the booze making it difficult for her to do either, "I told myself not to open the door. I didn't want to see anybody from Matheson, not even you. Nothing personal."

Magdalena folded her hands, placed them in her lap, and tried to stay still despite her nervousness. "Please tell me what happened."

"Every one of those places I worked in had their share of bad stuff. Juju, they call it, bad juju. All those doomed people, all that death. But Matheson was the worst. Maybe because it's so old, I don't know, but there's a lot of darkness inside those walls, Mags, whole lot of darkness."

"Joan said the look on your face…it was like you'd seen the Devil himself."

"Maybe I did." She smiled, but it was joyless. "Remember how every time there was a full moon the residents always got more agitated?"

"You really believe that—it was the moon?"

"Used to think so," Esther said. "After a few years, you get to wondering if there's more to what they say about near-death experiences, out of body stuff, crisis apparitions, all that shit. For me, the whole CNA thing started when I was a kid, just a little younger than you now. I was hanging with a tough crowd, and one by one, people I knew either ended up on the street, in prison, or dead. I'd already done a stint in juvie, never wanted to be locked up again. I wanted to change my life, and luckily they seal up juvie shit, so I got a job waitressing, slinging diner food for shit money and shittier tips. I wanted to do something else, something where I could help people. Didn't have any education except for high school, and I knew this chick that was a CNA. I figured that was for me. Always wanted to be a nurse when I was a little girl, and that never worked out, but this was at least in the vicinity, right? Anyway, I got my certification and started working nursing homes. Worked in three different facilities in Boston for fifteen years before I wound up at Matheson, and I was halfway burned out even then. And not just physically, okay? You know that elderly *Tales from the Crypt* shit can get to you after a while. Right before they die, they talk about dead spouses visiting, seeing angels, shit, even demons sometimes."

Magdalena knew exactly what she was talking about, but didn't want to interrupt her or get her off track, so she remained quiet.

"I started seeing shit out of the corner of my eye. Just fast, shadows, really. Been the same everywhere I worked. But Matheson, that fucking place was the worst. You know there was an old mill on those grounds back in the early 1900s, right? Place burned to the ground, lots of carnage, over fifty people burned to death. Couple years later they built what was then a state mental hospital there, and it was shut down and sold in the 1950s. Most of the buildings were demolished, but the main one was remodeled and turned into a nursing home. There's bad energy in a nursing home three months old, Mags, never mind one as old as that place, and with the history surrounding those grounds. You ask me, there's a real darkness in that building."

"What did you see that night?" Magdalena pressed.

Esther looked pained. "It gets worse every year, doesn't it?"

"What do you mean? The workload? The patients?"

"That too…"

Magdalena looked to the windows but the shades were drawn, casting the room in shadows, which at first hadn't bothered her but now seemed menacing. "What scared you so bad that night that you had to quit your job and leave right then and there?"

Esther seemed to be gathering her thoughts, but she was so drunk it was hard to tell what was going through her mind. Her gaze focused on the doorway to the adjacent room. "I've seen and heard a lot of things over the years, told you that, and you know that lots of strange shit happened at Matheson. Old people, the ones closest to death, they always got tales to tell. They see people in the walls, or standing at the foot of their beds. One woman insisted I leave her window open, even in winter, because her dead husband visited her the night before and told her that way her soul could fly away once it left her body. Like I said, it's no different in any of those places. The stories are always similar, but…"

"But what?"

She took another drink from the bottle. "Sometimes when it was quiet, I heard things there, like a radio droning on and on somewhere down the hall, but I could never find it. Most times I couldn't make out what the voices were saying, it's like it came from somewhere far away, and when I walked down the hall, I swore I heard the same voices coming from some of the patients' rooms. Then I'd peek in and there'd be nobody there but the poor soul snoozing in their deathbed." She threw up her hands. "That's how it was, at least at first anyway. Those old folks, it's like they see and hear things from the other side, and people like us, after a while we can…Mags, sometimes we can hear them too."

"Mrs. Gage was having experiences," Magdalena said. "And I think maybe whatever she was experiencing, whatever it was she was hearing and seeing in her room and in the hallways at night, I think...I think they're in my house now too."

Esther's eyes watered. She looked so hopeless in that moment, but Magdalena couldn't tell if the sorrow so clearly etched across Esther's face was for her or herself.

"I don't know anything for sure," Magdalena told her. "Not yet. But I need answers. I need to know that whatever's happening isn't something that will hurt my child. I need to know that I'm not the only one—"

"You're not the only one," Esther snapped. "I just fucking told you you're not. Jesus Christ, I'm the one drunk as fuck around here, try to stay with me. Are you even listening?"

"I need to know Kaley's safe. I swear to God I'll kill anything that hurts her."

The mention of Kaley's name softened Esther's expression, but she offered nothing more.

"Is she in danger, Esther?"

"We're all in danger, kid." She put her free hand to her face and massaged her temples with her fingers. "You know Mrs. Tucker?"

"Yes."

"There was something in her room the night I left. And I was working so you know I was stone cold sober. I may be a drunk out of work but I would never endanger those people or risk my license."

"Of course not," Magdalena said. "Just tell me what happened."

"She hit the call button and I'd just finished emptying a bedpan from Hell," she said. "So I went in thinking it was more of the same, right? But when I got there I felt this really bad vibe like...almost like we weren't alone in that room. She was sitting up in bed, eyes filled up, scared to death. My heart broke for her. She was terrified. I asked her what was wrong and she said they were coming back for her. I asked her who, and she said it was the voices again—she talked about them all the time—and you know, she's got dementia, so you roll with it, right? But this was different, Mags. The air in that room had changed. Other things were changing too. I could *feel* it. And the look in that poor old girl's eyes told me she could feel it too. So I comforted her best I could, got her settled in and stayed with her a while so she'd see everything was fine even though I knew damn well it wasn't. Eventually she got back to sleep. Let me tell you, I couldn't get out of that room fast enough. I'd just made it into the hallway when I heard it behind me. Just a single word, but I knew it didn't come from her. *Sleep...*"

A chill crept up over the back of Magdalena's neck. "That's when you ran?"

Esther's eyes filled with tears and her lips trembled. "Not right away. I was going to just walk away, ignore it because it was just more of that bad juju, spooky nursing home shit. I thought about my bills, how much money I need to cover them, told myself to just walk away, take a break, do my job. But I was scared, Mags. I still am. Maybe I'm just getting too old for that shit, but God help me, I didn't walk away. I turned around, and I walked back into Mrs. Tucker's room. I saw them. I fucking *saw* them. And they saw me."

"Who were they?" Magdalena asked, her voice trembling.

"You saw the drawings Mrs. Gage made."

"Jesus, Esther. Are you telling me—"

"I don't know what they are," she said in a loud whisper. "I don't know what they want. I only know I've been doing the job for years, and I've got the scars inside and out to prove it. My knees are giving out, my back's shot, but I—Mags, I've always had my mind." A tear spilled down her cheek. "I'll never work in a nursing home again. I'll never set foot in or anywhere near Matheson Manor as long as I live. Only thing is, *they* don't seem to care. I thought that would do it, but they come when I sleep now, when everything's quiet. Here, in this house. Do you understand? They're *here*."

"What are we going to do?" Magdalena's heart pounded against her chest so violently she was afraid she was about to have a panic attack.

"Me? I'm gonna sit here and drink." Esther held the bottle up as if in evidence. "I figure if I get shitfaced enough, they'll still be around, I just won't give a fuck. They'll either leave me alone or I'm dead, right? I'm too tired to run. I'll make my stand here."

"Esther—"

"I got nothing, nobody. But you have Kaley, so you should leave now."

"But I—"

"Run, Mags. Please. Go. Get as far away as you can. Take Kaley and just *go*."

"Go where? Where the hell are we supposed to go *to*?"

"Anywhere...nowhere...everywhere..." She looked at the corner drunkenly, as if something in the shadows had caught her attention. "Try not to sleep too much. And keep the fucking lights on, know what I mean?"

"We have to figure out how to—"

"Get out."

Magdalena blanched. "What?"

"You heard me, kid. Bounce. Get out."

"Esther, don't—"

"Get out of my house, Mags. I mean it. I'm not fucking around." She tried to get up out of the chair, but was so drunk she couldn't quite manage it. "I gave you everything I know. There's nothing else here but my broken-down bitch ass and the demons in my fucking head. I care about you, I always have. So go, while you still can. In my own fucked up way I'm trying to help you. Please. Just go."

Shaking, Magdalena rose from the couch and headed for the door. She looked back at Esther, but she was finishing off the bottle.

Just as Magdalena stepped out into the brutal cold, closing the door behind her, her phone pulsed. Moving toward her car, she slipped the phone from her purse and read the screen.

INCOMING CALL: GEORGE GAGE

# CHAPTER TWELVE

IN THE MORNING, AFTER talking with the funeral director and confirming the plans for his mother's cremation, which he'd arranged and paid for previously, George forced himself to make a series of unpleasant calls to the few people his mother knew that he thought should be informed of her passing. An only child, other than his parents, George had no real family to speak of. There were a couple cousins in the Midwest and another down in Florida, but he didn't know them at all and they'd never been part of his life. His father died in a car accident when George was just six years old, so although his memories of him were fond, they were also quite vague. A high school teacher, George remembered his father as a gentle, soft-spoken, well kempt man with dark hair and a mustache. When George was ten, his mother remarried. A loud and unpleasant man that sold cars, his stepfather Randall was never much interested in George, and they were never close. After only four years of marriage, just as George was about to begin high school, his mother divorced her second husband. After that, although his mother dated from time to time, she never married again. She worked for a large insurance company as a clerk for years, and after retiring, spent most of her time gardening and puttering around the same modest house George had been raised in. Unfortunately, because she failed to make prior arrangements to protect her assets, when it became necessary for her to go into the nursing home, the facility and state took nearly every dime she had, including her retirement and even the house. This not only left George with no inheritance to speak of, but also responsible for settling numerous bills she'd left behind and getting her remaining finances in order.

Now there were only memories. Most were good, but the last several years of watching his mother lose everything, including herself, while slowly fading away into oblivion had been devastating.

And now he had this madness with the phone to contend with.

At the small sandwich shop where he'd arranged to meet Magdalena, he sat at a booth that allowed him to see the entrance clearly, and then chose the side facing the door. After listening to the recordings on his mother's phone the night before, he didn't know who else to talk to about these things, and could only hope Magdalena might be able to shed some light on exactly what the hell was going on.

Before he could think more about it, he saw her through the front windows as she made her way to the entrance. She slipped inside from the cold, pulled free a pair of sunglasses, and looked around.

George raised his hand to catch her attention, and offered a guarded smile.

Once she'd seen him, Magdalena approached the booth with what could only be described as caution. She looked paler, more tired, drawn, and troubled than the last time he'd seen her, and after the night he'd had, George was certain he did too.

Rising to his feet, he extended his hand. "Thanks for meeting me."

Magdalena peeled off a pair of leather gloves and shook his hand. "I didn't mean to be weird on the phone, I just didn't expect to hear from you like that," she explained. "How did you get my number?"

"When we met you told me your full name." George motioned to the bench across from his. "So I Googled you and got your number online."

She seemed less than thrilled with this, but slid into the booth and gave a quick, self-conscious smile anyway. "Makes sense," she said softly.

"Believe it or not, back in the day there was this thing called privacy." George sunk back down into his seat and folded his hands on the table between them. "But that definitely seems to have gone by the wayside these days."

"I've always heard privacy was a myth anyway," she said.

George couldn't quite read her. She seemed so uncomfortable he wasn't sure if she was being snide, ironic, or making an attempt at humor. "Well, there's a good chance it is. Hell, maybe it always was."

Magdalena looked around, craning her neck. "I've never been here before."

"Thought it might be a good place to meet," he said. "I figured you'd be more comfortable in a public place."

"Thanks," she said, refocusing her attention on him.

"Not to mention they've got good breakfast sandwiches and decent coffee."

"I could use some coffee, didn't sleep that well last night."

"Me either."

"I don't doubt it," she said.

"How do you take your jitter juice?"

"Regular," she said, smiling. "Two sugars, please."

George got up, went to the counter and ordered. A moment later he was back with two Styrofoam cups of coffee. "As I mentioned on the phone," he said, settling back into the booth, "I listened to the recordings on the sleep app on my mother's phone last night. I'm assuming you've heard them too."

"Yes." Magdalena held her cup with both hands and stared down into the coffee before her. "I only downloaded it for her because she was having trouble with—"

"It's fine. I know you were trying to help her."

Magdalena nodded. "I didn't understand it really, I still don't, but I felt you needed to know. And like I told you before, I made your mother a promise that I'd tell you what she said."

"What the hell is going on in that place, Magdalena?"

"I don't know." She took a sip of coffee then returned the cup to the table. "But it's not just happening there."

George felt a rush of fear course through him, and he looked quickly at the entrance. Had something horrific been walking through those doors at that exact moment it wouldn't have surprised him in the least, and that was so troubling he didn't even know how to process it.

Eyes trained on the coffee, Magdalena explained what had happened with her daughter and her stuffed panda, choosing her words carefully. Now and then she glanced up, her eyes quickly returning to the coffee before her each time. "But there's definitely something happening at Matheson," she said once she'd finished explaining about the recordings Kaley had mistakenly captured. With a deep breath, she went on to explain as best she could about Esther.

"Jesus," George said.

"Yeah, I know." She was quiet for a while, and then she said, "To be honest, I wanted to be done with it. I wanted to keep my promise to your mother and tell you what she'd said, and then walk away from that place and all of this and get on with my life. But whatever it is we're dealing with didn't just follow Esther home, it followed *me* home too. And it involved Kaley, my *daughter*."

"How old is she?"

"Five."

"Is she all right?"

"Yeah," Magdalena said with a sigh. "She doesn't really understand any of it. She's too innocent to be frightened at this point."

George was glad to hear that at least. Magdalena was still a nervous wreck, but she, like most, was different away from work. She struck him as a more fully realized person in this setting, not so formal and unsure of herself, but still a troubled young woman with a daughter she loved and a life she was struggling to maintain. "This friend of yours—"

"Esther."

"Right, Esther. Did she care for my mother too?"

"Sure, she was on the same unit. But the night she quit and walked out she'd been caring for Mrs. Tucker. She suffers from dementia too. All she's got is a son that visits. Kind of a nerdy older guy about your age, I guess."

"Can't tell you how awesome it is to have reached an age where people refer to me as an *older guy.*"

"I'm sorry," she said. "I didn't mean to—"

"It's okay, just trying to lighten the mood." George sipped his coffee. "So this Mrs. Tucker, she was experiencing the same things my mother was going through?"

Magdalena gave another nod.

"Do you think talking to her might do any good?"

"We'd have to do it at Matheson. Since I don't work there anymore and you have no reason to be there now that Mrs. Gage is gone, I guess we could try to see her as visitors, but I'm not sure what the point would be in her condition."

George let a few passersby distract him a moment. "What do you think we're dealing with here, Magdalena?" he asked.

"Mags," she said. "Nobody calls me Magdalena."

"Make you a deal. You drop the Mr. Gage for George, and I'll go with Mags."

"Sure."

"So, *Mags,* what do you think we're dealing with here?"

"I honestly don't know. But I don't think it's anything good."

"I don't mean to be flippant," George said, "because I'm as disturbed by this as you are, but do you know if these...*people*...have caused any actual harm to anyone? I mean, I know they're frightening and this entire thing is unsettling, but could it be possible there's no real danger here?"

Magdalena gave him an incredulous look. "How can we know for sure if we don't know who they are, what they want, or what they're doing?"

"I guess we can't. I'm just saying, as far as we know, nothing has actually happened to anyone as a result of these, for lack of a better word, *visitations,* right?"

"I don't know that for sure either. But I'm not aware of anything specific."

George thought about that a while, and Magdalena apparently did the same, drinking her coffee without comment.

"Has anything else happened?" George finally asked.

"Not that I know of," she said, watching him with a discerning guise usually reserved for cops or lawyers. "But how do you mean? Like what?"

"Have you had any strange phone calls since this started?"

"No."

"My mother's phone rang last night," George said hesitantly. "At first it was just all this noise and distortion, but then I…"

"It's okay," Magdalena assured him. "You can tell me."

George wiped his mouth with the back of his hand and looked around. For what, he had no idea. He only knew he couldn't bring himself to look her in the eye when he answered. "I thought I heard a voice say the word *sleep*."

She swallowed so hard it was audible. "Did you recognize it?"

"I don't know, I—I'm not sure, but like I said, there was a lot of distortion and weird noises, but I've never heard a voice quite like what came through that phone. I couldn't even say for sure if the voice was human but—oh, Jesus!" It wasn't until he felt the burn that he realized his hand had begun to shake so badly he'd spilled some of his coffee on his wrist and onto the table. "Damn it, I—I'm sorry, I—what the hell is wrong with me?"

Magdalena plucked some napkins from a silver holder on the table and handed them to him. "You're frightened."

He eyed her with uncertainty as he mopped up the spill. This woman was nothing if not honest. "Yeah," he said quietly. "I guess I am."

"You think I'm not?"

George pushed the cup aside. He'd had enough coffee. "So what do we do?"

"*We?*" she said, arching an eyebrow.

"Am I being too presumptuous to think that we're in this together?"

She sat back and seemed to think about that a while. Remaining quiet for a minute or more as George twisted in the wind, Magdalena nibbled her lower lip and refused to make eye contact.

"Look, I know you're married, so if this is going to cause any problems for you at home, if you'd prefer, I can just leave you alone."

"It's not that," she said. "My husband, he's kind of out of the picture."

"I'm sorry."

"Don't be. We're both probably better off."

"Are you and your daughter all alone? No other family?" When she didn't answer, George feared he'd overstepped. "Sorry, I didn't mean to pry. It's none of my business. It's just that I'm a widower myself, my wife and I never had children and I have no other family to speak of, so I understand going through this without anyone else around, that's all I was—"

"It's okay," she said. "And I'm sorry about your wife."

"Thanks. I lost her a little over a year ago."

Magdalena grimaced. "You've been through a lot."

"Not going to argue that one with you," George said, attempting a smile.

"I've got an older sister, but she lives in California with her family, so we don't see each other much. And my parents moved to South Carolina a few years ago. Their politics are just to the right of Mussolini, so we aren't exactly close these days." Magdalena fidgeted in her seat like if she didn't get up and move around soon she was going to come out of her skin. "But this has nothing to do with them or any of that. I'm getting used to handling things on my own. I'm not a weak person."

"No, I'm sure you're not."

"I just don't know what to do with all this."

"That definitely makes two of us."

"I can't go back to Esther. She made it clear she wanted me to stay away."

"Do you think she knows more than she told you?"

"She might, but it's not an option, at least not right now." Magdalena sat forward, resting her arms on the table. "I might be able to get one of the other CNAs I know on staff to see if she could talk to Mrs. Tucker for us, but like I said, she's not lucid much, so I'm not sure there's any point."

"Didn't you say she has a son that visits her?"

"Yeah, I've seen him around. He tends to visit late, way after normal visiting hours usually, that's why. But I've only actually met him once or twice though. I'm trying to remember his name."

"Maybe he knows something. I mean, it's possible his mother could've—"

"Warner, I think," Magdalena interrupted. "No. Wait, that's not it. Winston. I think his name's *Winston*."

George recognized it immediately. "I know him. Well, I don't know him exactly, but I met him last night when I left Matheson. You know the little coffee place in the plaza across from the lights? I'd seen him on the unit earlier and ran into him there a while later. We actually spoke. Mostly we talked about how hard it was to have a parent with dementia. Little mousy sort of guy, right?"

"Sounds like him, yeah."

"And his mother's the one your friend Esther was caring for?"

"Yes."

"If Winston's mother is experiencing the same things my mother did, maybe she's told him about it."

"It's possible."

"Then maybe we ought to talk to him, see what he knows." George grabbed his phone and did a quick Internet search. "Strange, his name doesn't come up."

Magdalena checked her watch. "I left my daughter with a neighbor so I can't be gone all day," she explained. "But I can call the unit and try to get his contact info. I have a friend there, Joan, she's a CNA too, and she'd get it for me if I ask."

"Is that legal?"

"Nope," she said, sipping her coffee, "not at all."

*She's growing on me*, George thought. "I wouldn't want you to do anything that'll get you in trouble, Mags."

"What are they gonna do?" A subtle smile curled her lips. "Fire me?"

# CHAPTER THIRTEEN

"*THERE'S SOMETHING WRONG.*"

With a heavy sigh, Winston stood in front of the mirror and forced himself to take in his reflection. Earlier, completely out of the blue, he'd received a call from George Gage. Not only was he shocked, he was baffled as to how the man had gotten his number. Before Winston could gain the courage to engage with him, George made an uneasy attempt at small talk to make sure Winston realized who he was, and then apologized for bothering him. But it was what came next that hit Winston like a punch to the chest.

"There's something wrong at Matheson Manor."

"I don't understand," Winston said.

"It involves our mothers."

"My m-mother?" he stammered nervously. "What do you mean?"

What followed was so unsettling it forced Winston to consider leaving the relative safety of his home and venturing out to a place he'd never been before, a place where people drank liquor and danced and went looking for sexual partners.

*And God knows what else*, he thought.

Winston could only imagine what his mother would say about such an undertaking. Not that it mattered at that point. He'd already decided he was going, and he was doing it for her, though of course she'd never understand or see it that way. Regardless, he had to find out exactly what was going on, and George didn't want to discuss it over the phone. He'd been adamant about that.

*Smart*, Winston thought. *One can never be sure who might be listening.*

As he inspected himself in the mirror, straightening his sweater and adjusting his eyeglasses, he wondered if George's concerns had something to do with the strange car he'd seen parked in front of the house the other night.

*It's far more likely it has to do with Mother's care at Matheson*, he thought.

After all, George had said there was something wrong at Matheson and it involved their mothers. But George's mother had just died, so if it had to do with their care, how could it have anything to do with her now that she was deceased?

Winston remembered a news report he'd seen once about elder abuse at a nursing home in the Midwest. It sickened and enraged him all at once, watching the grainy and purposely blurred undercover footage of some defenseless elderly soul punched, slapped, and tortured by a healthcare worker.

The idea that such a thing might be happening to his mother was horrifying. But Winston was sure if it was anything along those lines his mother would've told him. Then again, with her dementia she might've become confused or not realized what was truly happening.

*I'm not a violent man, but if anyone ever hurt my mother, I'd…*

Whatever it was, George said it was something Winston needed to know.

He took a final look at his reflection. *Well, there's only one way to find out.*

The call had come in the morning, but George said he wanted to meet later in the day, so it was dusk when Winston left the house. Deciding it might be a good idea to take in some cold fresh air and clear his head, he decided to walk rather than take an Uber or the bus. His destination was a bar called January's, a place where the alcohol flowed from midafternoon until the wee hours of the morning.

The rains had washed away the snow, but most of the sidewalks in Winston's neighborhood were still covered with ice. With his dreams continuing to haunt him, he contemplated the long night ahead, wondering if he'd be able to sleep after this meeting. George had also mentioned a woman would be joining them, a CNA from Matheson named Magdalena. Winston had met her briefly on a few occasions, as she worked on his mother's unit, but other than that, he knew nothing about her.

As Winston moved carefully along the sidewalk, his breath tumbling from his nose and mouth in long plumes, he appeared to be alone on the street. Yet he thought he heard subtly odd noises—like barely discernable whispers—drifting toward him from the surrounding semidarkness. Sounds he could neither identify nor pinpoint. Keeping his eyes straight ahead, Winston continued on his way through the neighborhood, crossing to the next block.

The sudden cry of a lone crow sitting atop a nearby telephone pole startled him. He glanced up at the bird, and upon seeing it staring down directly at him, he looked away and pushed on into the cold.

In the distance a motorcycle roared, and from the other side of the street, just a bit farther up the block, a woman's voice called out from a third-story window, beckoning her child home to dinner. Winston searched for the child, but there was no one else there.

A gust of wind whipped down the street, slamming into him as once again the eerie whispers returned. This time, at the very outskirts of his hearing, he was able to make out a single word.

*Sleep...*

Winston stopped abruptly and looked around, his eyes slowly panning and scanning both sides of the street. Nothing but parked cars and snow drifts, quiet drab buildings with dirty dark windows, a gloomy side street to his right, and at the far corner, a weathered stop sign littered with what appeared to be several bullet holes.

Something deep within him, perhaps something instinctual, told Winston to keep moving, so he did, hurrying to the next corner, then down a narrow side street. Winston figured he could use it as a shortcut to get back to the main drag where the GPS on his phone said January's was located.

A plethora of thoughts flooded his mind: the odd man on the bus and the dark figure Winston had seen when he got off; the peculiar car parked in front of his house; a motionless silhouette sitting behind the wheel; the gun—it was never far from his thoughts these days—tucked away in that kitchen drawer. Those images swirled in his head the same as they had just before he'd finally fallen asleep last night.

Winston dreamed of his mother, but she wasn't the empty husk she'd become, rather the person she used to be. She was coherent and engaged in lively conversation with a CNA from Matheson named Esther, a woman he'd spoken to on several occasions while visiting his mother. Esther told him that despite the doctor recently increasing his mother's meds, she was still having trouble sleeping through the night. In the dream, Esther was just as he remembered her in real life, professional, matter-of-fact, and possessing an aura of strength that only served to enhance his own feelings of insecurity. She was also very good-looking, with auburn hair and startling green eyes. In real life, Winston couldn't look directly at her when they spoke, just stood there riddled with anxiety, uncomfortably mumbling his responses while keeping his head bowed so eye contact was impossible.

But in the dream, he lifted his gaze and looked right at her.

She smirked in response. Was she mocking him?

Women like Esther usually did. Winston had never garnered much attention from women, or even girls when he was younger. Years ago in school, only girls like Irene Sims, a freckle-faced kid that wore eyeglasses even thicker than his, paid any attention to him. The cheerleaders and pretty girls, the popular girls, all made fun of him, calling him a creep and a nerd and a dork, giggling and laughing cruelly when they walked behind him in the hall.

And they all had that same mocking look in their eyes.

Irene Sims once told him they were just mean girls. One day, she assured him, they'd be overweight and unhappy housewives, their glory days in high school long behind them and the only thing they'd have left to reminisce about fondly.

Winston liked Irene. She was pretty in her own way, and very smart, which Winston found attractive, so he took her to a school dance once. But after she tried to kiss him in the parking lot, he didn't call her again and eventually had to tell her he just wanted to be friends. She asked if he was gay. He said no, but Winston was never sure she believed him. Truth was he just didn't feel comfortable with intimacy.

And then, of course, there was his mother.

"Nice girls don't throw themselves at boys and use their sex appeal and bodies to lure them into sin and lascivious situations," she warned. "Kissing, petting, and sex should only take place after marriage, between couples that love each other and have a strong commitment. Even then, sex should be reserved for procreation, not recreation."

Winston had never gone on a date again.

Long ago, he'd resigned himself to the fact that he'd never marry. Except for his beloved mother, he'd spend his life alone, without a wife or partner and without children who'd carry on his name. But at a young age he learned to fantasize about such things, futures that would never be, with women in magazines, on television, or in movies. It was something he still did, since he knew his mother would never find out, but it was just a game he played, imagining what it might be like to have a girlfriend or wife, and to live a more usual life. Sometimes he even fantasized about sex, and not just with movie stars or other celebrities, but women he saw on the street or at the grocery store, and of course, online. He'd once even gone to a chatroom and tried to talk with some women, but it didn't go well as he had no idea how to keep their attention. He'd hoped under the anonymity of the Internet he might be able to hide his social limitations—after all, if there was anywhere he was confident, it was in the world of computers—but his nerves always got the better of him, and soon, the women he spoke with were gone, as disinterested and thoroughly unimpressed with him as those in the so-called real world.

Now and then he'd sneak onto porn sites once his mother had gone to bed, and was shocked and wildly excited to see how all these things worked and played out. But the novelty quickly wore thin for Winston. What he first found enticing soon became repellent. There was something ugly about those photographs and videos that made him uncomfortable. It wasn't like the sex in his fantasies, where everything was sweet and innocent and romantic. That, coupled with the guilt he felt each time he visited those sites, caused him to stop frequenting them. He'd still go a few times a year, to relieve himself of the sexual tension once it built to a point where he could no longer stand it, but none of it was enjoyable for him. In the end, it just made him sad.

But he still had his fantasies, and one of the women he often fantasized about was Esther. She wasn't a movie star, a singer, or any kind of celebrity, but Winston thought she was beautiful. And when he'd dreamed of her last night, the memories now flickering through his mind like a film, she seemed softer and more amicable somehow.

"It'll be all right, Mrs. Tucker," she said. "You just need to *sleep*."

His mother, clear-eyed, sharp, and articulate, answered, "I'm not afraid for myself, you understand. It's my son. Winston's a good and decent boy, but he's weak and timid, like a little church mouse. He's always been that way. What's going to happen to him once I'm gone? What will become of my son?"

"Who knows?" Esther shrugged, her beautiful eyes void of emotion suddenly. "Nobody knows a goddamn thing, can't you see that?"

Then the room darkened, and what sounded like a chorus of eerie voices began to whisper. "*Sleep...*"

A strange shape, perhaps a shadow, floated from the darkest corner of the room, its form slowly twisting and turning as it draped itself across his mother like a black cloud.

The whites of his mother's eyes pierced the shadows, glaring at him hopelessly. "Winston," she gasped. "Help me!"

He reached for her, but it was too late.

*Tell us what you see, Winston.*

Blood exploded from his mother's face—spraying from her eyes and nose and mouth—spattering the walls and white bedsheets and coating his face.

And as his mother was dragged back and away into that dark corner, swallowed whole by a curtain of blackness, Winston looked back at Esther, his mother's blood staining his clothing, smeared across his face and dotting the lenses of his eyeglasses.

But she was gone, and he was alone.

Alone, except for his screams.

Winston opened his eyes, released from that nightmare just as the horizon began to lighten. No dark beings scurried from beneath his bed and no voices whispered cryptic warnings from dark corners, yet that unsettling feeling of dread stayed with him throughout the day.

His mood brightened momentarily when an unexpected call came from George Gage, the same man he'd chatted with at The Hot Cup, and a person he'd felt comfortable sharing small talk with. He'd even fantasized about them becoming friends, but the happiness left with George's strange warnings about Matheson Manor. With reluctance, Winston accepted an invitation to meet George and Magdalena at January's.

He could just hear his mother. "You're meeting them at a *bar*, Winston?"

On the dark side street there were no sidewalks, but there also weren't any cars, and since it was only a short distance, he hurried down the middle of the street, negotiating the icy pavement as best he could. In his head, he replayed parts of the telephone conversation he'd had with George.

"I'm sorry to bother you," George told him. "I hate to intrude like this, and I appreciate your patience, but it's about your mother. It involves my mother too. There's something we need to talk about. It's important."

"Is it something I can speak with the doctors or nurses about? I'm not sure I'm comfortable discussing—"

"There's something wrong, Winston," George interrupted. His tone was stern but sounded more desperate than scolding.

"I don't understand."

"There's something very wrong going on at Matheson Manor."

"What are you saying?" Winston asked. "What are you referring to?"

"I know I'm not making much sense, but if you'll just—"

"What is this about?" Winston asked, his imagination getting the better of him as he peeked out the window to see if the strange car had returned. "And excuse me, I don't mean to be rude, but how did you get this number?"

"With the Internet and all, information's easy to find these days."

No car. Winston felt a sense of relief wash over him. "My information isn't listed on the Internet," he said. "I've seen to that."

"Look, I'll be happy to discuss it when we meet, all right? I know we don't know each other and this must seem awfully bizarre, but it's very important. If it wasn't, I'd never bother you like this."

The designated meeting place, January's, was only five blocks from Winston's home. He'd ridden or walked by it hundreds of times, but this would be the first time he set foot inside it, or any bar, for that matter. But then, that's where people met, wasn't it? At coffee shops and restaurants and—yes, Mother—even bars. Half-heartedly, Winston agreed, but he wouldn't drink. He'd just get a soft drink or something.

"Always remember that liquor dulls the senses and annihilates inhibitions," his mother had told him numerous times. "It lures otherwise fine, upstanding, moral young men and women to do the Devil's deeds, and leads to the ruin of countless souls."

*Last thing I want to do is ruin my soul,* Winston thought.

He'd order a ginger ale. Or maybe wine. What about wine? Would that be okay? After all, even the priests sipped it during mass on Sundays. How bad could it be? Jesus drank wine. Winston fantasized about holding a glass of wine and sipping it casually, savoring it before swallowing. *Just like a regular connoisseur,* he thought. *Maybe that's what I'll do. I'll order a glass of wine and see what George and Magdalena have to say.*

But there were so many different kinds of wine, and he'd never had any of them before. How would he know which one to order?

*Better stick to ginger ale.*

His mind shifted to Magdalena. He'd talked to her once or twice at Matheson. A petite, quiet woman, she always seemed nice to Winston, and she was very pretty. Not sexy like Esther, but pretty.

Winston laughed lightly. *Sexy,* he thought. *What do you know about sexy?*

What did Magdalena have to do with all this? Esther cared for his mother far more often.

As he continued along the icy street, Winston grew tense about entering a place like January's. Would the people there laugh at him?

*Look at this guy. Who's this nerd?*

*Ginger ale it is,* he thought. *Mother's right, I don't need my senses dulled.*

As his mind cleared and he focused on the street before him, Winston realized that while he'd walked this particular street many times, it had always been during daylight hours. He'd never been here this late. Dusk was dying, slowly morphing into night.

Ice crunched beneath his feet, and as he neared the end of the side street, he saw a few homeless men at the mouth of a nearby alley, not far from a boarded-up bodega. Like sentinels of the coming darkness, they huddled there, watching the sky as Winston walked by them quickly as he could without slipping. They didn't speak or acknowledge him in any way—they didn't even look at him—but the smell of alcohol and body odor wafted toward him as he rushed by.

*Poor souls,* he thought. *There but the grace of God go I, right, Mother?*

As he came to the end of the street he saw a city playground across the way, a few shadows ambling about through the dark.

*Probably teenagers doing drugs and looking for trouble,* Winston thought.

A stray cat sauntered across the road as if it owned it; bright yellow eyes fixed on Winston. As it escaped into the darkness of another alley, Winston stopped in his tracks. Something spooked him, but he couldn't figure out what it was. It was as if he'd seen that cat before, but how was that possible? All he knew was he no longer felt simply uneasy on these dark streets. He felt decidedly *unsafe.*

Strange, Winston liked animals. He wasn't afraid of them and actually liked cats. He'd had a cat as a child. Felix, he named him. He became so attached to him that when Felix died Winston never got another pet. It was too painful. He missed that little cat to this day.

Breathing in the cold air, he pushed his glasses up higher on the bridge of his nose then continued on his way.

Leaving the side street shortcut, he crossed the road and passed by the playground, gaze fixed on the blinking neon lights ahead. January's was in sight. His heart skipped a beat in anticipation. He hoped he looked all right. How did people dress when they went to bars? Winston wasn't sure. Hopefully his khakis and sweater were okay. He didn't need people laughing and making fun of him.

What if this was all a joke? Maybe they wouldn't even show up. Back in school, other kids played tricks on him like that all the time, inviting him to meet them at the local burger joint only to never show up and leave him sitting there like an ass. Later they'd laugh and poke fun at him for being so gullible.

*Like we'd hang out with you! Fucking loser!*

The wind picked up again, and Winston swore he heard that same awful laugher from all those years ago echo along the street behind him, drifting closer from the playground.

*Don't be ridiculous. This isn't high school. You're a middle-aged man. So is George. And Magdalena must be about thirty or so. Grownups don't pull tricks like that, and besides, what would be the point?*

No, this was no joke. This was important, that's what George said. So important he had to call him and ask him to meet them at a bar.

A flash distracted him.

Headlights rounded the corner up ahead. Although a distance away, there was something menacing about them. As they came closer he saw they were attached to a large black SUV, which turned the corner and sped in his direction. The windows were tinted, but Winston couldn't tell if the windshield was as well or if the growing darkness simply made it difficult to see through it.

Mist rose from the street, curling like ghostly fingers around the vehicle.

It was then that Winston realized the SUV was literally headed straight for him.

"What are you doing?" he muttered aloud.

Like a black bullet, it raced along the street then swerved to be sure it was in line with where Winston was standing. This had to be a mistake. Why would someone purposely try to run him down?

But the SUV didn't correct its course. Instead, it increased speed and rocketed closer, the blinding bright headlights bearing down on him.

Winston ran. Stumbling across the street, he reached the far side and slipped, nearly falling on the ice as he reached the sidewalk. Flailing his arms in an attempt to regain his balance, he tumbled forward and crashed to the pavement.

The SUV sped past him, a black blur cutting the darkness.

Pain shot through his palms and up his arms and shoulders as somewhere behind him a screech of tires sounded. The SUV had skidded to a stop.

Winston's glasses slid off, but he quickly scooped them up and pushed them back onto his face as he regained his feet. Staggering away, he looked back over his shoulder to see where the SUV was.

It was stopped where it had come to a halt, perhaps half a block away, the taillights burning bright red in the darkness like a pair of glaring demonic eyes.

A wave of dizziness swept through him, and Winston nearly fell again.

What *is happening?*

He wanted to scream, "Are you drunk? You almost killed me!"

Instead, Winston stood perfectly still and silently watched the SUV, his chest heaving with each labored breath.

The taillights went dark.

And then, slowly, the SUV began to turn around.

Winston frantically looked in both directions. The street was empty. No other cars, no other walkers. Even the teens at the playground were gone, and from where he stood he could no longer see much of the alley, so he wasn't sure if the homeless men were still there or not.

The SUV now facing him again, it sat there like some giant shiny black monster, the headlights burning ominously.

And then it took off, lurching forward as it came for him again.

Just as Winston was about to run, without warning a second vehicle—a dark sedan—burst from the mouth of the alley and cut off the other car, causing it to slam its brakes.

Once again, the SUV screeched to a stop.

Amazed, Winston remained frozen, watching this unfold. Then he realized something else. He knew that sedan. He'd seen it before.

The car outside his house the other night, it was the same one.

He was sure of it.

Before Winston could fully wrap his mind around that, the window on the driver's side of the sedan dropped partially open. A hand reached out and waved at Winston to go.

*Run—get out of here!* it seemed to tell him.

And he did. Without looking back, and ignoring the pain in his knee and scraped palms, Winston ran as fast as he could for what he hoped was the safety of the neon-lit bar just up ahead.

# CHAPTER FOURTEEN

ONCE A HOTSPOT FOR a younger working-class crowd, and known primarily for watered-down drinks, inexpensive greasy appetizers, and dancing, in recent years January's had become a bit more upscale, catering now to young professionals. The dancefloor had been converted into table seating, and the bar was completely renovated with a wider birth to accommodate the throngs of patrons three and four deep on busy nights.

This night, Saturday night, it was still early, not quite five o'clock. The big crowds had yet to arrive, and although January's was far from empty, within an hour or so, it would be mobbed.

George arrived first, smiling dutifully at a couple barflies surprised to see a man his age there, then chose a table in the farthest, darkest corner he could find. As he draped his coat over the back of his chair and settled in, he tried to appear at least somewhat comfortable, but he already stood out from the usual clientele with about as much subtlety as the neon signage out front.

Magdalena suggested this place, George had never been before, and now that he was here he knew why. *Maybe twenty years ago*, he thought.

Thankfully, Magdalena was punctual and arrived soon thereafter, quickly locating him in the sea of otherwise empty tables. "My *God*, it's cold out there," she said, slipping out of her coat and gloves. "That wind, Jesus. Find the place okay?"

"Yeah, didn't have any problems." George stood, waiting until Magdalena slid into a chair across from him before returning to his seat.

"I haven't been here in a couple years, not since before Kaley was born." Magdalena looked around. "It's changed."

George nodded. They sat in silence for a moment, both doing their best to appear unaffected and failing miserably.

A waitress so cheery she bordered on psychotic suddenly appeared at their table, rescuing them. "Hey, guys! What can I get you?"

"I'll have a Jack and Coke on the rocks," Magdalena said.

George was impressed. "Just a bottle of Heineken for me, please."

As the waitress bounced away, Magdalena put her gloves in her coat pockets, then folded her coat and placed it across her lap. She seemed somewhat more comfortable in his presence, but remained guarded. Not that he could blame her. George wasn't completely at ease with her yet either. But he was getting there.

"Do you think he'll show?" she asked.

"I hope so, but it's hard to know for sure. The guy's a little strange."

"A little?" She smiled coyly.

The waitress brought their drinks, set them down, then moved away once George paid for them.

"Here," Magdalena said, pulling a small purse from her coat, "let me give—"

"Don't worry about it, I got it."

"I don't expect you to buy me—"

"I know you don't," he said. "I'm happy to. It's really not a big deal, okay?"

Magdalena watched him a moment then put her purse away. "Thanks."

"You're not used to people doing nice things for you, are you?" George asked.

She shrugged but didn't answer.

"Well," he said, raising his bottle, "here's to better days."

"And quieter nights," she added, lightly tapping her glass against his beer.

Awkward silence returned, falling between them like a shroud.

George checked his watch. "Think I should try calling him again?"

Before Magdalena could respond, the front doors burst open and a man exploded through the entrance at breakneck speed. He smashed directly into the bar, bounced off, then tumbled to the floor, sprawled there as the patrons and employees—all stunned—tried to figure out what had just happened.

Startled by the noise, Magdalena turned and looked back at the bar.

"Holy shit," George said, slowly rising from his chair. "That's him."

Had Winston's entrance not been so violent, it might've been comical, but only one person at the bar laughed. Everyone else turned to see what was going on with expressions of concern.

George was already on his way to him when one of the bartenders, a scowling musclebound twenty-something, hurried over to where Winston had fallen.

"The hell's your deal?" he growled, grabbing Winston by the wrist and effortlessly yanking him to his feet. "We ain't about trouble in here, *bud.*"

"Hey, easy," a young woman at the bar said. "He's a lot smaller than you. And he might've hurt himself."

Winston was babbling incoherently and readjusting his glasses when George stepped in. "It's all right, he— I know him."

The bartender already had Winston nearly to the door, but hesitated and turned to George. "This guy's a friend of yours?"

"Yeah," George said, and then looked to Winston. "What's going on?"

Winston, flustered and beat-red, eyes wide, was still out of breath. "Someone in an SUV tried to run me down just now," he managed, holding his scraped palms up for them to see. "I fell on the sidewalk. They al-almost killed me."

"Was this someone you know?" George asked.

"No," Winston answered, "of course not."

"*Dude,*" the bartender said. Frowning at the injuries to Winston's hands, he released him then opened the front doors and looked out at the night. "The street's quiet. Yo, you get a tag, bro?"

Winston looked at him as if he'd spoken a foreign language. "No," he finally said nervously, realizing at that moment that everyone in the place was looking at him. "I just ran, I—I'm sorry."

The bartender closed the doors. "You want I should call 911?"

"I don't think..." Winston looked to George, as if for an answer. "No, I..."

"This person *deliberately* tried to run you over?" George asked.

Winston nodded.

"Then the police should probably be called. He could hurt someone else."

"I'm sure they're long gone by now," Winston said.

"Probably some jackoff kids fucking with you," the bartender said, strutting back toward the bar. "Trying to prank you, feel me?"

"I guess it'll be okay," George said to the bartender, taking Winston by the arm. "Could we get some water for him though?"

"Sure you don't want something stronger?" the bartender offered. "On the house, bro, my bad on the rough stuff, thought you were a tweaker or something."

"Maybe a soft drink," Winston said. "Do you have Sprite?"

"You got it."

As the bartender returned to his duties, George led Winston to the table at the far end of the room. "You remember Magdalena," he said, motioning to her.

"Yes," Winston said, bowing his head. "We've met before at Matheson."

"Hi. Are you okay?"

"I have some minor injuries, but yes, I think so."

As Winston sat down, George handed him his cocktail napkin. Winston looked at him questioningly. "To wipe your hands," he said.

"They need to be properly washed and sanitized, I've broken the skin and that could lead to infection." Winston removed his eyeglasses, wincing as he did so, and used the napkin to clean them instead. Once he'd wiped them off, he returned his glasses to his face with shaking hands. "Mother always says that one should *thoroughly* wash out all cuts and…" His voice trailed off, and his eyes filled, leaving him looking like a terrified child that had just awakened from a nightmare. "I…I just can't imagine why someone would do this to me."

"Hey," Magdalena said, exchanging a quick uncertain glance with George before resting her hand on Winston's wrist. "It's okay. Do you want to go to the restroom and straighten up, maybe wash your hands?"

Winston gently pulled his arm free, blushing as he did so. "I don't patronize public bathrooms. They're horrific. Mother says even when they appear to be clean, they are in fact hideous bacteria factories. She raised me to never— I'm sorry, I—I'm a little shaken. I've never experienced anything like this."

"You don't have to apologize, it must've been terrifying." Magdalena shook her head. "Who would do something like that?"

"I certainly don't know."

George waited until the waitress brought Winston's soft drink, then leaned in closer and said, "Can you tell us exactly what happened?"

After sipping some Sprite through a straw, Winston took a few deep breaths then explained the incident, his voice trembling throughout.

"And you're sure the other car was the same one in front of your house the other night?" George asked. "You're *positive* about that?"

"Yes," Winston said, still flustered. "I don't know what any of this means and I hurt my knee when I fell and now I— Why would anyone want to harm me? I've never done anything to anyone, I— Look, why did you want me to come here?"

"You need to try to calm down," Magdalena said evenly but with compassion, her skills as a caregiver emerging. "Just breathe and relax. You're safe now."

Winston nodded, sipped more Sprite.

"Do you have any existing medical issues?" she asked.

"I don't mean to be rude, Ms. Carlino, but—"

"I was only asking because sometimes in a fall you can never be sure what else it might trigger or—"

"My personal medical history is not something I'm comfortable discussing."

"Sure, okay." Magdalena sighed. "Forget it, none of my business."

"Do you want to go to the hospital?" George asked, hoping to diffuse the situation. He could tell Magdalena was irritated to the point where she might get up and walk out, and he didn't want to lose her. "I'd be happy to run you over to the ER if you think—"

"I just want to go home," Winston blurted.

George and Magdalena exchanged another round of troubled glances.

"Are you sure that's a good idea?" George asked. "If that other car was parked in front of your house the other night, then—"

"Whoever that was *helped* me," Winston said. "He probably saved my life. Please, just tell me what's wrong. You said something was wrong. I've had a terrible time and I—I'm not comfortable in this sort of place—I don't really go to bars."

"Let me guess," Magdalena said, throwing back some JD. "You don't drink."

"No, I do not."

"Is *Mother* against that too? She has so many *fascinating* opinions."

Winston appeared thoroughly unamused.

"I mean, I don't know about you, George, but I'd *love* to hear them all."

"On the phone you said something was wrong," Winston said, addressing George. "Something I need to know regarding my mother and Matheson Manor."

"Yes." George sipped his beer and shot Magdalena a quick sideways glance. He didn't know her well enough to be sure, but she seemed like someone that didn't drink much herself, since the Jack Daniel's was already obviously loosening her up. "This is going to be difficult to hear, Winston. It's going to sound insane, I know, but if you just hear me out…hear *us* out…I think you'll understand why we asked you to come here tonight. Some strange things have been happening. Very *disturbing* things we can't explain."

Winston sat perfectly still and listened intently as George shared what he and Magdalena had experienced and knew to that point. His expression remained blank throughout, and he gave no reaction whatsoever, so it was impossible to read him. But there was no doubt he'd heard each and every word.

The bar was picking up, getting busier. More patrons filed in every few minutes, and what to that point had been soft background music was now louder and more intrusive. As a series of track lights along the ceiling activated, the entire place, including the dark corner where their table was located, was suddenly bathed in a dreamy red hue.

"You're telling me, among other things, that Esther left her job at Matheson because of the things she saw and heard in my mother's room?" Winston finally said.

"Yes," Magdalena answered before George could, then she finished what little remained of her drink in a single attempt. "That's what he's telling you."

Winston's eyes found her briefly before returning to George. "Have you told anyone at Matheson about this, one of the charge nurses or an administrator? I would think they'd want to know about unauthorized people in my mother's room."

"That's just it," George said. He knew Winston was trying to hide it, but he was frightened. "I'm not sure that's what they are."

"You know Esther?" Magdalena said.

"I've met and spoken with her, yes, she cared for my mother."

"Does she strike you as someone that would be afraid of some unauthorized visitors? She'd throw them out so fast it'd make their heads spin. She didn't. She ran. She quit her job, walked off the unit, and hasn't been right since. She's on a tailspin drunk I'm not sure she'll ever find her way out of."

A nervous smile danced along Winston's thin lips. "I don't understand."

"Are you sure?" she pressed. "Are you sure you don't understand, Winston?"

"I remember you from Matheson, Ms. Carlino," Winston told her. "You were very nice and always professional. Quiet, actually."

"I don't work there anymore either," Magdalena said flatly. "I'm sorry if I seem aggressive and less than patient right now, *Mr. Tucker*, but as George just told you, the same things haunting your mother are now in my home, around my *child*."

Winston seemed to think this over for a moment. "Are you sure these people are a threat?"

"No," George said. "But these aren't people we're talking about."

"You mean not people as in..." Winston hesitated. "Not *human?*"

That potential reality dropped onto all three of them like an anvil.

George held his beer bottle in both hands, studying it as if searching for the answers within that pale green glass. "Yes."

"What then?"

"I don't know."

"Do you have any idea what they look like?"

George reached into his coat pocket and pulled out the pad his mother had drawn on in the days leading up to her death. Flipping it to the appropriate page, he placed it flat on the table and slid it over to Winston.

"This is what my mother claimed she saw in her room before her death," George explained. "She claimed this in her lucid moments. They were rare, but she did have them. I can also play the sleep recordings on her phone and you can hear them for yourself. Also, according to what Esther told Mags, these drawings my mother made are the same things *your* mother claimed to see in her room as well."

This time Winston's expression did change. He could no longer mask his terror and he was no longer trying. "We should leave now," he said abruptly.

"I'm sorry?"

"We should leave," Winston said again.

Magdalena leaned closer to him. "And go where?"

"I think somewhere private and not so noisy would be best."

"Can you tell us why?" George asked.

"Because," Winston said, scowling. "I think I've seen one too."

# CHAPTER FIFTEEN

FREEZING WIND WHIPPED THROUGH the trailer park as Magdalena unlocked her door. Kaley clutched the edge of her mother's coat sleeve with one hand, Amanda the Panda in the other. "Come on in," she said to George and Winston, both of whom shuffled in behind her. "Having some issues with the heat, supposed to be someone coming to look at it Monday."

Magdalena hoped they believed her. She was embarrassed enough bringing them to the shabby trailer; if they found out she couldn't pay her bills she'd be mortified. But once they were inside it became immediately apparent that it wasn't much warmer inside the trailer than it was outside.

George looked around curiously while Winston remained just inside the door, seemingly hesitant to step deeper into the trailer's interior. He looked so small to Magdalena, a lost and rather delicate soul riddled with confusion and uncertainty. *Such an awkward guy*, she thought, watching as he shivered a bit, his glasses sliding down the bridge of his nose.

"It's all right, Winston," she told him. "Just me and Kaley live here."

He pushed his glasses back into place. "I see."

"It's not much but it's clean. I sanitize everything because of my daughter."

"Don't worry," George said, clapping Winston playfully on the back. "You're not going catch anything, for crying out loud. We're all stressed enough as it is, no need to—"

"I'm well aware of that," Winston said stiffly. "I could've been killed tonight."

"Yes, well, we're all shaken by whatever the hell is happening," George replied, following Magdalena as she moved deeper into the trailer.

Winston remained where he was, glancing around awkwardly. "I've never known anyone that lived in a trailer," he said softly. "It's actually much nicer than what you see in movies and on those hoarder shows."

"Well, thanks," Magdalena said. "I think."

Kaley eyed the men, her gaze flickering to George and then back to Winston, taking in his scraped hands and pants torn at the knee and stained with crimson.

"Kaley, this is Mr. Gage and Mr. Tucker," Magdalena told her. "They're Mommy's friends and they're going to visit for a little while."

"Did you fall down?" Kaley asked Winston.

Winston cleared his throat, his eyes darting back and forth without ever settling on the child. "I did, yes. I did."

"Sometimes I fall down and scrape my hands and sometimes my knees too," Kaley said. "It hurts and I cry sometimes. Did you cry?"

"No," Winston said. "Well...not really."

"Were you playing and not paying attention? Mommy says you should always pay attention so you don't fall down and get hurt, but I still do sometimes."

Winston looked as if his head might explode at any moment, so Magdalena said, "Sometimes grownups have accidents too, sweetie. He's okay."

"Hello there, Kaley," George said, trying to shift her attention to him. "It's nice to meet you."

"It's nice to meet you, Mr.—"

"You go ahead and call me George, okay?"

"Okay. This is Amanda." Kaley held up the stuffed panda.

"How are you, Amanda?" George moved closer to the kitchen table where Magdalena stood holding her. "I've got to tell you, that is one beautiful panda right there."

"Yeah," Kaley said, as if this was blatantly obvious.

"It is rather cold in here," Winston said, still standing near the door. He glanced around nervously. "You do have *some* heat, don't you?"

"Of course," Magdalena said. "It just takes a long time to kick in. That's why they're coming to fix it Monday. Have a seat. I'll clear off the table." She quickly scooped up the stack of overdue notices and bills and shoved them between a cookie jar and a coffeemaker on the counter, unsure if she'd done so in time. She looked over at George. He smiled warmly as if to let her know it was all right.

*He knows,* she thought. *My God, I'm so embarrassed.*

"About a million years ago, before I was married," George said. "I lived in a trailer very similar to this, and I always had issues with the heat too. It's not that unusual with the propane heat in a lot of these old trailers."

"Yeah," Magdalena said, trying to force any emotion from her voice. "It happens."

"I'll just keep my coat on, if you don't mind," Winston said.

Magdalena put Kaley down then crouched before her and said, "I left your coloring book and crayons on the coffee table in front of the TV. Why don't you go color while I talk to my friends, okay? Be a good girl and later on, before you go to bed, we'll have hot chocolate, how's that sound?"

"Good," Kaley answered through a big smile.

"Hey, Kaley," George said, "would you mind leaving Amanda here with me for just a little while?"

"Do you want to play with her?" Kaley looked at George with wide eyes.

"Would that be okay?"

Kaley looked at Amanda a moment, thinking it over, then nodded and held her out for George. "Okay."

"Thanks, that's awfully nice of you," George said, taking the stuffed panda and holding it as if he could barely contain his excitement. "I promise I'll take good care of her."

"Go finish coloring that pretty princess you started last night," Magdalena told her. "Mommy won't be long with her friends."

The little girl scurried over to her coloring book and sat on the floor with it in front of the television.

"What a great kid," George said.

"Thanks, she is, isn't she?" Magdalena smiled. "Can I get you guys some coffee?"

"Nothing for me," Winston said. He still hadn't moved from the door.

George shook his head in the negative. "I'm all set, thanks."

"Do you want me to take a look at your knee, Winston?" Magdalena asked, noticing how he cringed at the idea. "Or can I at least get you some Tylenol or something?"

"I'd like very much to wash my hands, if you don't mind." Winston showed her his palms as if in evidence. "They're still quite sore, as is my knee. But I think I'll be fine if I can just sanitize the scrapes on my palms."

"Everything you need is right there," she said, pointing to a small sink where liquid soap, a roll of paper towels, and a bottle of hand sanitizer sat on the counter. "Band-Aids are in the top drawer. I tend to stash them everywhere with Kaley being so accident prone. Kids, you know."

Winston cautiously made his way to the sink, moving as if he expected to encounter quicksand at any moment. "Thank you," he said once he'd made it.

While he commenced to washing and disinfecting his hands like a surgeon getting ready to operate, George leaned close to Magdalena. "I don't mean to overstep here," he said, nearly whispering, "but you might want to give the community action center downtown a try. They have a heating assistance program you'd likely qualify for."

"I'll look into it," she said, feeling her face blush. "Things have spiraled out of control since my husband left and I—"

At that moment Winston appeared at George's side, silencing her. His wounds cleaned, he spoke quickly as he took in a nearby lopsided bookcase and the inexpensive kitchen table where George had set Amanda the Panda. "I'm sorry to interrupt your private conversation, but we're here for the purpose of discussing these incidents, are we not?"

"Yes, Winston," George said, rolling his eyes and moving to the other side of the table. "That's why we're here."

"Normally I would never agree to meet at a bar—or to come here— but I'm worried about my mother. After what happened tonight, quite frankly, I must confess I'm worried about myself as well."

"Listen to this," George said, pulling his mother's phone from his coat pocket. "This was my mother's. The recordings were made while she was asleep in her room at Matheson."

As he held the phone up so he and Magdalena could listen, the app came to life and the recordings played the eerie voices that had been recorded.

"There's more," Magdalena said. Retrieving Amanda from the table, she played the recordings the stuffed animal had captured as well, the odd monotone voices echoing through the trailer.

Winston's left eye began to noticeably twitch. He removed his glasses for a moment and pawed at his eye. "Were those recorded here?" he asked.

"In my daughter's bedroom," Magdalena said grimly.

"My mother, she's been talking about seeing and hearing things in her room at night. The same things, apparently, that made Esther leave her job so suddenly."

"And the same things on all these recordings," George added.

Winston returned his eyeglasses to his face. "As I mentioned earlier, the things your mother drew, I…I saw something similar."

"Go on," George said evenly.

Winston frowned, equal parts frustrated and frightened. "I feel as if I've fallen through the proverbial rabbit hole, although at this point it may not be quite as *proverbial* as one might hope. I don't have any recordings, but I have been receiving strange phone calls of late. Mostly just strange white noise and occasionally an electronic screeching, but it wasn't until the other night, when I was on my way home from visiting Mother at Matheson, that I actually *saw* something. "

As Magdalena and George listened, Winston fumbled through his story about taking the bus, the confrontation with the enigmatic man, and how when he'd gotten off, at the rear window there was a shadowy figure looking out at him.

"And you're sure that you, the driver, and this strange man in the hospital garb were the only people on that bus?" George asked.

"Positive," Winston said. "I couldn't see a lot of detail, but it looked a lot like those horrible things your mother drew."

"Okay, we know my mother experienced them before her death," George said, as if thinking aloud. "And now, Winston, your mother is experiencing them too."

"And so am I," Magdalena said. "Kaley's heard them too."

"There's no way to know for sure if what happened to me tonight is connected to all of this," Winston said. "It may or may not be, but I think it premature to rule it out one way or the other."

"So what do we do then?" George asked. "Where do we go from here? I ran a bookstore for years. I'm not exactly equipped for this kind of thing."

They all stood staring at each other as another burst of icy winter wind pummeled the trailer. Nothing seemed real, yet there was a strange familiarity to their gathering none of them could shake, and a profoundly disturbing feeling of dread descended upon them.

"I work in computers," Winston finally said.

Magdalena arched an eyebrow. "Okay, and?"

"Of course, I've never heard these specific recordings until this evening," he said. "But I have heard of such things happening before, and I have heard similar inexplicable recordings allegedly made while people were asleep."

George seemed genuinely surprised. "You *have?*"

"I hesitate to claim I believe in much of it, but I've always been something of a paranormal buff," Winston explained. "It's a hobby, I suppose, just something I find interesting. There are countless strange and unexplained audio and even visual phenomena out there. One only needs to know where to look. Numerous videos exist across the Internet.

YouTube and other such sites have an endless supply of them, though most of what you'll find there are hoaxes and amateurish fakes. One has to dig considerably *deeper* to find examples that may be real occurrences."

"I've honestly never put much stock in this kind of thing either," George said.

"Whatever we're dealing with is real," Magdalena insisted. "Winston, you've seen them. And now we've *all* heard them."

George nodded. "You're right. But I ask again, now what?"

"I have the ability to get onto sites and into areas most can't," Winston clarified guardedly. "And I can do it without anyone noticing. A special browser, a few encrypted numbers, and I can not only open a lot of otherwise locked doors, but I can do it undetected."

"Are you one of those hackers?" George asked.

"I am an IT professional," Winston corrected him.

A slight smile pursed George's lips. "You're a hacker."

Feathers ruffled, Winston blushed and shook his head. "We need to know more. We have to know if they're dangerous, if they'll hurt my mother, or Kaley, or any of us. Are you two familiar with what is commonly referred to as the *dark web*?"

"I've heard stories about it," Magdalena said. "But I've never actually seen it."

"Same," George told him.

"Many horrible people lurk there. Criminals, degenerates, sexual deviants, predators, pain freaks, pedophiles, human traffickers, and violent extreme political groups, just to name a few."

"Sounds charming," George said.

"There are a lot of very sick people in this world," Winston announced, as if this were news to anyone.

"Are you saying these things have something to do with the dark web?" George asked.

"I've no way to know that yet, of course. But, if that's where I conduct my research, whatever information I uncover is far more likely to be reliable." Winston wrung his hands. "I've seen things there, and once you learn of what's taking place in the darkest corners of the web, you can't unlearn them, do you understand? There's no erasing these things once you've seen them. Because there's the dark web, and then there's the *deep* web. It's even more disturbing, but it's also more reliable in terms of the authenticity of what you find there. It could hold the answers we're looking for. I have access to a browser that isolates any website I visit. It's virtually impossible to hack my IP with all the safeguards I have installed. I can't be tracked. I can't be *fingerprinted*, as it were. That's important because you've got to remain anonymous when you go that far into the dark."

*There's a lot more to this uptight little geek than I realized*, Magdalena thought.

"Do you have a computer, Mags?" George asked.

"I mostly use my phone these days, but there's a desktop in my bedroom," she said.

"How old is it?" Winston asked in a condescending tone.

"Seven or eight years, I guess. It's nothing fancy."

Winston laughed for the first time, his slender body quaking as he released a whiny chuckle. "That won't do at all, I'm afraid. I need to go home and use my equipment."

"I can't leave Kaley alone again tonight." Magdalena crossed her arms defiantly.

"No need," George said quickly. "I'll drive Winston back to his place, see what he's talking about and what he can find. You take care of Kaley. We'll be in touch soon as we know anything more. That is, if you're okay being by yourself tonight. If not, we can—"

"No, it's fine, go," she said, hugging herself. "Just be careful."

"If you have any…difficulties…go over to your neighbor's place. Make sure you bring your phone with you, and call us right away." George gave Magdalena a knowing wink. "Matter of fact, since the heating guy isn't coming until Monday, maybe you should spend the night at your neighbor's house anyway. It's awfully cold in here."

"We'll be all right," she assured him. "But if it gets too cold, we will."

The men made their way to the door. "Bye, Kaley!" George called to her. "Thanks for letting me play with Amanda!"

"You're welcome," Kaley answered. "Bye."

Winston gave a subtle, jerky little wave goodbye but said nothing more.

When they'd left and she'd closed and locked the door behind them, Winston's words about the dark web and all the crazies out there stayed with her, replaying in her mind. A moment later she heard George's car come to life and pull away.

Once they'd gone, she treated Kaley to the promised hot chocolate, then helped her into her pajamas and tucked her into bed, all the while trying her best to appear calm. She knew if Kaley sensed the fear Magdalena felt, she might become frightened as well.

Later, once her daughter had fallen asleep, Magdalena checked all the windows in the trailer, latching those that weren't already, and then, just to be sure nothing was out of place and no strangers were roaming around the property, peeked out the front window.

"Nobody out there," she whispered, thinking again about what Winston had told them. Maybe she couldn't get on something as exotic as the deep web, but she could pull up some YouTube videos on her phone.

Clicking on her browser, Magdalena found YouTube, then keyed in a search for DARK WEB VIDEOS.

The first link read: HAUNTINGS AND INTRUDERS

With a deep breath, she hit PLAY.

The video began with a pitch-black screen. After a moment, a man with a British accent began to speak in a slow, eerie, emotionless monotone.

"In 2010, a woman named Emily Sullivan, of Hartford, Connecticut, began to experience what she believed to be paranormal activity in her apartment. Ms. Sullivan, 28 years of age at the time, lived alone and was employed at a credit union just blocks from her apartment building. After experiencing what she described as strange, unidentifiable sounds while trying to sleep, and finding things misplaced around her apartment come morning, Ms. Sullivan decided to set up a video camera to record her bedroom while she slept. One particularly hot summer evening, Ms. Sullivan reported she had trouble sleeping and came awake very late at night. She claimed something she could not explain entered her room at that point and attacked her. Be warned, what you are about to see is the actual video Emily Sullivan recorded that frightening hot summer night. Viewer discretion is *strongly* encouraged."

A chill running up the back of her neck, Magdalena looked around quickly then returned her attention to her phone.

The black screen went to static and then suddenly to what looked like an old grainy surveillance videotape. Through the shadows, she could make out a small bed against a wall and a young woman sleeping on her side, facing the camera.

Very slowly, something near the foot of her bed separated from the shadows.

The woman seemed to come awake then slowly sat up, as if in a trance.

Suddenly, a close-up of Linda Blair's hideously ravaged face in *The Exorcist* filled the screen along with a loud screeching sound.

"Jesus!" Magdalena gasped, so frightened by the jump scare that she nearly dropped the phone. "Fucking assholes scared the shit out of me!"

Trembling, she closed the browser and put her phone on the counter. The whole thing was just a joke, but it had left her badly rattled, and as angry as she was frightened.

"Fuck this," she muttered, and quickly donning hat, coat, and gloves, hurried to Kaley's bedroom. Gently scooping her up, she wrapped a blanket around Kaley's tiny body, making sure her head was covered too.

"Mommy, I was dreaming," Kaley mumbled, barely awake. "What are you doing?"

"We're going to Mrs. Bucci's for the night."

"How come?"

"Mommy wants to wait for George and Mr. Tucker there. It's too cold in here."

"George is nice," Kaley muttered, her eyes closing as she drifted back to sleep. "And Mr. Tucker makes me laugh. He's funny."

As she crossed the kitchen with Kaley tucked beneath her left arm, Magdalena plucked a steak knife free of the wooden knife block on the counter with her free hand and carefully placed it in her coat pocket.

As she left the trailer, the wind picked up as if to welcome her. The cold air was jarring, but she hesitated and looked around. The park was dark, quiet, still.

But somewhere just beneath the howling winter wind, or perhaps from somewhere deep within her own mind, Magdalena was certain she heard an eerie whispering voice telling her to

*Sleep...*

# CHAPTER SIXTEEN

ALTHOUGH THE MOON WAS hidden behind heavy cloud cover, leaving the night exceptionally dark, and the already freezing temperatures had dropped even lower, the ride to Winston's house was uneventful. Due to the slippery roads, George kept his concentration focused on driving, but occasionally checked his mirrors for any dark and ominous SUVs that might be tailing them. After several failed attempts to engage Winston in conversation about what was taking place, George gave up. His replies were brief and distracted, leaving George to wonder if Winston was simply preoccupied with his own thoughts or only displaying further evidence of his social awkwardness. Either way, at least for now there seemed no point in pressing him.

*What a strange series of events,* George thought, as they rolled to a stop for a red light. *All of them leading me to this point, to this night, and to this man I barely know yet have no choice but to trust.* Never had George imagined spending his time this way in the days following his mother's death, but here he was, on this brutally cold and remarkably dark night, in the throes of a mystery so bizarre he couldn't even fully comprehend it.

"Take a left at the next block," Winston said.

When the light turned green, George continued to the following block, then turned onto a sketchy but quiet street, surprised to see how bad the neighborhood was. They'd been getting steadily worse for a few minutes now, and as George found himself in a part of the city he normally drove straight through on his way to other places, he tried to imagine Winston living here.

*How does he survive in a neighborhood like this?*

Due to the way he presented himself, George had expected Winston to live in a nicer area, perhaps one a bit more rural. Instead, following Winston's instructions, George pulled up and parked in front of an old and dated two-story house in what was clearly a largely forgotten but dangerous neighborhood. Most of the houses and walkups were in various stages of disrepair, with bars on the windows and steel front doors. Several homeless people were curled up nearby, lying on the sidewalks, their breath escaping them in dramatic, smoke-like plumes. Some had covered themselves in newspapers and used scraps of cardboard for beds. A couple of them were lucky enough to have actual blankets.

*My God*, George thought. *How can they last for long in this cold?*

"It used to be such a nice neighborhood," Winston said. He sighed heavily, looking out the window a moment as if working up the courage to get out of the car. "Now look at it."

George didn't know what to say, so he asked, "Have you lived here long?"

"Almost all my life," Winston said, gripping the door handle, his eyes still trained on the house looming over them. "The sidewalks are covered in ice, be careful not to fall."

George found the area creepy, and the house Winston called home even more so. As they both got out of the Chevy and walked around to the sidewalk, Winston hesitated and pointed across the street to where an empty space and a couple trash cans were located.

"That's where the strange car was parked when I first saw it on my way home," he said, then turned and pointed to an upstairs window facing the street. "And I saw it from that window too."

"So you got a good look at it more than once."

Winston nodded as if that should've been obvious from his statement, then moved across the sidewalk and up the porch steps to the front door, a ring of keys jingling in his hand.

Following, George stepped into a foyer which was dimly lit by a nightlight in the shape of a covered wagon plugged into a socket near the baseboards. He was immediately hit with the warmer air inside the house, along with a heady smell, some sort of cleaner that contained bleach. Beneath both, a faint but distinctly musty odor lingered, the kind one might expect to encounter in an old cellar. To his right was a living room outfitted with furniture that looked like new but was old and out-of-date, and straight ahead, just to the left of a staircase, laid an equally dated kitchen. Even at a distance, George could see it had a rooster theme. They were everywhere in there.

The place reminded him of a movie set from the 1950s.

Winston removed his shoes and placed them on a small mat just inside the door, then looked at George. "Please remove your footwear in the house."

"Oh," George said, quickly kicking off his slip-on Sketchers and dropping them on the mat next to the other pair of shoes. "Sure, no problem, my mother had the same rule growing up."

Hardly enamored with this information, Winston stared at him as if it were totally irrelevant. "Yes. At any rate..." He removed his coat and hung it in a nearby closet. "You may hang your coat here if you'd like."

George did, then glanced around a bit. While the outside looked terrible, the inside of the house was pristine. Almost too clean and tidy, George thought, to the point where it barely looked as if anyone actually lived here. "Nice place you've got, Winston."

"Thank you. Since I'm by myself now it's rather big, but it's my home."

"I know what it's like to come home to an empty house. It's not exactly something to look forward to. But at least you have a roof over your head and a lot of history here, I'd imagine. Good memories."

Looking uncertain regarding the intent behind many of George's comments, Winston guardedly replied, "Mostly wonderful memories. Of course, the house was much livelier and warmer when Mother was here."

"I bet," George said gently.

"Since she...well...I've done my best to maintain things as she'd want me to. But it's not the same."

"I understand." George wanted to drop a hand on his shoulder and give it a reassuring squeeze, but he knew with Winston that would likely make things even more awkward. "Believe me, I do."

"Having *truly* lost your mother, I'm certain you do."

"I lost my wife to cancer last year too."

Brow knitted, Winston frowned. "I'm very sorry."

"Thanks."

The two men stood there a moment, neither speaking.

"Do you, I mean, would you like anything?" Winston eventually asked. "I have coffee, tea, orange juice, and bottled water. I also have a package of Lorna Doone cookies."

*Jesus*, George thought, *I didn't know they still made those.* "I'm okay, thanks."

"They're quite tasty."

"It's okay, I'm fine."

Winston nodded but looked unsure. "I ah, I—I don't really have *guests*, per se, so I'm sorry if I—"

"Winston, you're good. We're both good. Everything's good."

With an intensely serious expression, he motioned to the staircase. "We should go up to my room and get started then."

George stifled a laugh. All he could think of was a horror movie where the unsuspecting visitor follows the socially awkward and peculiar momma's boy up to his room, only to be slaughtered in a fashion Norman Bates would be proud of. Of course, he had no real fear of Winston, odd as he was, and even the briefest of humorous thoughts were a welcome change from what had already been an intense evening. And George knew there was a good chance it might get a lot worse.

"Lead the way."

Winston's room reminded George of a space better suited to a preteen boy, with the exception of how extraordinarily clean and neat it was. Shelves were packed with an array of dated but pristine toys and gadgets, many of them still in their original packaging, and a small, neatly made bed, complete with a Star Trek comforter, filled one wall. Opposite the bed there stood a bank of computer equipment, most of it displayed across a sprawling desk unit. In addition to the monitors, keyboards, and standing towers, there were many pieces of equipment George couldn't identify.

"That's quite a command center you've got there."

This seemed to please Winston. "Yes," he said, smiling blandly. "It's not only my job, it's my passion."

*That and action figures from the 1970s,* George thought.

"Computers, that is," Winston added, noticing how George had looked at the old toys. "It's what I know."

George motioned to the equipment. "By all means then, do your thing."

Since there was only a single chair at the computer wall, Winston suggested George sit on the edge of his bed. As George did so, Winston sat in a high-backed leather swivel on wheels and got to work, bringing everything to life like some sort of crazed modern-day wizard. Lights and beeps and hums filled the room as the various pieces booted and powered up, and Winston was immediately someone else, unusually comfortable and confident as he maneuvered from one piece of equipment to the next, clicking away on three different keyboards before wheeling himself over to a piece on the far side of the desk, a contraption with several rows of blinking lights that looked like something out of the cockpit of a spaceship. It had the look of something Winston might have built rather than bought.

Once everything was up and running, he spun around in his chair to face George. "You have to understand this may take some time. I can get into certain rooms and other areas where people discuss these kinds of things. Normally such areas also have examples of various phenomena.

The difference between such sites on the Internet and those found on the dark web is that here, in the dark, there's nearly always some sort of agenda. There's also a reason—paranoia, imagined, genuine, or otherwise—as to why those involved are operating under what they believe is the cover of the deep web. I'm going to have to sift through a lot of information, most of which is likely of no use to us, and that takes time. But if there's any kind of trail that directly relates to what we've experienced, I'll find it."

George eyed the monitors. One appeared to be doing a search or scan of some kind, as rows of number sequences scrolled by at such a rapid pace he couldn't make out what any of them said. The second was dark but on, and the third had a single rectangular box sitting against an otherwise black background. "Okay," he said, suddenly oddly uncomfortable. "So, what exactly happens now then?"

Slowly spinning his chair back toward his desk, Winston began to click away on the nearest keyboard, the blue glow from the equipment bathing his face and reflecting off his glasses. "We take one giant step into the dark."

* * * *

It was the headache that came first. Starting behind his right eye, it moved with a rhythmic pulsing into his temple before slowly spreading down into his jaw. Along with the pain, there came a series of strange flashes and alterations of light. Like a prism, the lights rotated in various colors before his eyes, turning and slashing at the fabric of what he knew to be reality.

"There's something wrong," George heard himself say, his voice rough and strained, as if it took every bit of his energy to generate it. "Something's *wrong*."

*Tell us what you see...*

A crackling sound in his ears accompanied the flashes, and then everything before his eyes began to splinter. The only thing George could liken it to was the way a television signal, when interfered with or suffering from a poor signal, fragmented then regenerated in a series of tiles and electronic pulses. The world around him crumbled then reset, only to crackle and break apart again.

Clutching his head with his hands, George could no longer be sure if he was standing or seated. As quickly as the prisms had appeared, they were gone, taking all light with them. He'd gone blind, and all he could hear was the strange crackling sound, like a light socket on the verge of an electrical fire. The sound grew louder and louder, joining the pain already present and searing his skull as words came to him as if from very far away.

*It'll pass. You're okay. It's all you now.*

He thought for sure the pain would cause him to pass out, but suddenly it ceased, leaving only darkness and an eerie silence. Yet he was conscious, he could feel it, sense it. This was no dream. He no longer had any sense of his physical self, of up or down, left or right. Lost in the darkness, George had become an untethered entity of pure consciousness, free-floating in an all-encompassing nightscape.

All sound was gone, and he couldn't feel anything, not even fear. He simply *was*, existing now in a weightless nothingness, an empty void into which he'd been absorbed.

From the black came a hint of green. A small bar, like a computer prompt, flashing, as a seemingly endless series of numbers and strange symbols George didn't recognize began to fall through the darkness before him like rain. They just kept coming, falling in sheets and moving faster and faster, as whispers echoed all around him, muttering something as indecipherable as the green numbers and symbols racing past his eyes.

Or was it his mind's eye?

George could no longer be sure.

The fear returned, along with the pain, his screams of agony drowning out the mutterings and crackling until he was exhausted, and only the sounds of his labored breathing remained.

"Can you hear me?" a strange voice said, echoing through the dark chamber.

*Is that a human voice?* George wondered, because it sounded similar to a human voice. But something was wrong. Something was very wrong.

"What is the basis of reality?"

*Something's wrong.*

"George, can you hear me? Listen to the sound of my voice, George."

*Winston, something's wrong!*

"What is the basis of reality, George?"

*Winston is—is that you? Wait, that—that's not you!*

The sequences fell apart, the numbers and symbols separating and falling away, tumbling through the darkness around him as if someone or something had hit the sheets with a hammer.

Darkness…

In the distance, at the very edges of George's perception, an image emerged.

An old stone bridge over turbulent water, the forest beyond it dark…

"It's all right, George," a voice said. "You're okay. Come back."

\* \* \* \*

George sensed then saw light, as everything slowly came into focus.

"Do you mind?" Winston said, standing over him.

"What's happening?" George asked groggily.

"Would you sit up, please? I don't mind you sitting on my bed, but I'd prefer you didn't...you know...*recline*, as it were."

Realizing he was lying on his side, George sat up, still confused. "Sorry, I—"

"You fell asleep," Winston explained.

"I haven't had much lately, must've nodded off."

"Yes, it's very late." Winston pushed his glasses higher on the bridge of his nose and sighed. "Are you coherent now?"

"Yeah," he said, standing. "I was having the strangest dream."

"I'm not surprised. You were making odd noises."

Embarrassed, George asked, "Did you come up with anything?"

"Yes. In fact, I'm surprised at the amount of examples out there that could be connected to whatever this phenomenon is we're dealing with."

"Maybe this goes deeper than just us and some people we know."

"That certainly appears to be a possibility," Winston said, looking not only puzzled and drained, but frightened. "Of course, I can't be sure of the authenticity of most, but there is something I came across I think you need to see."

Cocking his head back and forth in an attempt to loosen the stiffness in his neck, George moved closer to the monitors. One in particular had a series of words emblazoned across its screen. They stopped him cold.

WHAT IS THE BASIS OF REALITY?

# CHAPTER SEVENTEEN

UNABLE TO BELIEVE WHAT he was seeing, George asked, "What is that?"

"A broadcast," Winston said, motioning to the monitor.

George read the title of the program again.

WHAT IS THE BASIS OF REALITY?

"That phrase," he said. "I saw it before, when I was dreaming."

Winston arched an eyebrow. "You mean just now?"

With a nod, George moved closer to the monitor. "How is that possible?"

Perplexed, Winston stood there a moment, then sat in his leather chair and quickly typed something on the keyboard. "I suspect the deeper we go here, the more we may be forced to rethink what is and isn't *possible*."

George focused on the screen. Had he somehow seen these words there before? Was it possible he came awake at one point, saw them without consciously realizing it, then fell back to sleep? How else could he have dreamed of them?

"The broadcasts cover a range of paranormal and government conspiracy topics," Winston said. "But this isn't your typical nonsense in that regard. The phrase you see is a code, a marker for those searching for this group's content."

"What are they exactly?"

"Recorded segments originally streamed live and still available out there if you know where to look, or, like in this instance, stumble onto them while searching peripheral themes."

"And who's behind them?"

Winston nervously fiddled with his glasses. "An underground dark web group that presents information anonymously, and far as I can tell, they're legitimate. The particular broadcast I have cued up concerns a man by the name of Jules Valentine, a former Roman Catholic priest. I was able to do some basic research on the man and found he was defrocked several years ago for what the church deemed *heretical views*. He was employed in a diocese in upstate New York at the time, but they moved him around quite a bit prior to that. Seems he was a bit of a problem case for some time. His specialty was working with the elderly and the dying. Most of his assignments were to nursing homes and hospitals, and he did a lot of hospice work. Beyond that, there isn't much personal information on him out there, which I suspect in today's day and age is not an accident. There are a couple links to utterly unqualified conspiracy theory fools on YouTube that mention him and his followers, but I found them to be of little use."

"When you say *followers*, are we talking online or literal?" George asked.

"Apparently, not long after Valentine was stripped of his priesthood, he and a small band of disciples he'd garnered by then fled to an undisclosed location and formed a sort of, well, for lack of a better word, *sect*."

"You mean like a cult?"

"I suppose that word could apply as well, yes."

"Terrific," George said, sighing.

"Valentine and his group didn't want the public to know where they were located, and this group doing the broadcast on him went to extreme lengths to conceal that. It took a while, but I was able to break through their security and safeguards. What you are about to see originated from northern Vermont." With an uncertain frown, Winston looked back over his shoulder at George. "But you need to understand, it's very disturbing."

Out in the dark, a cold winter wind blew, rocking the old house.

"At this point I'd expect nothing less," George said.

Winston hit the appropriate key and the broadcast began.

As the words dissolved away, absorbed into the black screen, the sound of something brushing against a microphone could be heard, like someone had drawn something across it before positioning it correctly. And then, gradually, something began to emerge from the darkness.

A wooded area, snowy and remote…

In the distance, a lone figure walked slowly down an incline toward the camera. As he approached, they could see it was a man. He appeared to be in his late sixties or early seventies, and once he was closer, it was his striking ice blue eyes they noticed first. Bald but for a neatly trimmed horseshoe of gray hair on the lower portion of his head, the man had a closely cropped silver beard and was clad in a brown robe similar to a monastic scapular. At first glance he looked like a mad monk from the

Middle Ages. Behind him, nestled in the snowy forest, was a small cabin, but it was difficult to tell much in the way of detail.

"That's Valentine," Winston said.

Off camera an electronically altered voice said, "Thank you for allowing us to come and speak with you. We believe what you have to say is not only important, but essential. We can only hope people will listen."

After several seconds of thoughtfully staring at the camera, the man finally responded in a deep, rich voice a radio announcer would've envied. "Whether they admit it or not," he said, plumes of breath dancing around him in the cold air, "most people have come to realize that things are not as they once were even a short while ago. They understand something has changed in our world, something fundamental and tangible. They don't feel the same as they once did. They're on edge, nervous, frightened, angry, and uncertain of the world around us. Nothing seems quite as familiar as it once did. Many of our memories no longer feel the same, as if we're remembering them incorrectly, even when we're certain we're not. Because they often no longer align with what we believed previously, they, like reality at present, are askew. We all know it. We all feel it. And this goes beyond politics or normal, expected changes that happen over time with each new generation. No. *This* is not *that*. *This* is different. *This* is alien to your experience on planet Earth. You know what it's like to be alive in our world, and suddenly that is—*has become*—something else, something *off*. Even a slight difference is enough to cause tremendous waves of stress and anxiety throughout our entire world. We can't identify it, can't quite put our finger on it, but we know it to be true. Nothing is the same. It's as if something has shifted. We feel a sense of unavoidable, inevitable dread—doom—and we don't know why. It's a horrible thing to wake up one morning and realize that the world you find yourself wandering through is not the same one it was when you went to sleep. You understand it may look somewhat similar, but profound changes have taken place. *Alterations* you failed to notice earlier. Why? Because they weren't there, that's why. This is new. *They* are new. And yet, they're older than time."

The man began to stroll, his footfalls crunching the frozen ground. The camera followed, the still slightly-out-of-focus snowy forest deepening behind him.

"I spent my life helping others transition to the other side," Valentine continued. "There were always things I couldn't understand, mysteries I couldn't solve. Anyone that works with terminal patients will tell you the same thing. But that's all they were, small mysteries, a phrase spoken near death, someone briefly claiming to see someone or hear something the rest of us couldn't. Visitations, messages from loved ones that had gone before them, these types of incidents have always taken place, they're nothing new. What's happening now is different. I've witnessed the changes firsthand, and searching for answers to what is really going on, and why, destroyed my former life. It's likely only a matter of time before it also destroys what life I have left, as well as the lives of those closest to me, those few who have not only seen the truth, but chosen to seek refuge with me. And that is not only despite our enlightenment, but more likely because of it."

As Valentine continued, George realized that although the man was speaking in vague terms, his words had nonetheless struck him as profoundly accurate. He *did* feel those things. He had for some time, and obviously he was not alone.

"What began subtly has become blatant," Valentine said, no longer looking at the camera but instead gazing off into the forest. "It's all right before our eyes, but we, as a society, have trained ourselves, through some false and absurdly arrogant sense of knowledge and greater understanding—neither of which most truly possess—to disconnect ourselves from the spirit world, from anything we cannot see, hear, touch, smell, or taste. Despite the fact that science long ago proved there is an entire realm that does not fall within the reach of our five senses, we have convinced ourselves otherwise. So why have we done this then? Have we concluded that while some things do exist beyond our capacities, they're unimportant? We know for a fact that our species can only see a limited amount of the light spectrum. Why, then, do we convince ourselves so adamantly that there is nothing beyond our means, in that enormous scope of vision, simply because we cannot see it? Here's the oddest part. We haven't. We know there exists an entire spectrum we cannot see—we know this—and yet we and others continually work to convince the world none of that matters. Whistling past the graveyard?"

Valentine returned his gaze to the camera, his expression more sorrow than fear. "Perhaps," he said. "The reality, whether we like it or not, whether it's convenient or fits nicely into our tiny box of knowledge we're so sure of, is that the spirit dimension exists alongside the material one, whether we can always see it or not. It's happening right now, all around us, at all times."

George and Winston watched as Valentine continued.

"Your broadcasts ask the question: What is the basis of reality?" Valentine's expression grew darker. "The fact of the matter is we are wired to know and experience these things. It's chemical. It's in our brains and literally part of our makeup as human entities. We can deny it all we'd like, but that won't change a thing. Facts don't care what you think or want to believe.

"Our brains are designed to receive this information," he continued. "But we have spent hundreds of years reprogramming ourselves to ignore that, to turn it off. What so many fail to see, however, is that those entities in these other realms—and they are many—could not possibly care less what we believe. They continue to do their work regardless."

A burst of wind muffled the microphone as several branches on the trees behind Valentine swayed and dumped snow to the already snow-covered ground.

"Know this," he said. "There are forces in this world that are well aware of these things, and they work diligently to keep them from the general public. Even now, with these recent shifts in our world, our reality, they use all of their powers to keep the proverbial genie in the bottle as best they can. They see that their efforts are weakening, but still they deny and deflect. Slowly, gradually, we are seeing more and more *modifications* to our reality, and make no mistake, these—*they*—are only *new* to our muddled consciousness. The walls are fading, crumbling, as it were, and while no one is exactly sure why, there seems to be no way to stop it. Despite our perceived intelligence and might, they are not at our mercy. *We* are at theirs."

The picture suddenly went dark then quickly came back into focus, but now Valentine was inside, presumably in the cabin they'd seen behind him earlier.

Sitting at an old wooden table, the only light coming from a couple candles placed before him, Valentine sat with his hands folded and his head bowed in prayer. Surrounded by shadows, his lips moved silently, and then slowly, he raised his head and looked directly into the camera again.

"If you've been led here and are watching me now," he finally said, his voice softer, "you must understand that you're here for a reason. You've found us on your own or someone has helped you find us, but you're here because you've seen and heard them too, or someone close to you has. You're here because you've noticed what's happening all around us in the shadows of our world, perhaps you've been confronted with it, and you've chosen to no longer look the other way because you no longer can. You've not only felt these beings, you've seen and heard them as well. They're standing right behind you even now, and when they realize you've noticed them, they tell you to sleep. More often than not that is exactly what you do, because the human mind would rather protect itself through sedation than face what might actually be happening. We tell ourselves they're hallucinations or nightmares, things seen and heard by damaged or dying, diseased minds. But you know now, or at a minimum suspect, that is not, and has never been, true."

Valentine shifted his position subtly, and George and Winston could see he was holding rosary beads, the crucifix at the end lying on the table before him. "We believe these entities come primarily, though not exclusively, to the sick and dying, to those struggling with mental health issues, or souls facing a spiritual or religious crisis. They do their work in the night, in darkness and shadows, when we're the most vulnerable and malleable to their intentions."

"Father," the man behind the camera says, voice still electronically disguised. "Who are they?"

"Not who," Valentine said. "*What*."

"All right, *what* are they then?"

"There are examples all over the Internet and documented in several books, but such things are generally written off as hoaxes and flights of fantasy. Many are just that. But we know the truth. Many are not." Valentine grimaced as if in pain. "I've *seen* them. I've heard their voices. On numerous occasions, many of us have *recorded* them." His blue eyes locked on the camera. "And I still haven't any idea."

Silence fell over the cabin a moment.

"I've had the audio recordings analyzed, as have others," Valentine said, sighing. "In every instance where the recordings were legitimate— that is to say, they were proven not to be tampered with or faked—audio experts have concluded these voices fall well beyond the normal range of human vocalization."

Shadows shifted to the former priest's right, indicating he and the man behind the camera were not alone in the cabin.

"What are their intentions, Father Valentine?"

"Neither they nor their intentions are human. Thus, it's not entirely clear."

"To anyone?" the cameraman prodded.

"I've no definitive proof, but it is possible that some deep within the darkest government projects have come closer to understanding what these things are and what they're doing than you or I ever will. Even now there are forces in our world working on and utilizing various technologies involving these alternate realms and merging them with neuroscience—neurochemistry and experimental psychology—and literal *machines*, so-called artificial intelligence and the like, so who can say?"

"People are frightened," the electronically altered voice said.

"They should be."

"Do these entities mean us harm?"

"Make no mistake. These beings are not benevolent. They want us to remain in the dark, asleep while they feed on us."

"*Feed?*"

The old man stared at the camera for what seemed a very long time. "They exist in darkness," he finally answered.

"To those watching this that need help, what should they do, Father?"

"Disconnect. Fall away from the world you now know. Pray. Meditate."

"And if that doesn't work?"

Valentine glanced off to his left, as if someone nearby had momentarily distracted him. As he turned back to the camera, the sorrow on his face returned. "Then try your best to wake up," he said softly. "And *run.*"

As a chill trickled along George's spine, the picture blinked and went black. After a moment the words dissolved back onto the screen.

WHAT IS THE BASIS OF REALITY?

"Jesus," George said. "Is that it?"

"Isn't that enough?"

"Maybe it's just me, but I get the feeling if we were sitting in front of this guy instead of watching some recording, he'd have more to say."

Winston got up to stretch his legs and stifled a yawn. "I concur."

"Can you find him?"

"I told you, the broadcast originated from northern Vermont."

"That's a lot of area. Is there any chance of pinpointing it?"

Winston looked at him like his question was ludicrous. "Yes."

The earliest beginnings of daylight seeped through the window.

It was nearly dawn. They'd been up all night.

"All right," George said. "Then do it."

# CHAPTER EIGHTEEN

NOT FAR OUTSIDE OF St. Albans, Vermont, about fifteen miles or so from the Canadian border, Magdalena turned onto a dirt road. Lofty pines and oaks lined each side of the narrow passage, a tall wooden cross positioned near its entrance. Rosary beads hung on the splintered wood, dead flowers and palms scattered on the snowy ground. Plastic relics of Jesus, angels, and the Blessed Mother were strewn about as if haphazardly thrown there, and something dark and crusted stained the cross.

Magdalena tapped the brakes and the car skidded slightly before coming to a stop. She took in the large cross more fully, her eyes no longer focused on the road but the dark stain along the crossbeam. Her stomach tightened, and she felt slightly nauseous.

"Somebody please tell me that's not what I think it is," she said softly.

"Well, it—it could be any number of things," George said from the passenger seat, though he sounded anything but convincing.

"It's clearly blood." Winston sighed and sat forward from the backseat. "The salient question is, where—and from what or whom—did it come?"

Random thoughts raced through Magdalena's head.

*This is insane. I promised myself to stop listening to men. I should have told them to do this without me. What the hell am I even doing here?*

"If this was a horror movie," she said, "now's right about the time you'd tell the characters to turn around."

This small area wasn't even a town, just forest and a few very old houses sprinkled throughout, many of which were abandoned and the last of which they'd passed more than twenty minutes ago. On the maps, the area was only designated by a series of numbers, not a name.

"Don't be absurd," Winston said. "We've just spent more than five hours on the road to get here, not to mention, with the exception of a brief and not terribly restful nap I was able to take while you were driving,

I spent all of last night and much of this morning gathering the information necessary for us to find this place."

George watched the cross. "We've got plenty of time until nightfall." He reached over and gave Magdalena's wrist a light squeeze. "It'll be fine."

"Please," Winston said irritably. "Continue on."

Magdalena shifted the car back into DRIVE. Moving slowly down the dirt road, ice crunched beneath the tires and shadows moved between the trees on either side of them, brief flashes in the corners of her eyes distracting her as they went.

*Just animals,* she told herself.

They'd encountered snow a few times on the trip, but when they'd first ventured down this strange, unmarked forest road, it had stopped. Now it began again, big fat fluffy flakes falling gracefully from a barren gray sky. Magdalena switched on the windshield wipers, glancing up at the massive trees through the snowfall. It was strange here, almost as if they'd crossed into some other reality. Every snarled branch, every shift of light or brief shadow became suspect—dangerous—frightening.

"Easy," George said, clearly sensing her discomfort.

As they continued on, deeper into the woods, they noticed more crosses lining either side of the road, these much smaller and draped with tattered fabric and rosary beads. A few had strange symbols painted or carved into them, and at the base of a large pine tree to their right, what appeared to be animal bones were scattered about. But when Magdalena looked again, they hadn't been scattered at all, they'd been positioned—purposely positioned—as if into some sort of makeshift talisman.

A half mile in, a crude sign stood beside one of the macabre memorials.

**DANGER**

"Great." Magdalena slowed the car to a crawl. "That sounds promising."

"Keep going." George pointed to the sky. "No way of knowing how bad this snow's liable to get. Up here it can come down for days. Let's get in, figure this out, and get back on a real road before we're stuck out here."

She drove on, increasing speed but only slightly. They passed another small, and what appeared to be a final, wooden cross. Lying beside it in the snow was a tattered old teddy bear that reminded Magdalena of Kaley. Exhausted and frightened, she bit her lip to prevent the emotion from getting the better of her.

*I'll be home soon, sweetie. Mommy loves you.*

"I knew it was going to be remote," George said, watching the forest around them. "I guess I just didn't think it would be quite *this* remote."

"It's only found on one map, and not an official one," Winston said. "I wasn't entirely sure it was even legitimate, but as I mentioned earlier, further research seemed to confirm its existence despite the fact that all mainstream and official maps show nothing out here but acres and acres of forest. All of this had to come from Valentine and his followers."

"If you're going to drop off the grid," George said, "might as well go all the way."

"We're certainly not the first people to try to locate Valentine and his headquarters," Winston continued. "A handful of others have as well, and according to the information I was able to find in various dark web chatrooms and message boards, a handful even ventured out here and found it."

"Was there any further word from those who did?" George asked.

Winston didn't answer right away. "Not that I was able to find."

"Jesus, Winston," Magdalena snapped. "You might've wanted to mention that before now."

Mumbling incoherently, Winston sat back and looked out the window.

Magdalena looked to George as a sudden gust of wind broke through the trees and shook the car. "We could just turn around now and go back."

"It's going to be all right. Keep moving."

Everything in Magdalena's being screamed at her to turn and run, to get as far from these woods as fast as possible.

But she drove on, deeper into the now swirling snow.

\* \* \* \*

Magdalena agreed to drive after George's call at just after five in the morning. He and Winston hadn't slept all night, and though she'd gotten a few hours herself, they were far from restful.

George explained about a defrocked priest named Valentine and how he had something to do with what was happening. He had information, answers they needed, and there was only one way to get them. They had to go to him.

He gave her Winston's address, told her to be careful on the road but to get there as soon as she could. There were things she needed to see and hear. Exhausted and gripped with fear, she found Mrs. Bucci rocking beside her kitchen window, a prayer card in her hand.

"Prayer to Saint Francis," the old woman said, smiling wearily as Magdalena approached her. "One of my cats is missing. Francis always helps."

"I'm sure he will."

"What's wrong, dear? I heard your phone ring."

"I've got to go somewhere. It's important. I might be gone until late tomorrow, I—I'm not sure. I hate to keep asking, but can I leave Kaley with you again?"

"Of course," she said with a faint smile. "What's better for an old lady to do than protect little cherubs and pray to the saints? Kayley makes me feel young again. Go, do what you need to do, and don't worry about the time. I've got plenty of food, it's nice and toasty warm in here, and I really don't want to be alone anyway, not now."

A strange memory—if that's what it was—of cherubs floating in the clouds flashed in Magdalena's mind, and for just a moment she felt lightheaded. As it cleared, she noticed Mrs. Bucci looked concerned. "Is something wrong?"

"I was just about to ask you the same thing."

"I'm fine, what's wrong?"

"Just some bad dreams, and now I'm afraid to go back to sleep. Isn't that silly? It's been happening lately."

Magdalena did her best to appear calm. "Are you sure that's all it is?"

Mrs. Bucci nodded. "I'll be fine."

Magdalena bent down and kissed the old woman's forehead. "Thank you."

"Keep praying," Mrs. Bucci said. "That's the key."

A moment later, Magdalena was off and into the darkness, driving down empty streets and finally to a bad neighborhood where her GPS said Winston lived.

Once inside, she watched the video and listened to the information Winston had gathered. "You're telling me you really want to go all the way out there to find this man, to a place in the middle of the woods that might not even exist?"

"Found some information," Winston told her. "Some posts allegedly by a few people that went to one or two of Valentine's *gatherings* out there. It's a little past St. Albans, almost at the Canadian border."

"How do we know he's even there?" Magdalena asked.

"We don't," Winston told her, his voice strained. "Supposedly it's a small village at the end of a long dirt road. No sign, no name, just a big old wooden cross before you turn."

"This is crazy." Magdalena looked to George, hoping he'd agree. "George, help me out here."

"You're right," he said. "It is crazy. I'm not exactly excited about making this trip either. But what's the alternative? To turn our backs and pretend everything's fine? We can't do that. Not now. Not anymore. Winston could've been killed earlier, and for all we know, whoever was behind the wheel of that SUV could come looking for us too. Ignoring these things and pretending they're not happening are luxuries we can no longer afford. I agree with you. I do, okay? This whole thing is nuts. But at this point, what choice do we really have?"

Magdalena sighed, unsure of what to say, as Mrs. Bucci's words whispered to her from the darkest reaches of her mind.

*Just keep praying...*

\* \* \* \*

About two miles in, the road widened a bit, and they noticed an old, dilapidated barn in a clearing to their left. No more wooden crosses, only forest and this clearing now. Atop the barn, several blackbirds sat perched, screeching at them as if on cue.

The snow continued to fall and swirl about in the wind, both of which had been steadily increasing over the last few minutes.

Just beyond the remains of the barn, they found themselves at a crossroads of sorts. At the center was a life-sized statue of a veiled kneeling woman, her hands clasped in prayer. Positioned ominously before four possible paths, her skeletal face was pointed right at them. The eyes were hollowed out into empty craters, and her mouth was little more than a thin grim line, but the workmanship was astounding. Another blackbird was perched on her thin shoulder, and dead leaves slick with ice had accumulated in the well of her lap.

Once more, Magdalena rolled the car to a stop.

"What the hell is that supposed to be?" George asked.

"I'm not entirely sure," Winston said. "Some sort of woman in the throes of prayer, from the looks. Could it be a saint?"

Magdalena rubbed her tired eyes then looked again at the stone sculpture before them. "She's not pointing anywhere, which way do we go, Winston?"

"According to the map, we need to go left. If my information is correct, there should be cabins less than a mile from here, the ones we saw in Valentine's video."

"A saint, huh?" George eyed the statue. "I'm hardly an expert on these things, but that doesn't look like any saint I've ever seen. The thing actually makes me want to go in the opposite direction."

"I'm sure that's what they had in mind," Magdalena said.

"Do you think it's a warning?" George asked.

Magdalena nodded, dropped the car into PARK, then cracked the window and pulled her cigarettes from her purse. "I'm pretty sure it's supposed to be the goddess Hecate."

George and Winston stared at her, baffled.

"She's the goddess of the crossroads," she said, stabbing a cigarette between her lips as she searched her purse for a lighter. "A deity of death charged with guiding souls to the underworld. Same way they say blackbirds sometimes do."

As if it had heard her—and perhaps it had—the raven on the statue's shoulder screeched and flapped its wings, but remained where it was. The sound eerily echoed through the forest around them, eventually replaced by the previous snowy silence.

"Some of her followers drank blood, sacrificed animals." Having finally located a lighter, she pulled it from her purse and lit the cigarette. "Some say even people. You know, when seasons changed and during full moons and eclipses. It's Pagan stuff."

George arched an eyebrow. "How do you know all that?"

"Always been interested in that kind of thing," she said.

"But Valentine is a Roman Catholic, not Pagan."

"So am I," she said, drawing on the cigarette then exhaling a stream of smoke out the cracked window. "But those paths are far more intertwined than most would have you believe. Hecate isn't a Catholic saint, she originated in Greece actually, but I had a grandmother from Italy that did what a lot of people from her time did. She mixed both Catholic and Pagan beliefs, because oftentimes both existed side-by-side in their culture. So she taught me not only about the saints, but about the gods and goddesses many worshipped long before them. A lot of the church's rituals originated with and are based directly on Pagan ones. Christianity isn't the only thing that came to the new world from the old countries, you know. Not by a longshot. Really dark shit came over too. Like her."

"So this all fits together into some sort of spiritual stew then?" George asked. "With all the crosses and rosary beads and now this statue, Valentine and his followers are out here meshing Christianity with Paganism and God knows what else?"

"They are described as a religious sect," Winston reminded them.

"I think people are drawn to places that mirror whatever makes them tick," Magdalena said. "Energy seeks similar energy, isn't that what they say? The law of attraction and all that, right?"

"At least at this juncture," Winston said, poking his head between the front seats again, "I don't see how our personal beliefs in these areas are relevant."

"Whatever they're doing out here," she said, catching a glimpse of Winston in the rearview mirror and flashing him a stern look, "they decided to do it in the middle of fucking nowhere. So they obviously don't want to be seen, and that's never good. What makes you think they're going to be okay with us just showing up like this?"

"From the looks of the things we've seen so far," Winston said, "I'm not sure there's anyone still out here. Except for these irksome birds, that is."

The snowfall intensified, turning the world white.

Magdalena smoked her cigarette, her hand trembling each time she brought it to her mouth. Her eyes scanned the ancient trees surrounding them. Odd streaks of black and gray darted along her peripheral vision, flashes of twisted faces.

*Just my imagination...they only come at night...*

"We need to keep moving," Winston said after a moment. "And please, could you put that cigarette out and close the window? It's freezing."

She flicked the cigarette away then closed the window and stared straight ahead.

Hecate stared back with her empty sockets, the blackbird serving as her eyes and watching them for her while teetering precariously on her shoulder. "You did say left, didn't you?" she said softly.

"Yes."

Magdalena dropped the car into DRIVE, then gently pressed the gas. The car slowly crept forward, passing the statue on the left. The bird remained where it was, but its black eyes followed them as they pulled onto an even narrower road.

She increased the speed of the windshield wipers in an attempt to keep up with the swirling snow, and just as Winston had said, less than a mile from the crossroad they came to another clearing, this one much larger.

Three cabins; the first. surrounded by several fallen trees, was dark and covered in snow, but looked reasonably intact. The other two were as well.

"That's the cabin in the video," Winston said, pointing to the first one.

George nodded. "It doesn't look like anyone's been here in a long while."

Winston threw open his door and started to get out.

"Hold on," George said. "We don't know who or what might be inside."

"But you just said—"

"I know what I said, Winston, but I can't be sure yet, so don't go bolting ahead like some kid charging into a candy store. Let's take a good look, make sure we're not walking into something we can't get out of. Then we go together, nice and slow, okay?"

Embarrassed, Winston shut the door, his face flushed bright red. "Fine."

"Mags, drive around the place," George said. "Let's see if there are lights or any sign of human life beyond these structures."

Magdalena slowly maneuvered the vehicle around the first cabin, noting no smoke streamed from the chimney and most of the windows were broken. Even the roof had sustained some damage, most likely from falling branches. Someone had at some point draped a blue tarp over it, but the elements had shredded it, leaving ribbons of blue strewn on the ground, hanging off gutters, and dancing in the wind. The closer they got to the clearing, she could see that the holes in the roof were deep and allowing snow to fall freely inside the cabin. "I don't think anybody's been here in a long time," she said, pulling around near the back of the first cabin. The back door hung off its hinges, like someone had hastily picked it up and propped it against the doorframe long ago. She peered into the dark interior beyond but couldn't make out much through the snow.

"Okay, park it," George said. "We can see all three cabins from here and still have a good view of the road out. This is as good a position as we're likely to find."

They exited the car, but before they could take a step, a bevy of blackbirds descended, landing on the roof of the cabin like a dark cloud.

"Jesus," George said. "It's like the damn things are following us."

"That's exactly what they're doing." Magdalena hugged herself.

"Don't they go south for the winter?"

"Apparently not," she said. "Nothing's right. Everything's off."

The birds sat in a row, silently watching them, *appraising* them.

"They're just birds," Winston said. "I suggest we ignore them and check inside."

Huddled together, the trio walked gingerly across the ice and snow until they'd reached the partially blocked doorway. From inside the cabin, a horrible stench wafted toward them.

"Smells like something died in there," George said, bringing a hand to his nose.

Winston made a face. "That is rather pungent."

"An animal probably crawled in there and croaked."

*That's no animal,* Magdalena thought.

She'd smelled death at work for years. She knew that smell. It was human.

*We need to leave. We need to get out of here. Now—we—we have to go now!*

George stepped forward and wrenched the door free of the snow, breaking Magdalena's train of thought. "Stand clear," he grunted. "This thing's a hell of a lot heavier than it looks."

As Winston and Magdalena stepped back, George wrestled the door away and threw it to the ground. It landed hard and sunk into the fresh blanket of snow.

Beyond the open doorway sat a wooden table—the same one Valentine had sat at in the video—a crucifix at each corner and an empty bottle of wine at its center. Even inside, perched along the tops of two empty and crumbling bookcases and along the remains of an old woodstove, several blackbirds watched them.

As they stepped inside, covering their noses against the awful stink, they were better able to see just how substantial the hole in the roof was. Snow fell inside the place, and the few pieces of old furniture still there—an overturned chair, a threadbare couch, and another smaller table—were already covered in snow. Between the tear in the roof and most of the windows being broken, the line separating inside from outside had become quite thin here.

A few old candles had melted into the table and the crucifixes were caked with what appeared to be blood, reminding Magdalena of the first cross they'd seen at the start of the road in. What was once a rosary dangled from the edge of the table, broken, beads strewn across the table and scattered about the floor.

Closer inspection revealed another smear of blood across the top of the table, and two more narrow swathes on the floor nearby.

"The hell happened here?" George asked, looking around.

Behind the thick lenses of his glasses, Winston's eyes darted from one end of the cabin to the other then back again. "Whatever took place resulted in a fairly substantial amount of blood loss."

Something caught the light coming through the windows and open roof, and whatever it was clacked and rattled like a dull chime. Magdalena turned toward it, her eyes squinting, trying to register what she was seeing.

Several bones had been strung together with some sort of filament and hung from a jagged piece of glass in a window on the far wall. Beneath it, written in what appeared to be blood, was a single word.

**SLEEP**

"Those bones," Winston said. "They, they're human, they—they look human."

Magdalena blessed herself and stepped back, closer to the doorway.

Dark splotches momentarily blotted out the light above them, and when it returned several more blackbirds had descended through the hole in the roof and taken up position on the rafters overhead. They began to squawk and screech, setting off those already in the cabin as well. The noise was deafening, and as Magdalena took another step back, one red-eyed crow broke free of the group and took flight, soaring right at her.

Before she could duck out of the way, its beak pierced her cheek. Screaming and flailing at the bird, she staggered back, and in a whirlwind of feathers and snow and flapping wings, it flew up and out through the open roof.

"Are you all right?" George ran to her and took her by the shoulders.

"The fucking thing *bit* me!" She touched her face. Her fingertips came back bloody. "Jesus, I—I'm bleeding!"

George cocked his head, moving her closer to one of the blown-out windows so he could get a better look at her in the light. "Actually doesn't look too bad."

"It's just a scratch from the looks." With an expression of both concern and fear, Winston pulled a neatly folded handkerchief from his pocket and held it out for her. "Here, use this."

"Thanks," she said, taking it from him and pressing the cloth against her cheek. She was grateful, but wondered who the hell carried handkerchiefs these days. *Leave it to Winston,* she thought. *Of course he does.*

George had gone pale. "I've never seen anything like this."

There were countless birds in the cabin now, some flying back up through the roof and others coming in. It wasn't quite a frenzy of motion, but it was uncomfortably close. At any moment, if they all attacked, Magdalena knew they'd be in serious trouble.

"We need to get out of this cabin," she said.

"What about the other two cabins?" Winston reminded her. "Maybe we should split up and—"

"No," George said. "We stay together."

"We need to get out of this cabin," Magdalena said again. "There's blood that's probably human and bones that definitely are. We're standing in a crime scene I don't think anyone else has found before us."

This seemed to register with George and snap him back to reality. With a sullen nod, he gently took her by the arm. "All right, very slowly, so as not to agitate these bastards any more than we already have, move to the door."

A heavy gust of wind tore through the cabin, and as Magdalena shivered uncontrollably, a closet door at the rear of the cabin suddenly creaked open.

Hovering within, a dark form appeared, arms waving about as though conducting the chaotic flight of the blackbirds. The roof began to groan as more snow fell through, tumbling into the cabin.

Even before she could scream, Magdalena and the others realized what they were looking at. A corpse, a frozen corpse not standing, but hanging by its neck in the closet; the wind had caused it to sway and appear as if its arms were moving.

"My God," George said, bringing a hand to his mouth.

Winston stood frozen, staring at the body, his mouth hung open in shock.

Moving slowly, Magdalena approached the closet.

"What the hell are you doing?" George reached for her, but she was already beyond his grasp. "Don't go near that thing!"

But Magdalena wasn't listening. She'd seen dead bodies before, plenty of them, as a CNA. Never any in this kind of condition and decay, but it had been a long time since a dead body had disturbed her. This though, this was something different than what she was used to. This was someone who had hanged themselves in this closet probably weeks ago, if not longer. The body was frozen and blackened in parts, and when she got closer she realized the wrists had been slashed as well. The blood had long congealed and frozen along the floor and from the wounds, an old-fashioned straight razor still lying where it had been dropped, just beyond the blackened, frostbitten bare feet of the dead man.

"It's him," she said, just above a whisper. "I—I'm pretty sure it's him."

"Valentine…"

She looked back at George and Winston and nodded.

"It looks like his body's been here for a while," George said.

"It's a guess—I mean, I'm not a doctor—but I'd say a week or more. He slit his writs with a straight razor and then hanged himself."

George winced. "Why would he do that?"

"Whatever the reason, he wanted to make sure there was no turning back, no chance of survival. Why else would he go to those lengths?"

"Where are the others?" Winston asked.

"Maybe they're in the other cabins," George said. "This could've been one of those death or suicide cults. Don't most of those things eventually end that way?"

Although repelled by the sight of it, she took another look at the corpse. It was in bad shape, but it did resemble the man she'd seen in the video. Written on the inside of the door in his blood was the phrase: IT'S ALL A LIE

Winston motioned to the words. "What do you suppose that refers to?"

"I don't know, but it was obviously important enough for a dying man to write it on the back of that door in his own blood."

"You were right before," George said. "We need to get the hell out of here."

"Shouldn't we—I don't know—call someone? The cops or—"

"And tell them what?"

"I don't have any idea. But we can't just leave him here, he's a human being."

"Not anymore, Mags."

Magdalena knew he was right on that count. She took another look at them. Both men were horrified. "I know you guys aren't used to seeing dead bodies, but I am. We can't just leave his corpse here without telling anyone. It's wrong."

"Yes, it's a sin," Winston said softly. "Mother would say we had to do something, I—I agree. Only, I don't—I don't know, I...I don't know…"

"Take a deep breath, Winston." George was trying his best to maintain some semblance of calm, but was failing miserably. "Maybe we can discuss this outside?"

"Y-Yes," Winston stammered. "I think that would be best."

Magdalena took the handkerchief from her cheek. The bleeding had stopped.

But the birds were still watching. They'd stopped screeching and become oddly silent. Didn't animals sometimes get that way right before they attacked?

"Back out of here carefully," she said, "and very slowly."

Together, they inched their way out through the doorway and into the snow.

Trees stood like giant sentinels lording above them, snow flying about in the deep gray sky. And even more blackbirds had congregated now, sitting along the roof of the cabin, while others took flight, circling overhead through the sea of tumbling snowflakes.

George stood staring at the ground, looking like he might vomit.

"Are you all right?" Magdalena asked him.

He nodded but said nothing more.

"I think we should check the other cabins," Winston said, equally upset.

George whirled around, facing him. "For what, more bodies?"

"Yes. There were others, Valentine had followers. Maybe they're here too."

"We're leaving," George said. "Now. Let's go."

"You two go wait in the car." Winston reached into his coat pocket, took something out, and held it down against the side of his leg. "I'm going to go look."

Magdalena stared at him, incredulous. "Is that a *gun*?"

"It is."

"Is it loaded?"

"Of course it's loaded. Why do people always ask such a nonsensical question? What possible good is a gun if it isn't loaded?" As Winston shook his head, his eyeglasses slid down his nose a bit. He pushed them back into place with his free hand. "Honestly, who carries around an unloaded revolver? I am wholly unaware of anyone doing such a thing, and if they did, what would be the point exactly?"

"He had it at his house," George explained sheepishly. "We thought it might be a good idea to bring it along in case of—I don't know— trouble."

"Well, we've found plenty of that, haven't we?" Through eyes tearing from the cold, Magdalena turned back to the car. But something else, something beyond it, grabbed her attention, something facing them from the dirt road leading into this awful place.

She looked back to George and Winston, but there was no need to alert them.

They'd seen it too.

A black sedan.

# CHAPTER NINETEEN

"THAT'S IT," WINSTON SAID, the revolver still at his side. "That's the car that saved me when the SUV tried to run me down."

Before anyone could say more, the driver's door swung open and someone stepped out of the car. Their gender was not immediately evident, but they were of average height and build, and wore an ankle-length dark wool coat, black winter hiking boots, and a knit hat pulled down low on their brow. Reaching up, the driver slipped the hat free and tossed it into the car, releasing curly brown hair specked with gray that hung just shy of their shoulders. As the person walked through the falling snow to the front of the car, their face came into clearer view. It appeared to be a woman somewhere in her middle forties, pale and void of makeup, with steely gray eyes, a long aquiline nose, a small circle of a mouth, and a pronounced chin. At first glance she looked like she'd been hastily assembled using a variety of wildly opposing and exaggerated parts.

"Who are you?" George demanded.

"My name's Oakley. Nyx Oakley. I would've made contact sooner but it wasn't safe." The woman's voice was deep, her delivery rapid-fire and anxious. "Truth be told, it still isn't. But this was my best chance, so I took it. I've been tracking you for some time now."

"*Tracking?*" George exchanged worried glances with Magdalena and Winston. "What the hell does that mean?"

"Call it observational surveillance." Nyx fidgeted about nervously, like she expected others to arrive at any moment. "It's clinical. I'm a doctor, a scientist."

"You saved me," Winston said suddenly. "The SUV—"

"I did what I could, but we don't have much time. They're still on your asses."

"Who are *they?*" George asked.

"You need to get in your car and follow me," Nyx said. "We can't stay here."

"We're not going anywhere with you," Magdalena snapped. "Are you out of your goddamn mind?"

The woman almost seemed amused. "That's always a distinct possibility."

"I have a gun," Winston announced, showing it to her in his best attempt at being intimidating. "And I am in no way afraid to use it."

Nyx stared at him a moment, then shook her head wearily. "Yeah, uh, okay. Anyway, here's what I need you to understand right now. I'm trying to help you, but we're not safe here. You saw what's in those cabins."

"We saw what's in this one," George told her. "What's in the other two?"

"More of the same," Nyx answered, suddenly spellbound by the birds lining the roof of the cabin. "This is a place of the dead now."

"We don't even know who you are," Magdalena told her. "Why should we trust you? Why *would* we?"

Nyx gave a sad and ironic little smile as her strange gray eyes shifted from the birds to Magdalena. "I can't really blame you if you decide not to. But know this. That SUV is on its way here right now, and they don't give a shit either way, so I'd suggest—"

"Who are they? What do they want with us?"

"We don't have much time. Our only chance is to get out of here and go somewhere we can talk for a while."

"We need answers, not conversation."

"Trust me, I'm here to give the answers you're looking for," Nyx said. "But the clock's ticking and we need to go."

"Look," Magdalena said, stumbling toward her through the accumulating snow. "If you've got something to tell us, then let's hear it!"

"Not here. I'm leaving. With or without you, it's your call, but I'm gone."

Magdalena turned to the others. With a frown, Winston slid the revolver back into his coat pocket. George held her gaze a moment then offered a subtle nod.

"Okay," Magdalena said reluctantly. "Go. We'll follow."

\* \* \* \*

"What in the *hell* is happening?"

It was the only thing anyone said, but George said it three times during the course of driving back down the snow-covered road through the forest. The entire time they sat with their own thoughts and watched

GREG F. GIFUNE & SANDY DELUCA

the road up ahead, fearful the SUV might appear at any moment and block them in. But it never did. Instead, they carefully made their way back through the storm, onto the main road and eventually to the state highway, where they followed the sedan for nearly another ten minutes.

Finally, Nyx pulled into the parking lot of an old roadside motel.

"Okay," Magdalena sighed, taking in the run-down and dated rectangular building. "Fucking *now* what?"

There was only one other car and an eighteen-wheeler in the lot. Otherwise the place was quiet and appeared empty. The snow was still coming down but seemed a bit lighter here, blowing about in the wind and sweeping across the lot and adjacent highway in slinking, serpentine lines.

"Keep your eyes open," George said, as Magdalena followed the sedan around to the rear of the motel. "I already don't like the looks of this."

"That makes two of us."

"Three," Winston muttered from the backseat.

Nyx parked near two large dumpsters.

Magdalena pulled in alongside her, first making sure she'd turned the car around so it was facing out. If they needed to get out of there quickly, it was better to have a straight shot back to the front of the motel and waiting highway.

Beyond the small paved area behind the motel was nothing but woods.

"Damn near anything could come at us from those woods and nobody'd ever see it," George warned. "And be sure to keep an eye on the corner of the motel to make sure no one else comes back here and blocks us in. No matter what she says or does, everybody stick close and stay alert."

They climbed out of the car. Magdalena left it running.

With snow continuing to blow about in thick curtains, the sound of nearby traffic bleeding around to the rear of the motel, and the wind whispering through the trees to their right, Nyx emerged from her sedan. Once at the rear of the car, she leaned back against the trunk and folded her arms over her chest.

"Okay, we did what you asked," George finally said. "So get to it, the smell back here is enough to gag a maggot. Who the hell are you?"

"Like I said, I'm a scientist." Nyx drew a deep breath then exhaled it as a cloudburst in the cold air. "My specialty is the human brain. Hell, I'm just an old hippie at heart, man, always was. My parents were too, it's how I was raised. All I ever wanted to do was help people, make the world a better place. Thing is, I was gifted in science, medicine, mathematics, one of those wunderkinds recruited right out of college by intelligence agencies buried so deep in all the bullshit and red tape only a handful of people even know they exist. Exactly the kind of fascist assholes I despised and wanted to stay away from. But they lured me in. It's what they do. Mouse to cheese, dig? Only I didn't know then I was the fucking mouse and it was cats setting the trap. Probably should've, but I didn't. All I saw was what I could have access to, the places we could go, the lengths to which they were willing to take this thing, and that clouded me—corrupted, I guess you could say. I'm ashamed to tell you I got just as drunk on all that as the rest of the nerds they recruited."

"What's any of this got to do with us?" Magdalena asked.

"When I first started out, I was so jazzed, you know?" Nyx said, ignoring the question. "I mean, this was wild, cutting-edge shit, and all of it served to me on a silver platter with none of the usual restrictions scientific studies are bound by, be it ethical or financial. All that mattered was results, and same as the others that were onboard with me, I was naïve and believed we were actually doing some good in the world, so why rock the boat and chance losing that, right? Sure, it was all behind the curtain, and we knew just like everything else the federal government covertly funds, particularly with potential military and intelligence applications, there'd be any number of aspects most of us wouldn't be comfortable with or approve of. But it was a trade. It always is. You learn that fairly quickly, and once you get that straight in your head you start to make exceptions. Pretty soon those exceptions become the norm, and by then it's already too late. It's gotten away from you and there's no getting it back. You're compromised. Even if you want to stop it, you can't, because believe me when I tell you they have the means to obliterate you if you decide to suddenly rediscover your principles and stop playing ball. The worst part is you're so completely blown away by what you're into, you don't even care about the ethics of it anymore. Right and wrong goes right out the fucking window."

Somewhere out on the highway, a car horn blared then faded away.

Nyx stuffed her hands into her coat pockets and pulled it in tighter around her, the snow whirling about in an otherworldly blur. "I worked at a number of universities over the years. Always with some bullshit front designed to conceal the things we were really up to. They generally kept us moving every decade or so. I eventually landed at a private but federally funded institute. To this day they'll tell you it doesn't exist and never did. I'm talking about clandestine research projects with secret but formal approval and funding from the federal government."

"And precisely what did these projects entail?" Winston asked.

"Our work was supposed to be about *furthering* mankind, not only through the expansion and deeper understanding of consciousness, but so-called reality itself. Some of that actually happened, just not the way we imagined it might. No one realized what we were going to find, the horror we were about to step into, and the lies it concealed."

George tried to mask his fear, but the words written inside that closet door in Valentine's blood flashed before his mind's eye like a neon sign.

IT'S ALL A LIE

"Nobody knew about The Bridge, and the power it held."

"What bridge?" George asked.

Nyx pushed away from the car, but kept her hands in her coat pockets, the guilt and fear on her face evident. "Any of you know what Dimethyltryptamine is?"

"It's a chemical substance naturally found in plants and animals." Winston removed his eyeglasses and wiped away the snow. "Including the human animal."

"Winner-winner chicken dinner," Nyx said. "Also known as DMT, it's a hallucinogenic narcotic with a long history. Some call it the spirit molecule due to its strong psychedelic effects. But long before it became a modern-day recreational drug, it was a common spiritual tool in a few South American and Mexican cultures. They prepared it as an entheogen for shamanic rituals, used it for eons. Turns out they knew a hell of a lot more about this shit than we did. They understood the things it could do, what it could bring about in the mind and beyond. More importantly, they knew why it so commonly exists in nature, and even inside *us*."

Freezing, exhausted, and frightened, George didn't know how much more of this he could take. "Lady, you better get to some kind of point real soon."

"DMT was a big part of our program," Nyx explained, pacing back and forth in front of the sedan now, her head bowed. "The shit's usually smoked in a pipe, or by the older cultures consumed orally. We used injections. The idea was to give it to unknowing human subjects to see exactly what kind of documentable effects it had on consciousness. We expected results similar to the effects of LSD, and at first, that's essentially what we got. People were tripping balls bigtime, dig? But then something else started to happen. Test subjects began to have *encounters*, seeing all sorts of crazy shit—gnomes, aliens, demons, insectoids—you name it, they were at the freak party. So we started increasing not only the potency of injections, but the frequency. It wasn't safe, and we all damn well knew it, but we did it anyway. The result was something we hadn't anticipated and couldn't explain away as just more supercharged drug trips. The encounters became more focused, and instead of a wide array of disturbing beings, there was only one. A single *species* of nonhuman entities, and without exception, every single test subject came into direct contact with them whether they wanted to or not."

The word *entities* made George cringe as the horrific beings his mother had drawn and claimed to see prior to her death returned to him in a rush of memory.

"But what we needed to know for sure was if the subjects were literally crossing over into an alternate reality and encountering these entities, or simply having identical hallucinations." Nyx's expression revealed how badly she was struggling to tell them these things. "So we upped the ante."

Although the snow kept falling, the world suddenly fell eerily quiet. Even the sounds from the highway and the whistling of the wind had ceased.

"I'm going to go ahead and assume you've heard of the pineal gland," Nyx continued. "Little cone-shaped structure in the center of our brains that secretes melatonin? Sometimes called the third eye? It's actually part of our endocrine system, which regulates things like metabolism, among others, through the release of hormones. Mystics and spiritualists have written about and described it since forever. They believe it to be a sort of metaphysical connective tissue between the physical and spirit world. Descartes called it the *seat of the soul*. Turns out he was wrong, in that he believed it was where all thoughts were formed. We know now that's the neocortex, but what the pineal gland *does* do is synthesize melatonin. Its production is what determines wake and sleep cycles. It's all about light and dark, dig? The more light the brain detects, the less melatonin is produced. The more darkness it detects, the greater amount it produces. That's why it helps us sleep, because levels are highest at night. The pineal gland is also where DMT is produced. Creativity, imagination, dreaming, extreme isolation and trauma, starvation—just to name a few—all these things produce compounds in our brains that result in varying levels of hallucinatory and altered states. Compounds like DMT. What we didn't know before the experiments was the degree to which large quantities can alter our brains. They become super receivers that operate on a much higher plain. They weren't experiencing hallucinations like the others. We're not talking some evil clown from a bad acid trip—no, these fuckers are *real*. And that meant the subjects weren't tripping. They were transcending our reality for theirs."

With his head reeling, George pictured his poor mother's face, frightened and confused by the things haunting her. They had to be the same entities Nyx was talking about, but how could she have known his mother was experiencing these things too? Surely some elderly woman ravaged with dementia hadn't been one of their test subjects?

"At first we thought we'd mistakenly opened a gateway, a door through which these things could also pass into our reality," Nyx said. "But we were wrong. That gateway's always been there. We just figured out something those on the other side have known since forever, and that's how to shine enough light on it to see the bridge that exists between the two."

"Bridge," Magdalena said. "You used that word before."

Nyx nodded. "That's what we called the project, The Bridge."

George motioned to Winston. "Our mothers, they've seen these things too."

"So has my daughter," Magdalena added. "I've heard them, I—I have their voices on tape, I—"

"You think you're unique?" Nyx leaned against the trunk of her car as if she might otherwise fall over. "Trust me, you're not. It's like going to bed at night and waking up because you feel a bug crawling on your skin. So you turn on the light to swat it, only to realize the entire room—the entire house—is overrun with these bugs, thousands of them covering you and your bed, the walls, the ceiling, the floor, dig? These fucking things are everywhere, all around us. Once we used that bridge, the walls between us and them became thinner. Eventually they fell. When that happened, people started to see and hear them too, and not just those in the project, but everywhere. It bled through. *They* bled through. The drugged, the drunk, the mentally ill, those with intellectual disabilities, even the autistic in many cases, the sleeping, the dreaming, the elderly, children, all those with a lower capacity to filter it out or a higher capacity to sense these things, those who were in the throes of an altered state of consciousness, *all* of them are especially vulnerable. Those close to death are even more so. But it's getting worse. It—they—are spreading, and the more they do, the more those on this side are coming to understand what's actually happening. Valentine and his followers figured it out, and when they did, you saw the result."

"But those people took their own lives," Magdalena said. "They weren't murdered."

"Exactly, and what does that tell you about the truths they found?"

"That death was preferable."

"And there you have it."

"What are these things?" Magdalena asked.

"I can tell you they're far more powerful than we are, but beyond that I—"

"Are they angels, demons, ghosts—what?"

Nyx shrugged hopelessly. "I have no idea."

The answer struck them like a blow to the face.

"What *aren't* you telling us?" George said.

"You can start with the SUV," Winston said.

"If they wanted to kill you, they would have. Their goal was to frighten you, to scare you off the path. Since that didn't work, now all bets are off."

"How did they know I was anywhere near a path to the truth?"

"The same shady black ops groups that funded us took it all away once we'd established what was happening. And then one by one they eliminated the test subjects that couldn't be blinded along with all the scientists and doctors that participated. They're working together now, in conjunction with these things."

"Why?" Winston asked. "For what purpose?"

"They know the truth, and as horrible as it is, to those types it's better to play ball and hold power than not. The way they see it, the rest is all window dressing."

"You're saying they *blinded* the test subjects?"

"Not literally. It means to reprogram through the use of alternate drugs."

"You mean making them forget," Winston said. It wasn't a question.

"Usually seems more like nightmares and strange memories to the subjects, but they bury it all so deep it's unlikely those memories will ever be fully recovered. Sometimes they have glimpses and pieces here and there but none of it makes a lick of sense to them. Sometimes the blinding takes. Sometimes it doesn't. When it fails, well, that's when they move to the second solution, which is termination. I'm the last surviving doctor involved, been on the run for a while now, trying to help when and where I can, because in those instances when the reprogramming starts to slip or doesn't fully take, they move. They can't let any of this out. People can't know what The Bridge actually revealed about our reality, and theirs."

George arched an eyebrow. "And what is that?"

Nyx's pale face watched them through the rage of snowflakes. "It's all a lie."

"What does that mean?"

"It means reality—our reality—is not what we think it is."

"What is our reality then?"

"We'll get there, just not quite yet."

George turned away, shaking his head. "This is ridiculous."

"You don't understand yet—not fully—and these are matters that need to be handled delicately from here on out. I don't want to do more harm than—"

"I'd say that ship has sailed, lady."

"I'll ask again," Winston said. "How did they tie us to any of this? Valentine was putting information out all over the web, and a great many of the vulnerable you mentioned include my mother, George's, and many others at the nursing home. But the three of us, we're everyday people. How did they know to come after us?"

"I'm sure you've figured it out," Nyx said, her strange gray eyes blinking slowly. "Right about now some of this should start to solidify in your brains and begin to sound strangely familiar. You're a smart little bugger, Winston, always figured you'd get it first. You want to tell them or should I?"

George looked to Winston, horrified by the realization clearly striking him.

"They knew to come for us," Winston said softly, bringing his hands to his head. "Because...it had to be because..."

"*Because*," Nyx said, finishing for him. "You were all test subjects."

# CHAPTER TWENTY

*THE SKY—WHAT—WHAT'S wrong with the sky? What have they done to the sky?*

Everything is a blur, a tangle of flashes and sounds hunting and circling like so many hungry wolves.

*It's on fire.*

Darkness then light strobe back and forth, nothing in focus or quite complete as familiar but distant voices speak frantically, the words slurred, swirling around her like snow, there then gone then back again.

*I can put her on the Bridge temporarily, but this is the only way.*

*Nyx...*

*Then do it.*

The last one, is it her voice? Did she hear herself just then?

*Mags, listen to me. Don't let this maniac do this.*

*You heard her, it's the only way.*

*I can put you there long enough for you to see, to understand.*

*Mags—*

*Just do it!*

The world slams to darkness, a total, endless, all-encompassing void of night. No sound, no senses, only a sea of incomprehensible nothingness. And as she floats away, like an astronaut broken free of her tether, silently spiraling and drifting deeper and deeper into the infinite void of space, there comes a sudden rain of color, a kaleidoscope of colors...

*Nyx, are you still here?*

A little girl opens her eyes and finds herself in a dimly lit room. Deep within the shadows surrounding her, strange white dots swirl, pulsing and winking in then out. Groggily, she sits up, and as the little girl pushes back layers of blankets and sheets, she catches a glimpse of herself in a mirror over a dresser against the far wall. Tousled dark hair falls in soft ringlets over her shoulders, as wide eyes stare back at her questioningly. But it is the dollop of blood on her cheek that draws her attention. She reaches for the wound with tiny fingers, brushes against it gently.

Magdalena winces in pain, remembers the bird that attacked her when she was much older, in a place of the dead. A crumbling old cabin deep in the woods, the roof lined with screeching ravens.

But that was only a dream. Wasn't it?

*None of us are really here.*

"Who am I?" she asks her reflection in a little girl voice. "*What* am I?"

Her reflection grins mischievously, and points to the wall.

Frightened and confused—reflections can't do that—Magdalena follows her finger, her eyes panning slowly across the room to the wall, and the words written there with a spidery hand in what can only be blood.

*A lie…*

The girl scrambles out of bed, stumbles to the window.

*Where are you?*

Beyond the window are darkness and a field of ash as far as the eye can see. The skies above it churn, ablaze with fire. A dead tree, branches gnarled like scorched bone, stands alone amidst the hellish landscape. On its lowest charred branch sits a big blackbird, watching her. Things she cannot quite make out glide along the black mirror gloss of its obsidian eyes, like souls trapped and writhing in darkness, reflecting things only it can see.

There's something wrong with this bird. It…

*Wait. That's…*

The little girl backs away, trembling.

*That's not a bird! My God, what is that?*

Screams echo, and flashes of dark figures closing in around her fill her head, as the world again blurs and spins out of control.

*I'm remembering…I think I—I think I'm remembering…*

A parking lot comes into view, as if she's hovering somewhere in the sky above it. A black sedan and her car parked at the rear of an old roadside motel.

*Where are you? George…Winston…Nyx Oakley…*

Hurrying through a door, over a worn carpet, scratched and dated furniture all around, an old tube television on a cart in the corner…

*Were you ever really here?*

Someone touches her wrist.

*Who's there?*

An oddly familiar voice answers, but it's so faint she can't make out any of the words. Before she can try again something pulls her back, down and away from that sky of fire and into a place she knows, a place she's seen before but can't remember.

*Long hallways littered with the dying and forgotten, the doomed...*

Before she can bring it into full focus it changes, and she is alone in a strange old dance hall, where ice-covered trees sprout up from the cracked floors, and old wooden crosses stand alongside them. Broken rosary beads dangle from frosty branches and feral red eyes glare at her from the shadows.

Faded cherubs and gods, chipped, worn, and looking down upon her sadly from the derelict fresco ceiling, seem to move and float of their own accord, but she can't be sure if it's just her blurred vision. Impossibly, snow begins to fall through the ceiling, blanketing the old ballroom in thick white drifts.

Positioned along the dancefloor are open caskets housing skeletal bodies long dead, their mouths open as if in mid-scream, old cracked tubes and tattered wires running from things attached to their skulls and chests, rusty syringes still protruding from their arms.

"What is this?" she asks, her voice raspy and raw, her throat sore, as if she's swallowed crushed glass. "Where am I?"

The questions echo through the empty hall, unanswered.

"Where am I?" she screams.

This time, there comes a reply.

*Home...*

Magdalena shakes her head, staggers away. "What did you give me?"

*What do you see?*

Visions of Winston and George fill her head, lying on metal tables, and her with them, tubes and wires swelling from their flesh.

*Cross the bridge, Magdalena. Cross the bridge and see...*

\* \* \* \*

The darkness moved like liquid, her eyes blinded to anything else.

"Jesus Christ, what are you doing to her?"

*George?*

"Don't touch her," Nyx said. "She needs to fight her way through it."

Magdalena tried to speak, but it came out garbled, like she'd forgotten how. "I can't—I can't see."

"You *can* see," Nyx told her. "Remember the third eye, Magdalena. Look across the bridge and *see.*"

Her vision cleared, the darkness fell away, and she was back in that old motel room. She knew the others were there, but the only one she could make out was Nyx, who was bent over the bed and looking down at her.

Before she could say anything, more the room began to shake. As it became more and more violent, Nyx slowly backed away and out of her view, and Magdalena heard her say, "Everything's okay—she's all right— she's going back through."

"Are you sure you didn't give her too much?"

*Winston?*

The walls began to crumble and fall as huge and hideous tentacle-like appendages broke through and whipped about, searching for purpose. A deafening screech sounded, tearing through her, and spikes of sharp pain slashed through her skull like a razor, blasting out from behind her eyes with such force she was certain they'd explode from the sockets.

"You're killing her!" George screamed.

"No," Nyx said from the shadows. "*She's* killing the barriers."

"Stop this!"

"I can't. She's on the Bridge. It's all her now."

\* \* \* \*

*I'm here… We're here…*

Light shifts as a familiar room comes slowly into focus.

Pink-flowered wallpaper changes to yellow daisies. A woman crouches by the nightstand, veiled, hands blistered, bleeding, while a blackbird pecks at her flesh, its beak stabbing her fingers, leaving them raw.

The woman raises her head, revealing a face drawn and pale and near death.

*Mommy, is that…is that you?*

The woman looks to the ceiling. Blood seeps through, leaving behind an enormous stain that occasionally drips to the floor below.

*Or is that…me?*

Shivering as the ghosts crawl across her skin, Magdalena wraps her arms around herself. "What's happening?" she cries in a little girl's voice.

The old woman cocks her head to the side, indicating the shadows in the corner of the room. "Sleep now," she says. "Let them do their work."

"You're not my mommy, you're only pretending." She presses tiny hands to her head as a cascade of rainbow streaks burst across her peripheral vision. "My mommy's dead."

*Your mommy never was.*

"You know who I really am, don't you?"

Through her tears, everything blurs, and she clenches shut her eyes.

It isn't until she opens her eyes again that Magdalena realizes the room and the woman are gone. Instead, she stands in darkness, her head resting on a man's shoulder.

She pulls away, gazing at his face. Is it her father?

"Is it really you?" she asks, feeling as if she's done this and been here with him countless times before.

"It doesn't matter," he whispers. "You need to stay very still and let them do their work."

She nods slowly, feeling the familiar folds of his clothing, his smell—tobacco and cologne—it's as if he's come back to life before her eyes. As if neither of them has aged a day beyond this point.

"Stay very still now," he whispers. "Just think about and remember the good times, okay?"

His eyes twinkle as he strokes Magdalena's cheek, and then he pulls his hand away and looks to the shadows. He sees something, grimaces and looks away.

Suddenly dizzy, she leans against the man, still not sure it's truly her father, but he and all of this feels so familiar, like it's played out a million times before.

"I've got to get home," she tells him. "My daughter's waiting for me."

"You're just a little girl," the man says. "Sleep now."

It's then that she smells them. It is a rancid smell, like the rotting flesh of things long dead and buried.

Dark forms separate from the shadows, move closer. They are not human.

*How did I get here?*

She feels one of them touch her cheek, something similar to fingers scurrying like spider legs across her flesh, finding the wound...

*You've always been here.*

Magdalena put her head against her father's chest, but beyond him, on the wall, an old mirror, smudged and cracked, reveals the things standing on either side of her. One holds her still while the other carefully threads a large bone-white needle. The thread is a brilliant sparkling gold, and when it moves, little sparks of light fall away from it like raindrops.

"Stay very still..."

The thread presses into her cheek, but there is no pain. Her eyes still trained on the mirror behind them, she watches as one of the entities weaves the thread in and out of her flesh, pulling it taut with each pass, stitching it into her face with slow but deliberate precision.

*Sleep…*

The faces, so hideous and dark, watch her, their heads cocked and studying her the way scientists study lab rats.

*Sleep…*

"Who we are and what happens to us is up to them," her father whispers. "They eat everything that's holy. That's what monsters do."

"Am I dead?"

"Death is simply the fifth dimension. There is no time here. We are free of it, as time exists at once. We can move in and through time because it's all set forth before us. It's the perspective that matters, child, and from ours, it appears like replication, all of it available to us at any time. There is no magic, only perspective."

*It's a game…*

"They've chosen to heal you for now."

*A god damn simulation, like some kind of twisted fucking cosmic video game.*

"Sometimes the cat allows the mouse to live so they might play another day."

The golden thread absorbs into her cheek and is gone, along with the wound.

*A sick game, that's it, isn't it?*

Calendar pages drift past, riding a hellish wind, years past and days to come falling around them before they all burst into flames and turn to ash.

Apparitions without names, lost in time, tumble through oblivion.

*A game of demons, that's what it is.*

It seems like years have passed, events swirl through her mind, a date with a man named Mitch, the birth of a child named Kaley, strange and horrifying apparitions moving through the hallways of the nursing home, George and Winston walking the hallways, visiting their mothers as she watches from the shadows, a cabin in northern Vermont, lying on a steel table in a white room, wires protruding from her arm, then lolling her head to the side and seeing the others there too, strapped to tables of their own.

*It's all a god damn game.*

"I've lived every second of this before, haven't I?" she whispers to herself, holding her hands in front of her face, child hands, small and dimpled, her palms caked with the bloody feathers.

She waves her hands and the feathers fall away like crimson snowflakes.

*Sleep...*

And then she's alone again, lying on a mussed bed in a dirty old motel.

# CHAPTER TWENTY-ONE

IT SEEMED A PECULIAR time to think of the motel, but Magdalena wasn't sure she could still control the visions, sounds, and memories flooding her senses.

With her vision clearing, and the horrible noises of the crash still ringing in her ears, she tried to move. Relieved to find she could, though her body was sore and she was still disoriented, she realized she was lying on her back.

Rolling onto her side, she felt the cold, hard, uneven ground beneath her. Snowflakes fell from the colorless sky as vague memories of pushing open the driver's side door and tumbling free from the car flashed before her.

And then it all came rushing back.

Rather than using the highway, they'd decided to primarily use backroads in the hopes of remaining more inconspicuous. But they'd only gotten a few miles along one particularly rural road when Magdalena spotted the black SUV in her rearview. Just as she warned George and Winston, the SUV surged forward and pulled alongside them, its windows and windshield tinted black to conceal the identity of its occupants. It looked for a moment like it planned to pass and get in front of them, but it suddenly turned directly into their path instead.

"Jesus!" she screamed, swerving into an open, snow-covered field. "Hang on!"

Now, outside the car and lying on her side, she saw the forest, perhaps fifty yards or so in the distance. Best she could tell, the area was deserted, but where were the others, and where was the SUV now?

Lolling her head in the other direction, Magdalena saw her car several feet away, sitting at an angle in the field where it had abruptly come to a halt. Footprints in the snow led straight to her, but it took her a moment to realize they were hers.

Her mind whirled along with the sea of snowflakes blowing about, further disorienting her as she slipped back to what had come before, at the motel.

* * * *

Wet snow slapped the windows, blurring the world outside.

"Drink it. It's okay, it's just water. You're awake now, it's done."

Magdalena took the paper cup Nyx had filled from the bathroom sink and brought it to her lips. Her mouth and throat were so dry, swallowing had become difficult.

"Cotton mouth," Nyx said with a humorless chuckle. "It's a side effect."

From her position on the edge of the bed, Magdalena scanned the room. "Where are the others?"

Nyx cocked her head toward the window.

"Are they all right?"

"Sure."

"*Sure?*" The casualness of Nyx's response irritated her.

"It's not like they didn't go through it with you. They did. But this is your journey, Mags. It always has been."

"Are they okay?"

"Are *you?*"

The room had a musty smell, and the only light came from the draped windows, which left most of the already dingy room in shadows. Magdalena took another sip of water then placed the paper cup on the nightstand next to the bed. "Feels like I've been run over by a truck three or four times."

"It'll pass."

Magdalena looked around. She gauged everything she could see and hear now, weighing its validity. "I don't know what's real anymore."

Nyx moved over to a table against the far wall and closed a small case she'd brought with her, shutting away the syringes and liquids and rubber tubes. With a heavy sigh, she walked over to the bed and gently rested a hand on Magdalena's shoulder. "I have to go."

"So you show up, do your damage, then walk away. Just like that, huh?"

"I'd like to think I'm making up for some of that damage now."

Magdalena looked up at her. "Well, that's certainly convenient, isn't it?"

"It's only a matter of time before they catch me and stop me. I know that. But until that happens, I want to help as many as I can."

"And you think sending me on more of your drug trips is *helping* me?"

"You agreed to do this, no one forced you."

"But only this time, right?" Magdalena shook her head, disgusted.

"You wanted the truth." Nyx stood by the door. "That's what you came in search of. I gave it to you. It's not what either of us want it to be, but it *is* the truth."

Despite her lightheadedness, Magdalena pushed herself up and onto her feet. "What truth would that be? The truth that existence is all a game—a simulation—manipulated by mysterious beings from God knows where doing God knows what while working alongside some dark government agency to control and keep it all from us? *That* truth, Nyx, is that what you're talking about?"

"You're a survivor, and now you have knowledge. There aren't that many."

"And whose fault is that?"

"I'm doing what I can to make it right with those that have made it this far."

Magdalena rubbed her eyes. Her vision was clearing, focusing up. "You're like a man that beats his wife and then takes credit for trying to help heal the wounds he inflicted on her in the first place."

Nyx's shoulders slumped forward, like the words had hit her in the gut and knocked the wind from her. "You'll come to understand that I don't have any more control over this than you do. I only thought I did. None of us ever had a chance."

Magdalena stumbled over to a nearby chair. Her coat lay draped across it. "I'm going home," she said. "I'm going to take my daughter and we're going as far away from all this as possible. I'm throwing that toy away and forgetting about nursing homes and nightmares and all the rest. I'm going to forget about *you*. I'm going to pretend none of this ever happened, and I'm going to start over. Just Kaley and me, we'll start a life far away, where none of this matters."

The door opened, flooding the room with light. Nyx stood there a moment, holding her case. "Sleep as little as possible," she said, her voice laced with genuine sorrow. "And stay in the light as much as you can. I think they're afraid of it."

"Can I ask you something?"

Nyx nodded.

"What kind of name is Nyx?"

"In Greek mythology, Nyx is a goddess," she said. "She's the daughter of Chaos. The name itself means *Night*."

Magdalena shook off a chill, turned her back and pulled on her coat. "Ironic."

"For whatever it's worth at this point, Mags, I truly am sorry. Good luck."

When Magdalena looked back, Nyx was gone.

Like melted wax running the length of a burning candle, everything began to drip and blur and run. She tried to stop it, but the world was already transforming before her, wrapping everything in a cocoon of darkness.

* * * *

"Are you all right?"

Magdalena wasn't sure who'd spoken, or if she'd even heard the words at all. Squinting, she brushed hair from her eyes and saw someone move around the side of the car and lumber toward her.

*George…*

"Mags," he said, sliding to a stop and crouching next to her. "Are you okay?"

She nodded, unable to get the words out before George's surprisingly powerful hands took hold of her and lifted her to her feet. Still a bit disoriented, a dull ache pulsed through her body, but she wasn't seriously hurt.

"Can you stand?" he asked, looking quickly behind him through the snow.

Her strength was returning, her mind clearing. "Yes," she managed.

"Come on," George said, spinning her in the direction of the distant woods. "Hurry, we've got to hurry!"

The next thing Magdalena knew, she was running through the snow, trudging through the accumulated drifts with some difficulty but still moving at a good pace. They'd probably only gone about thirty yards or so, but in the snow, it felt like a mile. With the world tilting and blurring through the flurry of flakes, she saw someone else running up ahead of them.

Just as she realized it was Winston, he looked back over his shoulder and waved at them to follow without ever slowing his pace. He'd nearly reached the trees when he fell. His impact with the ground set off an explosion of more snow, and shot a misty cloudburst high into the air that further concealed him from view.

Still clinging to George, and he to her, they continued on until they'd reached him. Winston hadn't moved, and lay face down partially sunken into the snow.

"Don't stop!" George called to her above the wind, pushing her toward the trees. "Go! Go!"

Magdalena did, staggering through a larger bank of snow at the edge of the forest before bounding between the trees. Once she'd made it to the forest, she stopped and leaned against a tree. With labored breath, the icy air causing her eyes to water, her nose to run, and her lungs to burn, she looked back at the field. Visibility was not optimum, but she was able to see George crouch next to Winston as he struggled to get him to his feet.

Moving back toward the tree line and still trying to catch her breath, Magdalena squinted through the snow in the direction they'd come. Despite her watery eyes, she was able to make out the SUV in the distance, parked on the side of the road.

Two dark silhouettes stood next to it, watching them but not moving.

Suddenly George and Winston were coming right for her, stumbling into the forest together, their arms entwined. And Magdalena could tell from Winston's expression that he wasn't just scared. He was in pain and leaning heavily on George.

"Is he all right?"

"I don't know!" George said breathlessly. "But keep moving!"

"They're still by the SUV," she told him. "They're not chasing us."

"Look again," he said as they hurried by her, his voice barely audible above a howl of wind whipping through the trees.

George was right. They were coming now, sprinting across the field, and one was carrying something that looked like a rifle.

*My God*, Magdalena thought. *Winston didn't fall.*

He'd been shot.

# CHAPTER TWENTY-TWO

SNOW FELL BETWEEN THE trees, but otherwise the forest had become oddly quiet. They were the intruders here, trampling the otherwise untouched snow as they hurried deeper into the woods. Although Winston was still conscious, his body had gone limp, his feet dangling lifelessly as George struggled to hold him upright and drag him along. Magdalena pulled up the rear, running hard as she could through the heavy snow and looking back over her shoulder now and then to keep track of their pursuers. She hadn't seen them the last two times she'd stolen a glance, but they were there; she could feel them.

Just when it seemed she couldn't run another step, they stumbled into a large clearing. In the center of it, impossibly, there stood an old house. It had two stories, a pitched snow-covered roof, and two large dark windows facing them, the old wood shutters long since gone. There was no porch, only two narrow, crudely fashioned stone steps and a badly worn wooden door. The entire structure looked impossibly old, like something out of the 1700s, but seemed sturdy. On the second floor, two more windows faced them. In one, the shutter hung precariously by its corner. In the other, it was intact but badly scarred and pitted.

"What the hell?" Using one hand to hold Winston, George quickly wiped snow from his face with the other. "How is that— Why would there be a *house* here?"

"I don't know," Magdalena said. "But nobody's lived in it for a long time."

"Hurry," George said, heading straight for it. "I can't run anymore, and Winston's barely conscious. We've got no choice. We'll have to make a stand here."

Magdalena nodded, shivering from the cold. "Where's the gun?"

Instead of answering, George held Winston tight and stumbled toward the house. Magdalena followed, passing them and moving up the stone steps first. When she tried the door it swung open easily, releasing an earthy, raw smell. The interior of the first floor looked empty, but it was impossible to know for sure because, except for small patches of light near the windows and door, nothing but darkness awaited them.

Fumbling in her coat pocket, Magdalena found her cigarettes and a lighter. Sparking the lighter, she led the way, doing her best to see as much of the first floor as she could as George carried Winston up the front steps. Far as she could tell it was empty, but for several cob and spider webs and dirt and debris from the forest that had blown in through the open windows. Snow had now spread along the floor near them as well.

Satisfied there was no danger inside, Magdalena kicked the door closed, then hurried to one of the windows and looked out at the forest.

George, out of breath and exhausted, lowered Winston to the floor once they were only a few steps inside. Winston let out a groan, kicked his legs a bit, then lay still. Even in the limited light Winston's face had become deathly pale.

Careful not to jostle him further, George reached into Winston's coat pocket and pulled out the revolver. It was cold as ice in his hand.

"I don't see them," Magdalena said, trying to shake a feeling of familiarity that had sidled up alongside her terror. This window, the view of the forest, she couldn't have seen it before, she'd never been here. Yet that's exactly how it felt. *More madness*, she thought, *more side effects of The Bridge*. "They were right behind us."

"I'll take the window." George got to his feet. "You need to look at Winston."

Magdalena switched positions with him. Dropping to her knees, she carefully opened then peeled back Winston's coat. Blood had already soaked the front and sides of his shirt. A lump formed in her throat. She took one of his hands in hers and leaned closer. "Winston, can you hear me?"

His eyes blinked rapidly then seemed to settle on her. His bottom lip trembled like a child's, and he opened his mouth, but at first no words came.

"It's okay," she said. "Don't—"

"I…can't…get…a…breath."

As Winston struggled to breathe, Magdalena could hear a rattling sound, a wheezing wetness gurgling up and emanating from his throat. "Don't try to talk," she told him. "And take short little breaths if you can. I have to reach underneath you and feel the wound. It's not going to be comfortable."

Even before she slid a hand beneath him and pressed her finger against his blood-soaked back, she knew this was a bad sign. The sounds he was making likely meant the bullet had pierced one of his lungs.

Winston was drowning in his own blood.

"Still nothing," George said quietly, his eyes trained on the forest.

As Magdalena's index finger located the wound, she slipped her fingertip into the hole. Hot blood pumped out around it. Winston's eyes widened, looking at her in helpless agony. Slowly, she slid her hand free. It came back covered in blood. "Don't try to move or speak," she said, gently stroking his forehead with her other hand. "I'll be right back."

He clutched at her hand with more strength than he appeared to have, which was the only good sign she'd seen thus far.

"It's all right," she said, slipping her hand free of his. "I'm not leaving you. I'll be right back, I promise. I just have to talk to George."

Magdalena pushed herself to her feet, staggered to the window, and crouched next to George. "Any sign of them?"

He shook his head no then looked at her. She could tell he knew what she had to tell him was not good. "It's bad, isn't it?"

"The bullet hit him in the back, and I'm pretty sure it punctured one of his lungs," she said softly. "He's already lost a lot of blood. If we don't get him to a hospital soon, he'll die. It might already be too late, I—I don't know."

"Isn't there anything you can do?"

"It's a bad wound. I don't think so."

George gritted his teeth. "God help us. What the hell is happening?"

"I'll try my best, but I'm not a doctor. I'm not even a nurse."

"Do what you can. I'll watch for them. They're still out there. They're probably just trying to figure out their best move at this point.

"They have to kill us now, don't they?"

"Maybe we'll kill them first."

She motioned to the gun in his hand. "Can you do it?"

"I'm a long way from the bookstore. Seems like a whole other life." Darkness washed over George's face. "But don't worry. If I get the chance, I'll kill them both."

Magdalena believed him. With a quick nod, she dropped a hand on his shoulder, gave it a reassuring squeeze, then scuttled back over to Winston, who had again begun to make disturbing gurgling sounds.

*I've got to stop the bleeding or he has no chance*, she thought.

"I'm sorry," she said, "but I have to move you."

Without waiting for him to try to respond, Magdalena carefully maneuvered Winston into what she'd been taught was the recovery position, turning him onto his side with his top leg bent at a right angle. Once she got his coat off, she took hold of his bloody shirt and tore the back open. The wound was steadily pumping blood. She knew of only two ways to stop the bleeding. One was to apply lots of pressure. The other was to somehow seal the wound or apply a tourniquet.

Heart racing, Magdalena frantically pushed her hands against the wound. They made a horrible squishing sound, but the blood continued to pump out along the sides of her palms. She knew then it was useless, but she kept trying, applying so much pressure that Winston eventually fell forward onto his chest. This time there was no groaning or kicking, only that horrible gurgling and sucking sound as his body bucked and another spray of blood escaped between her fingers.

"God damn it," she muttered.

Carefully, she rolled Winston back over. His eyes had gone duller now, and his face was ghostly white. As he blindly reached for her with a trembling hand, she realized his eyeglasses were gone. Taking his hand in hers, she looked around as best she could but the glasses were nowhere in sight.

"Winston," she said, just above a whisper, leaning in closer to him. "I'm here."

"M-Mother," he said, gagging.

Blood poured from his mouth and down over his chin. He tried to speak again but couldn't manage anything other than a groan. His grip weakened and then his hand went limp.

Winston blurred through Magdalena's tears. "I'm sorry, I…I can't do anything more, I…I'm *sorry*, Winston."

A final breath left his mouth, sending a misty spray of blood into the air. His body bucked once more, and then he was silent and still.

Falling forward, Magdalena let her forehead rest against Winston's chest. "George," she said, her voice strangled with emotion.

He turned from the window. "No, don't tell me, I—"

"He's gone."

George stood up, apparently no longer worried about being seen. With the pistol at his side, he stepped closer and looked down into the shadows. There was so much blood it was almost beyond belief. He choked on a dry heave, his anger clearly rising, pushing aside the terror and confusion in favor of rage.

He moved back to the window and fired a shot into the forest. The sound was deafening. "Come on!" he screamed. "Come on, you fucks! Do it! Come get us!"

Magdalena pushed herself away from Winston's body, quickly grabbed his coat and draped it over him. She was covered in his blood. Hands shaking, she wiped them on her jeans, then wiped her eyes and steeled herself as best she could.

*Hold it together,* she told herself. *We're getting out of this. I'm going to see Kaley again. Nothing—no one—is going to stop me from getting back to her.*

A sudden but brief creaking sound interrupted her thoughts.

Magdalena looked up and slowly backed away, closer to George.

"What the hell was that?" he asked.

"Someone's in the house," she whispered, pointing to the ceiling. "Up there."

\* \* \* \*

Crouched near the window, they waited.

"How did they get in on the second floor?" George whispered.

"I don't know, but there's definitely someone up there." Magdalena looked out at the forest. It was getting dark out there. In here, it already was. "Maybe it's not those guys."

She could tell by the look on George's face he knew exactly what she meant.

"Give me your lighter."

Realizing she'd left it by Winston, Magdalena scrambled over to his body and ran her hands along the dark floor until she located it. Rather than give it to George, she ignited it, watching as the flame slashed a flickering hole in the darkness.

Rising to her feet, Magdalena took another step toward the back of the house.

Along the wall was a staircase. From what little she could see, it was mostly rotted, and a section of it had long ago collapsed to the floor. Raising the flame higher, she took another step toward the base of the stairs.

The flame flickered, but it wasn't strong enough to illuminate the landing on the second floor.

"Careful," George whispered from behind her.

"Just watch the window," she said, moving the light toward the floor to make sure the area was clear of debris. It was, so she raised the flame higher and took another step, her eyes straining to see through the darkness.

"Mags," he said, no longer whispering. "*Mags—*"

"What?" She looked back over her shoulder.

George was facing the window, and through it, at the edge of the clearing, she saw the two men, the one with the rifle slightly ahead of the other.

Both came to an abrupt halt as they entered the clearing.

Again, a strange feeling of familiarity washed over her. She was afraid, but she'd known this fear before. She knew that window. Somehow, she knew it.

"What are they doing?"

"I don't know, they just sort of stopped." George widened his stance and leveled the pistol out in front of him. "But we've got the element of surprise this time. They don't know we have a gun. And I've got a clean shot at both."

"They killed Winston," Magdalena said. "Do it."

As George aimed for the one with the rifle, Magdalena was disturbed not only because he was about to kill another human being, but by the steadiness of his hand.

Just then the man without the rifle raised a hand to his ear. He was speaking as well, but was too far away to be heard. He then turned to the other man and together, they began walking back into the forest. They'd been called off.

George fired anyway.

The man with the rifle yelped, stumbled forward, dropped the rifle, then arched his back and twisted around, trying to reach for the wound with his hands. Spinning, he fell to his knees, looked to his partner with shock, and then collapsed forward into the snow and lay still.

The second man made no move to help his partner or retrieve the rifle that now lay in the snow a few feet away. Instead, he stood staring at the house, expressionless.

George fired again.

The round missed, tearing into a tree next to him, the bark exploding along with a spray of snow. The man raised his hands. Despite the snow, like his partner, he wore dark sunglasses, and for that, Magdalena was grateful. Had she been able to see the man's eyes, she wasn't sure she'd be able to let George pull the trigger.

*He's surrendering*, Magdalena thought. *He's giving up.*

Those were the last words that went through her head before George shot the man, this time hitting him directly in the forehead.

A shower of blood, bone, and brain tissue exploded from the back of his skull.

The man dropped, and a slowly widening blanket of gore surrounded both corpses, turning the snow a dark crimson.

"I killed them," George muttered. "I…"

Suddenly horrible pain tore at Magdalena's hand. Recoiling, she dropped the lighter, realizing it had heated up to the point that it was burning her fingers. The lighter clattered to the floor, plunging them back into darkness. She located it at her feet, frantically flicked it back to life, then swept the flame around to the stairs.

*Stay in the light as much as you can.*

As the flame danced along the wall and up the stairs, something separated from the darkness above her. Silhouettes of beings gathered on the second-floor landing stared down at her with glowing red eyes.

*I think they're afraid of it.*

Trembling, Magdalena pushed the lighter ahead of her, widening its reach.

In unison, the beings stepped back, red eyes extinguished as the darkness from which they'd come devoured them.

"It'll be dark soon," George said flatly. "The sun's going down."

"George," she said, trying to hold her voice steady, her ears still ringing from the gunshots. "George!"

He snapped out of it and looked at her.

The lighter began to burn her again, so Magdalena let the flame go out.

Just as their eyes met, darkness closed in around them, and the ceiling creaked once more.

"Run."

# CHAPTER TWENTY-THREE

WIND PUMMELED THE OLD house, and somewhere in the distance, Magdalena swore she could hear the ticking of a clock. The sun was falling quickly, and they needed to get out of this place. They needed to get back to the car, to the road.

Run...

She could no longer see George in the darkness. "George..."

Her head hurt, and a sudden pounding in her temples set to the beat of her heart left her even more disoriented.

*Damn you, Nyx, you really fucked me up.*

Stumbling toward what little light was still coming through the blown-out window, she heard movement behind her.

*Those things...*

Had George already gone? Was he already running through the forest?

Magdalena threw open the door and stepped out onto the stone steps. The snow was still coming down, but the wind had gotten worse, blowing the trees back and forth and whipping the snow into a whirling frenzy.

There was no sign of George, and as she hurried down the steps and sunk into snow past her ankles, she ambled through the heavy accumulation, moving as quickly as she could toward the tree line.

Coming to an abrupt halt, she pulled her coat in tighter around her and stared at the ground just up ahead. Baffled, she shook her head, as if this might help, and tried to make sense of what she was seeing. Or *not* seeing...

The bodies of the two men George had shot were gone.

Magdalena spun back toward the house, watching it through the snow. The door remained open, as she'd left it, but from this distance she could no longer see inside. Her eyes lifted, found the windows on the second floor.

Dark figures watched, silent and unmoving.

In her mind, she replayed fleeing the house. Winston's body, covered with his coat, as she'd left him, was directly behind her once she'd turned from the stairs and told George to run. Yet when she'd fled herself, she went straight to the door. She never stepped over his body or made her way around it.

*Because it was no longer there, Magdalena, don't you understand?*

"The Bridge," she mumbled, shivering in the cold. "It changed things…"

As if in answer, in the windows, and now in the doorway as well, the dark shapes became clearer, taking form as though an invisible painter had rendered them detectable on an otherwise black canvas.

*No, it wasn't The Bridge, was it? It was you…those things.*

"I can feel you," she said to them. "In my mind, I—I can *feel* you."

*Mom…*

Magdalena followed the sound of the voice.

Up ahead, in a small opening between a pair of towering oaks, a tiny finger pointed at her as snow swirled, revealing a child—her child—eyes wide, small body shivering.

"Kaley!"

*Mom…*

It was her, but the voice coming out of her was not the voice of her daughter. It was all wrong, it—it was no longer the voice of her little girl.

As Kaley turned and ran back into the forest, soft laughter trailed her.

Magdalena followed, charging down a spiraling pathway through the woods. But she'd only gotten a short distance when she realized how dark the forest had become. She'd lost sight of Kaley, and could no longer hear her.

She plucked her lighter from her pocket and flicked it to life. The wind blew it out just as it passed over a series of jagged low branches that seemed to thrust at her like knives. She tried again, but it was useless. The wind was too strong now.

Hoping she was still going in the right direction, Magdalena put her hands up around her face to block the low branches and ran through the forest.

Overhead, the trees lorded, partially blocking a dying, darkening sky, as things unseen scurried across the treetops, keeping pace with her like jackals running down their prey. Continuing on, she looked straight ahead, trying not to see those things above her, crashing down now through the trees, breaking the branches as they came, descending upon her.

Something caught her foot and she launched forward, crashing to the ground.

The snow broke her fall, the freezing cold of it against her face and sliding down her neck snapping her up and back to her feet.

But the forest was behind her now.

Before her stood a street, the yellow light from lanterns lining either side glowing eerily in the night. A large owl was perched atop the nearest streetlight, its eyes fixed on her, and a woman clad in blue scrubs that looked vaguely familiar stood beneath another, smoking a cigarette and speaking softly on a cell phone.

"I have to go," the woman said, giving Magdalena a sideways glance. "She's here."

"Who are you?" Magdalena asked, voice shaking. "Where am I?"

The woman slid the cell phone into her pocket and smiled. "It's me, Joan."

Magdalena frantically wiped the snow from her eyes. "You... You're not Joan."

"It's okay." She jerked a thumb behind her. "Go ahead, they're waiting for you."

*Mom...*

"Kaley?" She spun toward the sound of the voice. "Where are you?"

Her eyes scanned the dark street. Up ahead, a little girl stood waiting. Once Magdalena had seen her, she turned and ran, her hair blowing about in the wind.

Joan winked and cocked her head, as if to say, *Go ahead and follow her.*

And Magdalena did.

*The Bridge...it's closing.*

Running as hard and fast as her aching and exhausted body would allow.

*You're running out of time. Time you never had.*

Although still a good distance ahead of her, the child suddenly stopped and held her arms out to her sides. Blackbirds circled above her in the night sky, screeching, and the snow began to swirl around her, forming a small cyclone.

*Because Time has never belonged to you, it belongs to us...*

Spinning faster and faster, Kaley disappeared into it as the tornado of snow dissipated to reveal a spinning merry-go-round. Painted horses shook and rattled as they spun, deformed, eyes missing, legs broken, graffiti scrawled across their bodies, the word *SLEEP* written on limbs snapped off and discarded in the snow. The carousel spun, its unoiled gears squeaking and groaning and spewing crimson droplets into the air, staining the snow.

Discordant music filled the night as the carousel turned faster still. So fast that only a dizzying blur remained. And then it disintegrated, came apart and floated away on the wind, little more than smoke and ash.

"None of this is real," Magdalena gasped, trying to gain her bearings. "Nyx, what did you do to me? Kaley, where are you?"

*I'm right here, Mom.*

Kaley, just up ahead, turned and ran through the falling snow, her little feet pounding on ice, dead leaves, and fallen branches.

Going after her, Magdalena kicked up snow, feeling the sting of branches against her face. She was back in the forest but—but how was that possible?

Before she could make sense of it, the forest gave way, and she found herself standing on the manicured grounds of Matheson Manor.

*Back where you think it all began…*

The dimly lit windows, the car parked in the small lot, everything was as she remembered it. Except for the roof, there was something wrong happening up on the roof.

*But we know the truth, don't we, Magdalena?*

People were standing on the roof, out in the snow and cold, barefoot and dressed only in hospital johnnies. Countless elderly souls stood shoulder-to-shoulder looking to the night sky, mangled hands reaching for the darkness, their twisted bodies swaying in the wind, some crying out in pain, others mumbling incoherently, their faces blank and pale, as if already dead.

*And now, so do you.*

Dark winged things flew overhead, barely discernible in the black sky.

Until they swooped down and plucked one and then another of the old souls from the roof, carrying their broken bodies up into the sky, disappearing into the clouds beneath the moon.

*Mom—*

Below at the entrance, Kaley had stopped. She looked back then waved her hand for Magdalena to follow.

Shuffling along after her, Magdalena followed her daughter into the nursing home.

Smells of antiseptic, stale coffee, and death wafted all around her.

A man, a visitor, leaned on the receptionist desk, speaking softly with a nurse, his face twisted in anguish and sorrow.

"George?"

He seemed to neither see nor hear her, and though she wanted to stop, she couldn't seem to do it, and instead continued on, following Kaley down the long hallway.

Glancing into the open doorways on either side of her, Magdalena saw old men and women sleeping, their televisions muted but on and flickering light across the otherwise dark rooms. And in the shadows, something more watched, waited, and whispered.

Halfway down that hall, in a room where a small statue of Jesus sat on a nightstand, Magdalena spotted Nyx. Dressed in scrubs and holding a syringe, she was whispering softly into a prone woman's ear as she injected her. When she realized she was being watched she looked up, and Nyx's eyes met Magdalena's. Slowly, she brought a finger to her lips.

*Shhh…*

Again, Magdalena wanted to stop but couldn't. She no longer had control of herself now, and could not prevent herself from continuing on down the hallway after Kaley.

In the next room, an old woman sat upright in bed, holding a tiny gray cat. The two seemed to be having a conversation, eyes locked on each other. "Such a tiny child," the woman said. "I want to keep you safe." The kitten let out a delicate meow and the woman pressed it to her chest. "But you have to keep *me* safe, don't you?"

Another black cat rounded the corner. And just then Winston appeared, emerging from the room across the hall. His head down, he mumbled to himself, "Need more hand sanitizer in Mother's room. More disinfectant wipes. We can't have unnecessary germs—"

"Winston! You—you're alive, you—"

He walked right by her.

Magdalena looked into the room she was approaching, and saw that Kaley was in there.

"It's all right," her daughter said in that strange adult voice. "You need to get some sleep."

Gentle hands took hold of Magdalena from behind, lifted her higher then guided her onto crisp white sheets. From the corner of her eye, she saw a pretty young woman unfurl a blanket and place it over her.

The woman pushed a wheelchair into the corner beneath a window and then turned back to Magdalena, smiling as if she knew her.

Snow fell just beyond the window, as dark things slid from the shadows and gathered around Magdalena's bed. "They're here," she whispered, trembling.

The woman hesitated a moment in the open doorway, then slid a hand along the wall and turned off the lights.

A scream died in the base of Magdalena's throat, a choking sound escaping her instead as the things around her bed reached for her, their wings exploding from their backs and flapping hideously, red eyes glowing and glaring down at her.

"God help me!" she said, gagging and unable to move.

Something fetid and wet touched her face. With breath hot and horrible against her flesh, in a growling voice it whispered, "We *are* God."

# CHAPTER TWENTY-FOUR

MOTION...

Magdalena had no idea where she was, but she could feel movement, and as the darkness parted and sound and sight slowly returned, she found herself in the passenger seat of a car.

A little ceramic angel on the dashboard wiggled with the motion of the car, a small wire running from its hand to form a bubble above it that read: YOUR LITTLE ANGEL LOVES YOU.

*Kaley, she...*

Her daughter had picked it out for her at a store a year or so before, and Magdalena had kept it attached to her dashboard ever since. This was her car, it had to be. But they'd crashed and gone off the road—

"Mags," George said breathlessly, his hands gripping the wheel tightly as he sat forward, peering into the night and oncoming snow crashing the windshield. "Are you all right?"

Trying to shake the cobwebs free, she rubbed her eyes and pushed herself up from her slumped position on the seat. "What happened, I—"

"We were running and you fainted. I carried you back across the field to the car and managed to get it going and back on the road."

"How long have I been unconscious?"

"Only a few minutes," George said, glancing at her. "I don't know how far we're going to get, your car's running really rough. It sustained damage in the crash. I'm not sure how bad, but I'm just going to push it as far as I can. We need to put as much distance between that forest and us as possible."

Magdalena realized then how badly her car was shaking and rattling, and the degree to which George was struggling to keep the wheel straight. Snow zoomed at them from the darkness like something out of a video game, the flakes large and spattering as they hit the windshield and the frantic motion of the wipers.

"Where are we?" she asked, a pain firing through her temple.

"Not sure. I've been looking for signs for the state highway. So far, nothing, the storm's gotten worse and visibility is—well—you can see for yourself."

She could, and she wasn't sure how he was even driving in this mess. They literally could not see more than ten feet or so ahead of them. Even with the headlights poking holes in the dark, most of the beams' effectiveness was cancelled by the pitch-black night and oncoming snow.

"I'm still not right after that shit Nyx gave me," Magdalena said, rubbing her temple until the pain faded. "Winston, he…"

George gave her a quick sideways glance before returning his attention to the road. "There was nothing you could do," he reminded her. "You said so yourself."

"This is a nightmare."

"If only."

Magdalena nodded even though George wasn't looking at her. The heater was on and blowing smothering waves of hot air directly at her. As she leaned forward to drop the heater to a lower power, the car skidded a bit, the tail of the car gliding back then forth on the icy road.

"Hang on," George said. "Steering's getting more difficult."

Pulling her phone from her coat pocket, Magdalena tried to make a call but there wasn't enough of a signal. "I need to get home," she said. "I have to get to Kaley."

"I couldn't get a signal."

"Me either." The car shook more violently and skidded a bit again.

As George slowed the car, it only shook worse, and he couldn't prevent it from gliding closer to the side of the road. "Shit," he snapped. "I've got to pull over. Hold on."

Magdalena braced herself as he fought the wheel.

After several harrowing seconds, George managed to get the car to the shoulder of the road. It continued to shake and rattle violently until he brought it to an eventual stop, and by then smoke had begun to billow up and out from under the hood, mixing with the snow like a ghost in the darkness.

"Now what do we do?" Magdalena asked.

George looked like he was about to break down. "I'm sorry," he said, running his hands through his hair. "I don't know a lot about cars, I— Christ, I—I can't take any more. I don't know, all right? I'm sorry. I don't know what the hell to do."

His hands were still gripping the wheel, so Magdalena reached over and touched his wrist. "We either have to hunker down in the car and ride out the night, hope for the best, and come morning we—"

"What's the other option?"

She looked out at the snow dancing in the headlight beams. "We leave the car and take our chances out there, keep trying our phones or hope we find something out here in the middle of nowhere. A gas station or diner or…"

"If we lose our way or get stuck in the storm, we'll die out there, Mags."

Magdalena dropped her hand. "I know."

"Things changed so quickly," he muttered. "A couple days ago I was…"

"They changed things," Magdalena said, and when he looked at her questioningly she added, "Those creatures, they—they changed things."

George shook his head and pinched the bridge of his nose up near his eyes, as if a headache was setting in. "I don't know what's real and what's in our heads anymore. None of it makes any sense. I just need it to stop."

The windshield wipers were still on but losing the battle against the snow.

"Nothing's going to stop me from getting back to my daughter," Magdalena said. "I'm sure those two you shot aren't the only ones hunting us down. What's to say they won't try to go after Kaley to get to me? I can't sit here all night and ride out the storm. I have to get to Kaley. Or die trying."

George nodded. He understood but didn't like the odds any more than she did. "All right," he said quietly. "We'll take our chances in the storm."

"You still have the gun, right?"

"Yeah," he said, removing it from his coat pocket and holding it up so she could see it. "There are only two bullets left."

"Then let's hope they all travel in pairs. That's one bullet for each of them."

The glow of the dashboard washed over George's face. "Or if it gets bad enough, one for you and one for me."

She knew he was right but didn't want to consider that now, so she pushed open her door and stepped out into the storm.

The temperature had dropped considerably, the snow was coming down heavier and faster than before, and the wind was deathly cold, slamming through her. Surrounded by darkness, she could make out nothing beyond a small patch of the road ahead that the headlights were illuminating.

George got out and walked around to the front of the car. Smoke was still pouring out from under the hood. He pulled his phone out and turned the flashlight on. It did virtually nothing in the heavy snowfall. "We best get moving," he said. "Temperature's dropping."

"Give me one second," she said, trying her phone again. "I've got a bit of signal. Not much, but it's worth a shot."

Hand shaking and the screen wet, Magdalena's first two attempts didn't work, but she tried again. This time the call connected and began to ring.

"You got anything?" George asked.

She held a finger up then put the call on speaker, listening as the ringing continued. Eventually there was a click and a male voice answered.

"Hello?"

A man answering Mrs. Bucci's phone was the last thing Magdalena had expected, but she didn't care, she'd gotten through and that was all that mattered. "Hi—hello—can you hear me?"

"Barely, you're breaking up," the man said, the line crackling. "Who is this?"

"It's Magdalena, I—"

"Who?"

"Magdalena!" she shouted above the wind. "I need to speak to Mrs. Bucci!"

"*Mrs. Bucci?*"

"Yes, this is her phone, isn't it?" *Shit*, she thought, *did I misdial?*

"Is this supposed to be some sort of joke or something?"

"Do I sound like I'm joking to you? Let me speak to her."

"Lady, look, I—"

"Right fucking now, goddamn it!"

The screen blinked and the call disconnected.

"Shit," Magdalena cried, holding the phone out in front of her. "He hung up."

"You must've called the wrong number." George looked behind him, as if he'd heard something, then back at her. "We've got to get moving, Mags. We can't just stand out here, we'll freeze to death."

Magdalena brought the phone up close to her face and checked the number on the screen. It was correct. "Let me try one more time," she said. "I don't want to risk losing what little signal I have."

Rather than press the individual numbers again, just to be certain, Magdalena went to her contacts list, found Mrs. Bucci's number, and hit it.

The call went through, but didn't connect.

*Please*, she thought. *Please work.*

She watched the screen, blinking rapidly to keep the snow out of her eyes. After several seconds it began to ring. "I got it!" she said, hitting the speaker again. "It's ringing!"

"Yes?" the same male voice answered irritably.

"Please don't hang up on me again! I'm broken down on the side of the road in the middle of nowhere and I don't know if I'll get the signal back! Please, just let me speak with Mrs. Bucci! She's watching my daughter Kaley! They need to get out of there! She needs to take her somewhere safe!"

"Lady, I don't what your deal is, and I'm only getting every other word, but what are you trying to pull here?"

"Where is my daughter?" she asked the man. "Please just let me speak to Mrs. Bucci!"

"Are you talking about the old Italian lady with the cats, *that* Mrs. Bucci?"

"Yes!"

"Are you nuts?"

Magdalena looked to George, frantic. He stared at her, baffled.

"I just need to speak with her!"

"Well, good luck with that," the man said, his voice crackling through the phone speaker. "I bought this place from her years ago when she had to go into a nursing home. She hasn't lived here in decades. In fact, she hasn't lived anywhere in decades. Mrs. Bucci's been dead for years."

"God almighty," George said, bringing a hand to his mouth.

Magdalena was shaking so badly she nearly dropped the phone. "Where is my daughter? Where is Kaley?"

"Lady, get some help, okay? You're obviously really confused."

"Where's my daughter!"

"I'm hanging up now."

The call disconnected, and her phone went dark. Mouth open, she swayed in the wind, still staring at her phone. "I don't understand," she said in a tiny, shaken voice. "I…I don't know what to do, I…George…I don't know what to do."

He pulled the gun from his coat. "Come on," he said, stepping out of the path of the headlights and into the darkness. "We've got to get the hell out of here."

*Stay in the light.*

Without warning, something swooped down from the sky, thrashing about violently, a large shadowy thing with dark wings cloaked in night and an endless spinning wall of snowflakes.

"George! Get back in the light!"

With impossible speed, George was snatched away in a blur of snow and shadows, the echo of his scream gone as quickly as he was.

It was as if the night itself had come alive and taken him.

Finally broken, Magdalena dropped to her knees in front of the car, the headlights blinding her. Alone and lost in the storm, she began to weep.

\* \* \* \*

"Mom, don't cry," a woman's voice said from somewhere behind her. "Don't cry, Mom, it's all right. Why are you crying?"

Hands touched her shoulders, gave them a gentle, reassuring squeeze. Hands Magdalena knew but couldn't quite place.

"The snow," she said. "I'm lost in the snow."

"No," the woman's voice said sweetly. "You're inside, Mom. It's snowing outside, but you're safe and warm in here, see? Look. Look and see."

Magdalena opened her eyes and looked up at a large fresco ceiling stretched out above her like a false sky, cherubs and angels with forlorn faces gazing down at her from faded painted clouds. She recognized the ceiling from the dance hall in her nightmares, but it wasn't really a dance hall. A recreational room, that's what they called it here. A room where low-cost singers came and sang standards on Saturday nights, and where residents gathered to play bingo or other games during the week.

"Where's my daughter?" she asked, her mouth dry and her throat scratched.

But the woman was gone. Magdalena was alone in the rec room, staring up at that strange ceiling as she'd done so many times in the past here at Matheson Manor. Moving carefully, she turned and stepped out into the hallway.

Something swept past, a large shadow, there then gone.

But for the emptiness of the hallways, nothing had changed here. The noises were the same, the smells, the sights—all of it was just as she remembered it. Day in and day out, night after night, shift after shift, nothing ever changed here, except for those who left covered from head to toe in sheets. Like a factory—the old and dying, the forgotten and damaged, those no longer wanted or capable of caring for themselves— they came steadily like products on a conveyer belt, each one for sale, each one a profit for some and a loss for others. And somewhere beneath all the red tape and laws and insurance grabs and medical billing, there existed the remnants of beings once fully realized, fully human, and, if they were among the fortunate, those who still loved them. Here then gone, each one quickly replaced, their deathbeds cleaned and starched and filled with another ready to die so that the machine could keep running and the money flowing.

Magdalena walked along the empty hallway. Outside, the snow was turning to rain. Thunder rumbled. *How strange*, she thought, *to hear thunder in the dead of winter.*

A light from a room at the end of the hallway bled into the shadows ahead, luring her forward. But as she took another step, something in another room, one to her immediate right, distracted her.

As a boom of thunder shook the building, Magdalena saw a man on the floor of the otherwise empty room, lying in a pile of his own bloody entrails, trying desperately to hold them in place and gasping for breath.

Mitch? *My God*, she thought. *Is it really you?*

Gagging on his own blood, the man reached for her. "Mags…help me…"

She cocked her head in confusion. Was this a dream?

Behind him, the lone window in the room blurred as icy rain ran its length, spraying against it as more thunder sounded.

Magdalena reached a hand out to take his, but suddenly shadows swarmed.

Snatching her hand back, the shadows fell across him as if from thin air, black wings flapping excitedly as they tore him to pieces, devouring him before her eyes.

Magdalena cupped her hands to her ears in a futile attempt to block the horrible screams and gurgling, gagging sounds emanating from him. As Mitch's body exploded in a feeding frenzy of blood and gore, she backed away then staggered down the hallway.

*You're killing her!*

Falling against the wall, she looked back in horror.

*No. She's killing the barriers.*

"Stop," Magdalena whispered. "Please stop this."

*Only you can do that. You're on The Bridge. It's all you now.*

Clinging to the wall, Magdalena slid along the hallway, trying to remain conscious and keep her knees from buckling. The light at the end of the hall, that's where she needed to go. She didn't know why, or if in her exhausted and battered state she could even make it that far, but that light—that room—was summoning her.

*Look…*

Closer now, she pushed away from the wall and fell against the open doorway, the warm light from the room washing over her.

*Look and see…*

An old woman sat in a wheelchair by the window, the glass and night beyond blurred by icy rain sluicing along the pane. Next to her, a CNA and another younger woman were speaking softly to the woman, but Magdalena couldn't make out what they were saying.

Behind her, things screeched in horror.

*Some days the cat keeps the mouse alive, as that is its cruel pleasure.*

Distracted by visions of golden threads sewing her wound, she didn't look back.

*But in the end, the cat always kills the mouse.*

Couldn't look back…

*Always, Magdalena. Always.*

Instead, with shaking hands she wiped the tears from her eyes and stepped into the warm light of the room at the end of the hall.

# CHAPTER TWENTY-FIVE

SHADOWS DRIFTED, SLID ALONG the wall. The old woman in the wheelchair saw the things concealed within those shadows, but there was nothing she could do now. "I'm lost," Magdalena said in a raspy weak voice she barely recognized as her own. "In the snow, on a highway, I'm lost. I'm all alone now."

"You're inside," a woman said from somewhere behind her. "And we're here with you. Everything's okay, you're safe and warm."

Magdalena was so weak she could barely draw a full breath. "I need to find my daughter," she said. "I have to find Kaley."

"I'm Kaley," the woman said, crouching next to the old woman's wheelchair and taking her hands. "It's me, Mom. *I'm* Kaley."

"You're not my daughter." Magdalena turned, her neck sore and stiff, and looked into the eyes of a stranger. "She's just a little girl."

"Not for a long time, Mom," Kaley said patiently. "I'm a grown woman now, with a family of my own. Do you remember your grandchildren?"

"My *grandchildren?*" Magdalena said, staring at her through cataract-ravaged eyes. "I'm thirty-one years old."

The other woman in the room, a pretty middle-aged CNA with auburn hair and green eyes, stepped into view. Wearing colorful scrubs, she smiled and put her hands on her hips. "Atta girl," she said with a wink. "I'm barely a teenager myself."

Squinting, Magdalena tried to bring her into clearer focus. "Esther?"

"The one and only, darlin'," she said. "About time for bed, okay?"

Kaley stood up, gently cupped her mother's face, then turned to Esther. "She recognizes you but not me." She sighed heavily. "This is so difficult."

"Some days she has no idea who I am either," Esther said. "Just the way it worked out tonight, is all. I know it's rough. I'm sorry, kiddo."

Magdalena wanted to get up and out of the wheelchair, but she didn't have the strength. Why were they talking about her like she wasn't even in the room? "I can't stay here, I left my daughter with Mrs. Bucci and I need to—"

"Wow, there's a name I haven't heard in a long time." Kaley smiled at Esther. "She lived next door to us when I was a kid. She used to babysit me a lot, had all these cats. What a sweet lady."

Shaking, Magdalena looked away, focusing on the black window before her. In the reflection, she saw a man standing in the doorway behind her. Covered in blood, he stared at her desperately, his hands still clutching the huge wound in his abdomen, his intestines hanging free like bloody eels.

"Mitch," she whispered.

Esther arched an eyebrow.

"She's really going through the mental registry tonight," Kaley said. "Mitch was my father's name. He was killed in a motorcycle accident when I was a kid."

"Oh, I'm sorry."

"It's fine. He left when I was really little, I barely knew him." Kaley turned back to her mother. "Mom, I've got to get going, but I'll be back to see you in a couple days, okay?"

Magdalena looked at her hopelessly. *I have no idea who you are.*

"I love you," Kaley said, leaning in and kissing her mother's forehead. "Get a good night's sleep and I'll see you soon."

Returning her gaze to the window, Magdalena searched for the reflection of Mitch, but it was gone. He was gone. Everything was gone.

"Don't you want to say goodnight to Kaley?" Esther asked, wheeling her from the window to the bed. "She's heading home now."

Kaley stood in the doorway, eyes moist. When Magdalena said nothing, she gave a little wave then slipped into the hallway and was gone.

"They changed things," Magdalena muttered.

Esther locked the wheelchair in place, then went to the bed and pulled back the fresh sheets and blanket. "Who changed what, darlin'?"

"You know exactly what I'm talking about. You've seen them too."

"There's no reason to get upset before bed, okay?"

"Am I still on the Bridge?"

"You're in your room at Matheson Manor." Esther smiled.

An alarm somewhere down the hallway sounded.

Before Magdalena realized what was happening, Esther had lifted her from the wheelchair and gently placed her in bed.

*My God*, she thought, *there's nothing to me. I must weigh eighty pounds.*

Esther pulled the covers up over Magdalena and tucked her in, smoothing out the edges and making sure she was securely in bed. "Do you want me to put the TV on for you?" she asked. "Maybe watch one of your programs while you fall asleep?"

Magdalena shook her head no.

The alarm down the hallway continued to sound.

"Apparently I'm the only one working tonight," she cracked. "You sleep tight, darlin'. If you need anything, hit the call button."

Magdalena watched as Esther hesitated in the doorway. "Sweet dreams," she said, and then turned off the lights.

The room went dark, but light from the hallway allowed Magdalena to see enough. The black shapes moved about freely now. Comfortable in darkness, they surrounded her bed, their black wings tucked in tight and their fiery eyes glowing.

*This is your journey, Mags. It always has been.*

Paralyzed with terror, Magdalena closed her eyes, no longer wanting to see. "What have you done?" she whispered, her heart racing as pain rose in her chest. "What have you done to me?"

*Sleep...*

Something told her to open her eyes, and despite the fear, she did. Between those at her bedside, there was enough space to see the doorway.

Esther stood watching, eyes wide in disbelief and a trembling hand to her mouth.

"Help me," Magdalena whispered, the pain growing worse.

But the CNA was already gone, hurrying off into the shadows in the hallway and leaving Magdalena alone in the dark.

*I didn't know then that I was the fucking mouse...*

Alone, but not by herself...

*...and it was cats setting the trap...*

Somewhere close, so close Magdalena could almost touch it, the endless sands of time swept across an open plane, beyond which a long-dead forest stretched as far as the eye could see. At the farthest reaches of her hearing, what began as whispers became song. Ancient and otherworldly, a female voice sang to her, drifting eerily through the trees, beckoning her in a language she'd never heard before and didn't understand.

*Sleep...*

As the forest caught fire, the flames rising amidst the dead trees, Magdalena closed her eyes, banishing the creatures to true darkness.

*The barriers are burning away...*

The ethereal voice slowly faded, and Magdalena started across the plane. Into the forest she strode, venturing deeper and deeper into this place of the dead, where a black sun burned in the gray sky, dripping ash like charred snowflakes.

On the stump of a burned-out tree, a single raven sat watching her with its dark eyes.

But Magdalena was not afraid.

*It's all you now...*

An illusion...a lie...a simulation...government experiments gone wrong...the twisted memories and confused dreams of a lonely old woman hopelessly drowning in dementia...

None of that mattered now.

On the other side of consciousness, the dreams, nightmares, and the anger of angels resided in patient oblivion. It was there—once she'd crossed the forest, the ground still hot and simmering beneath her bare feet—that the night returned.

*Sleep...*

But soon, the first flickers of light pierced that darkness, and she awakened to the sound of a baby crying.

In that moment—that all-too-brief, precise and profoundly beautiful moment in the vast halls of space and time—Magdalena realized the tears were her own.

The Bridge lay before her.

She was free.

# ABOUT THE AUTHORS

GREG F. GIFUNE is a best-selling, internationally-published author of several acclaimed novels, novellas and two short story collections. He has been described as "The best writer of horror and thrillers at work today" by author Christopher Rice, "Among the finest dark suspense writers of our time" by author Ed Gorman, and "One of the best writers of his generation" by author Brian Keene. Working predominantly in the horror and crime genres, Gifune's work has been translated into several languages, received starred reviews from *Publisher's Weekly*, *Library Journal* and others, and is consistently praised by readers and critics alike. A feature film based on his novel LONG AFTER DARK is set to go into production in 2022/23. His novel THE BLEEDING SEASON, originally published in 2003, is still popular and in print in several languages, has been hailed as a classic in the horror/suspense genres, and is considered by many, including *Famous Monsters of Filmland*, to be one of the best horror novels of its kind ever written. Greg resides in Massachusetts with his wife Carol and two English Labrador Retrievers, Dozer and Dudley. He can be reached online at gfgauthor@verizon.net or on Facebook, Twitter and Instagram.

SANDY DELUCA has written novels, several poetry and fiction collections and a few novellas. These include critically acclaimed works such as *Descent* and *Messages from the Dead*. She was a finalist for the 2000 Bram Stoker Award® for poetry, with *Burial Plot in Sagittarius*, accompanied by her cover art and interior illustrations. A copy is maintained in the Harris Collection of American Poetry and Plays at Brown University, 1976-2000. She was also nominated once more in 2014, with Marge Simon, for *Dangerous Dreams*. Her visual art has also been published in books and magazines. It has been exhibited throughout New England and in New York's Hudson Valley.

Sandy lives in Rhode Island with several feline companions, including a black cat named Gypsy and her two sons, Gemini and Leo. She is currently working on a new novel and a series of large-scale expressionistic paintings. She spends some of her free time volunteering at a local food pantry, photographing abandoned buildings and perusing secondhand shops.

Lightning Source UK Ltd.
Milton Keynes UK
UKHW010658300822
408063UK00001B/129